Enter the world of crime and punishment, cops
and killers, madmen and murderers, with today's
top writers!

Mystery and suspense in the first degree!

PRIME SUSPECTS

EDITED BY BILL PRONZINI AND MARTIN H. GREENBERG

IVY BOOKS • NEW YORK

Ivy Books
Published by Ballantine Books
Copyright © 1987 by Bill Pronzini and Martin H. Greenberg

Library of Congress Catalog Card Number: 86-91845

ISBN 0-8041-0125-6

Manufactured in the United States of America

First Edition: June 1987

Acknowledgments

"Quitters, Inc.," by Stephen King. From *Night Shift*. Copyright © 1978 by Stephen King. Reprinted by permission of Doubleday & Company, Inc.

"You Can't Be Too Careful," by Ruth Rendell. Copyright © 1976 by Ruth Rendell. First published in *Ellery Queen's Mystery Magazine*. Reprinted by permission of Literistic, Ltd.

"People Who Kill," by Loren D. Estleman. Copyright © 1987 by Loren D. Estleman. An original story published by permission of the author.

"The Sweetest Man in the World," by Donald E. Westlake. Copyright © 1967 by Donald E. Westlake. First published in *Ellery Queen's Mystery Magazine*. Reprinted by permission of the author.

"Just for Kicks," by Ed McBain. Copyright © 1958 by H.S.D. Publications, Inc.; renewed 1986 by Hui Corporation. First published in *Alfred Hitchcock's Mystery Magazine* as by Richard Marsten. Reprinted by permission of Evan Hunter and John Farquharson, Ltd.

"Smuggler's Island," by Bill Pronzini. Copyright © 1977 by Davis Publications, Inc. First published in *Alfred Hitchcock's tery Magazine*. Reprinted by permission of the author.

"Wild Mustard," by Marcia Muller. Copyright © 1984 by Marcia Muller. First published in *The Eyes Have It*. Reprinted by permission of the author.

"Tex," by John Jakes. Copyright © 1955 by Flying Eagle Publications, Inc. First published in *Manhunt*. Reprinted by permission of the author.

Acknowledgments

"The Vanishing Men," by Edward D. Hoch. Copyright © 1979 by Edward D. Hoch. First published in *Ellery Queen's Mystery Magazine* as "Captain Leopold and the Vanishing Men." Reprinted by permission of the author.

"The Dettweiler Solution," by Lawrence Block. Copyright © 1976 by Lawrence Block. First published in *Alfred Hitchcock's Mystery Magazine*. Reprinted by permission of the author.

"The Unholy Three," by William Campbell Gault. Copyright © 1956 by Flying Eagle Publications, Inc. First published in *Manhunt*. Reprinted by permission of the author.

"The Girl Who Loved Graveyards," by P. D. James. Copyright © 1983 by P.D. James. First published in *Winter's Crimes 15*. Reprinted by permission of Roberta Pryor Inc. and Elaine Greene Ltd. (England).

"The Killer," by John D. MacDonald. Copyright © 1954 by Flying Eagle Publications, Inc.; copyright renewed © 1983 by John D. MacDonald Publishing, Inc. First published in *Manhunt* for January 1955. Reprinted by permission of the author.

Contents

Introduction   1

Quitters, Inc., Stephen King   3

You Can't Be Too Careful, Ruth Rendell   28

People Who Kill, Loren D. Estleman   46

The Sweetest Man in the World,
Donald E. Westlake   60

Just for Kicks, Ed McBain   72

Smuggler's Island, Bill Pronzini   85

Wild Mustard, Marcia Muller   106

Tex, John Jakes   118

The Vanishing Men, Edward D. Hoch   129

The Dettweiler Solution, Lawrence Block   153

The Unholy Three, William Campbell Gault   170

The Girl Who Loved Graveyards, P. D. James   192

The Killer, John D. MacDonald   211

Introduction

The crime story is as old as storytelling itself. Tales told around campfires frequently involved intrigue and murder, as did the earliest recorded stories and plays of dynastic struggles. One has only to read Shakespeare to realize that the crime story was not merely popular in his day, but in the proper hands could—and still can—be elevated to the level of fine art.

With the rise of modern police agencies and the development of scientific techniques in the apprehension of criminals, mystery and detective stories as we know them today were born. In the 1840s, Edgar Allan Poe, often called the father of the mystery story, anticipated every major plot device associated with the form: the tale of detection, the psychological detective story, the locked room enigma, the puzzle story, the secret agent story. And he also invented the use of the red herring, cliffhanger chapter endings, and the least-likely-suspect-as-guilty-party. Decades later, in the 1880s, Sir Arthur Conan Doyle refined Poe's inventions and introduced the first—and perhaps the greatest of all—private investigators in Sherlock Homes.

During the twentieth century, the crime story has undergone numerous other refinements and updatings, reflecting its times perhaps better than any other form of popular writing, and thus has not only continued to flourish, but has "grown up" to take its rightful place as a major part of world literature. Today its popularity is at an all-time high, owing in no small part to the large number of talented and innovative writers working within the (no longer confining) parameters of the field.

Prime Suspects #1 is the first of a series of anthologies

1

devoted to bringing you some of the best—and at the same time undeservedly neglected—criminous stories by these talented writers, and by such other major names in popular fiction as Stephen King and John Jakes. In future volumes you will find stories by John D. MacDonald, Ed McBain, Donald E. Westlake, Ruth Rendell, Lawrence Block, Loren D. Estlemen, P. D. James, Marcia Muller, and others featured in this first book, as well as stories by such other luminaries as Isaac Asimov, Stanley Ellin, Sara Paretsky, James McClure, Harry Kemelman, Antonia Fraser, John Lutz, Edward Gorman, Brian Garfield, and Ellis Peters—literally, the very best mystery and suspense writers working today.

Our pleasure was in selecting these fine stories; the pleasure from now on is all yours. Enjoy.

—Bill Pronzini and Martin H. Greenberg

Quitters, Inc.

•

Stephen King

Stephen King is the publishing phenomenon of the 1970s and 1980s, perhaps even of the twentieth century. Everything he writes turns to bestselling gold: novels such as The Shining, Pet Sematary, *and the recent* It; *collections such as* Night Shift *and* Skeleton Crew. *Nearly all of his work is in the fantasy/horror vein, but occasionally King has turned his hand to fictional crime, as in this macabre tale of an organization that helps people quit smoking—a story reminiscent of Roald Dahl in both flavor and mordant bite. If you smoke, "Quitters, Inc." may be the answer you've been looking for; then again, it may not be . . .*

Morrison was waiting for someone who was hung up in the air traffic jam over Kennedy International when he saw a familiar face at the end of the bar and walked down.

"Jimmy? Jimmy McCann?"

It was. A little heavier than when Morrison had seen him at the Atlanta Exhibition the year before, but otherwise he looked awesomely fit. In college he had been a thin, pallid chain smoker buried behind huge horn-rimmed glasses. He had apparently switched to contact lenses.

"Dick Morrison?"

"Yeah. You look great." He extended his hand and they shook.

"So do you," McCann said, but Morrison knew it was

a lie. He had been overworking, overeating, and smoking too much. "What are you drinking?"

"Bourbon and bitters," Morrison said. He hooked his feet around a bar stool and lighted a cigarette. "Meeting someone, Jimmy?"

"No. Going to Miami for a conference. A heavy client. Bills six million. I'm supposed to hold his hand because we lost out on a big special next spring."

"Are you still with Crager and Barton?"

"Executive veep now."

"Fantastic! Congratulations! When did all this happen?" He tried to tell himself that the little worm of jealousy in his stomach was just acid indigestion. He pulled out a roll of antacid pills and crunched one in his mouth.

"Last August. Something happened that changed my life." He looked speculatively at Morrison and sipped his drink. "You might be interested."

My God, Morrison thought with an inner wince. Jimmy McCann's got religion.

"Sure," he said, and gulped at his drink when it came.

"I wasn't in very good shape," McCann said. "Personal problems with Sharon, my dad died—heart attack—and I'd developed this hacking cough. Bobby Crager dropped by my office one day and gave me a fatherly little pep talk. Do you remember what those are like?"

"Yeah." He had worked at Crager and Barton for eighteen months before joining the Morton Agency. "Get your butt in gear or get your butt out."

McCann laughed. "You know it. Well, to put the capper on it, the doc told me I had an incipient ulcer. He told me to quit smoking." McCann grimaced. "Might as well tell me to quit breathing."

Morrison nodded in perfect understanding. Nonsmokers could afford to be smug. He looked at his own cigarette with distaste and stubbed it out, knowing he would be lighting another in five minutes.

"Did you quit?" he asked.

"Yes, I did. At first I didn't think I'd be able to—I was cheating like hell. Then I met a guy who told me about an outfit over on Forty-sixth Street. Specialists. I said what do I have to lose and went over. I haven't smoked since."

Morrison's eyes widened. "What did they do? Fill you full of some drug?"

"No." He had taken out his wallet and was rummaging through it. "Here it is. I knew I had one kicking around." He laid a plain white business card on the bar between them.

QUITTERS, INC.
Stop Going Up in Smoke!
237 East 46th Street

Treatments by Appointment

"Keep it, if you want," McCann said. "They'll cure you. Guaranteed."

"How?"

"I can't tell you," McCann said.

"Huh? Why not?"

"It's part of the contract they make you sign. Anyway, they tell you how it works when they interview you."

"You signed a *contract*?"

McCann nodded.

"And on the basis of that—"

"Yep." He smiled at Morrison, who thought: Well, it's happened. Jim McCann has joined the smug bastards.

"Why the great secrecy if this outfit is so fantastic? How come I've never seen any spots on TV, billboards, magazine ads—"

"They get all the clients they can handle by word of mouth."

"You're an advertising man, Jimmy. You can't believe that."

"I do," McCann said. "They have a ninety-eight percent cure rate."

"Wait a second," Morrison said. He motioned for another drink and lit a cigarette. "Do these guys strap you down and make you smoke until you throw up?"

"No."

"Give you something so that you get sick every time you light—"

"No, it's nothing like that. Go and see for yourself." He gestured at Morrison's cigarette. "You don't really like that, do you?"

"Nooo, but—"

"Stopping really changed things for me," McCann said. "I don't suppose it's the same for everyone, but with me it was just like dominoes falling over. I felt better and my relationship with Sharon improved. I had more energy, and my job performance picked up."

"Look, you've got my curiosity aroused. Can't you just—"

"I'm sorry, Dick. I really can't talk about it." His voice was firm.

"Did you put on any weight?"

For a moment he thought Jimmy McCann looked almost grim.

"Yes. A little too much, in fact. But I took it off again. I'm about right now. I was skinny before."

"Flight 206 now boarding at Gate 9," the loudspeaker announces.

"That's me," McCann said, getting up. He tossed a five on the bar. "Have another, if you like. And think about what I said, Dick. Really." And then he was gone, making

6

his way through the crowd to the escalators. Morrison picked up the card, looked at it thoughtfully, then tucked it away in his wallet and forgot it.

The card fell out of his wallet and onto another bar a month later. He had left the office early and had come here to drink the afternoon away. Things had not been going so well at the Morton Agency. In fact, things were bloody horrible.

He gave Henry a ten to pay for his drink, then picked up the small card and reread it—237 East Forty-sixth Street was only two blocks over: it was a cool, sunny October day outside, and maybe, just for chuckles—

When Henry brought his change, he finished his drink and then went for a walk.

Quitters, Inc., was a new building where the monthly rent on office space was probably close to Morrison's yearly salary. From the directory in the lobby, it looked to him like their offices took up one whole floor, and that spelled money. Lots of it.

He took the elevator up and stepped off into a lushly carpeted foyer and from there into a gracefully appointed reception room with a wide window that looked out on the scurrying bugs below. Three men and one woman sat in the chairs along the walls, reading magazines. Business types, all of them. Morrison went to the desk.

"A friend gave me this," he said, passing the card to the receptionist. "I guess you'd say he's an alumnus."

She smiled and rolled a form into her typewriter. "What is your name, sir?"

"Richard Morrison."

Clack-clackety-clack. But very muted clacks; the typewriter was an IBM.

"Your address?"

"Twenty-nine Maple Lane, Clinton, New York."

"Married?"

"Yes."

"Children?"

"One." He thought of Alvin and frowned slightly. "One" was the wrong word. "A half" might be better. His son was mentally retarded and lived at a special school in New Jersey.

"Who recommended us to you, Mr. Morrison?"

"An old school friend. James McCann."

"Very good. Will you have a seat? It's been a very busy day."

"All right."

He sat between the woman, who was wearing a severe blue suit, and a young executive type wearing a herringbone jacket and modish sideburns. He took out his pack of cigarettes, looked around, and saw there were no ashtrays.

He put the pack away again. That was all right. He would see this little game through and then light up while he was leaving. He might even tap some ashes on their maroon shag rug if they made him wait long enough. He picked up a copy of *Time* and began to leaf through it.

He was called a quarter of an hour later, after the woman in the blue suit. His nicotine center was speaking quite loudly now. A man who had come in after him took out a cigarette case, snapped it open, saw there were no ashtrays, and put it away—looking a little guilty, Morrison thought. It made him feel better.

At last the receptionist gave him a sunny smile and said, "Go right in, Mr. Morrison."

Morrison walked through the door beyond her desk and found himself in an indirectly lit hallway. A heavyset man with white hair that looked phony shook his hand, smiled affably, and said, "Follow me, Mr. Morrison."

He led Morrison past a number of closed, unmarked

doors and then opened one of them, about halfway down the hall, with a key. Beyond the door was an austere little room walled with drilled white cork panels. The only furnishings were a desk with a chair on either side. There was what appeared to be a small oblong window in the wall behind the desk, but it was covered with a short green curtain. There was a picture on the wall to Morrison's left—a tall man with iron gray hair. He was holding a sheet of paper in one hand. He looked vaguely familiar.

"I'm Vic Donatti," the heavyset man said. "If you decide to go ahead with our program, I'll be in charge of your case."

"Pleased to know you," Morrison said. He wanted a cigarette very badly.

"Have a seat."

Donatti put the receptionist's form on the desk, and then drew another form from the desk drawer. He looked directly into Morrison's eyes. "Do you want to quit smoking?"

Morrison cleared his throat, crossed his legs, and tried to think of a way to equivocate. He couldn't. "Yes," he said.

"Will you sign this?" He gave Morrison the form. He scanned it quickly. The undersigned agrees not to divulge the methods or techniques or et cetera, et cetera.

"Sure," he said, and Donatti put a pen in his hand. He scratched his name, and Donatti signed below it. A moment later the paper disappeared back into the desk drawer. Well, he thought ironically, I've taken the pledge. He had taken it before. Once it had lasted for two whole days.

"Good," Donatti said. "We don't bother with propaganda here, Mr. Morrison. Questions of health or expense or social grace. We have no interest in why you want to stop smoking. We are pragmatists."

"Good," Morrison said blankly.

"We employ no drugs. We employ no Dale Carnegie people to sermonize you. We recommend no special diet. And we accept no payment until you have stopped smoking for one year."

"My God," Morrison said.

"Mr. McCann didn't tell you that?"

"No."

"How is Mr. McCann, by the way? Is he well?"

"He's fine."

"Wonderful. Excellent. Now . . . just a few questions, Mr. Morrison. These are somewhat personal, but I assure you that your answers will be held in strictest confidence."

"Yes?" Morrison asked noncommittally.

"What is your wife's name?"

"Lucinda Morrison. Her maiden name was Ramsey."

"Do you love her?"

Morrison looked up sharply, but Donatti was looking at him blandly, "Yes, of course," he said.

"Have you ever had marital problems? A separation, perhaps?"

"What has that got to do with kicking the habit?" Morrison asked. He sounded a little angrier than he had intended, but he wanted—hell, he *needed*—a cigarette.

"A great deal," Donatti said. "Just bear with me."

"No. Nothing like that." Although things *had* been a little tense just lately.

"You just have the one child?"

"Yes, Alvin. He's in a private school."

"And which school is it?"

"That," Morrison said grimly, "I'm not going to tell you."

"All right," Donatti said agreeably. He smiled disarmingly at Morrison. "All your questions will be answered tomorrow at your first treatment."

"How nice," Morrison said, and stood.

10

"One final question," Donatti said. "You haven't had a cigarette for over an hour. How do you feel?"

"Fine," Morrison lied. "Just fine."

"Good for you!" Donatti exclaimed. He stepped around the desk and opened the door. "Enjoy them tonight. After tomorrow, you'll never smoke again."

"Is that right?"

"Mr. Morrison," Donatti said solemnly, "we guarantee it."

He was sitting in the outer office of Quitters, Inc., the next day promptly at three. He had spent most of the day swinging between skipping the appointment the reception ist had made for him on the way out and going in a spirit of mulish cooperation—*Throw your best pitch at me, buster.*

In the end, something Jimmy McCann had said convinced him to keep the appointment—*It changed my whole life.* God knew his own life could do with some changing. And then there was his own curiosity. Before going up in the elevator, he smoked a cigarette down to the filter. Too damn bad if it's the last one, he thought. It tasted horrible.

The wait in the outer office was shorter this time. When the receptionist told him to go in, Donatti was waiting. He offered his hand and smiled, and to Morrison the smile looked almost predatory. He began to feel a little tense, and that made him want a cigarette.

"Come with me," Donatti said, and led the way down to the small room. He sat behind the desk again, and Morrison took the other chair.

"I'm very glad you came." Donatti said. "A great many prospective clients never show up again after the initial interview. They discover they don't want to quit as badly as they thought. It's going to be a pleasure to work with you on this."

11

"When does the treatment start?" Hypnosis, he was thinking. It must be hypnosis.

"Oh, it already has. It started when we shook hands in the hall. Do you have cigarettes with you, Mr. Morrison?"

"Yes."

"May I have them, please?"

Shrugging, Morrison handed Donatti his pack. There were only two or three left in it, anyway.

Donatti put the pack on the desk. Then, smiling into Morrison's eyes, he curled his right hand into a fist and began to hammer it down on the pack of cigarettes, which twisted and flattened. A broken cigarette end flew out. Tobacco crumbs spilled. The sound of Donatti's fist was very loud in the closed room. The smile remained on his face in spite of the force of the blows, and Morrison was chilled by it. Probably just the effect they want to inspire, he thought.

At last Donatti ceased pounding. He picked up the pack, a twisted and battered ruin. "You wouldn't believe the pleasure that gives me," he said, and dropped the pack into the wastebasket. "Even after three years in the business, it still pleases me."

"As a treatment, it leaves something to be desired," Morrison said mildly. "There's a newsstand in the lobby of this very building. And they sell all brands."

"As you say," Donatti said. He folded his hands. "Your son, Alvin Dawes Morrison, is in the Paterson School for Handicapped Children. Born with cranial brain damage. Tested IQ of forty-six. Not quite in the educable retarded category. Your wife—"

"How did you find that out?" Morrison barked. He was startled and angry. "You've got no goddamn right to go poking around my—"

"We know a lot about you," Donatti said smoothly. "But, as I said, it will all be held in strictest confidence."

12

"I'm getting out of here," Morrison said thinly. He stood up.

"Stay a bit longer."

Morrison looked at him closely. Donatti wasn't upset. In fact, he looked a little amused. The face of a man who has seen this reaction scores of times—maybe hundreds.

"All right. But it better be good."

"Oh, it is." Donatti leaned back. "I told you we were pragmatists here. As pragmatists, we have to start by realizing how difficult it is to cure an addiction to tobacco. The relapse rate is almost eighty-five percent. The relapse rate for heroin addicts is lower than that. It is an extraordinary problem. *Extraordinary.*"

Morrison glanced into the wastebasket. One of the cigarettes, although twisted, still looked smokable. Donatti laughed good-naturedly, reached into the wastebasket, and broke it between his fingers.

"State legislatures sometimes hear a request that the prison systems do away with the weekly cigarette ration. Such proposals are invariably defeated. In a few cases where they have passed, there have been fierce prison riots. *Riots,* Mr. Morrison. Imagine it."

"I," Morrison said, "am not surprised."

"But consider the implications. When you put a man in prison you take away any normal sex life, you take away his liquor, his politics, his freedom of movement. No riots—or few in comparison to the number of prisons. But when you take away his *cigarettes*—wham! bam!" He slammed his fist on the desk for emphasis.

"During World War I, when no one on the German home front could get cigarettes, the sight of German aristocrats picking butts out of the gutter was a common one. During World War II, many American women turned to pipes when they were unable to obtain cigarettes. A fascinating problem for the true pragmatist, Mr. Morrison."

"Could we get to the treatment?"

"Momentarily. Step over here, please." Donatti had risen and was standing by the green curtains Morrison had noticed yesterday. Donatti drew the curtains, discovering a rectangular window that looked into a bare room. No, not quite bare. There was a rabbit on the floor, eating pellets out of a dish.

"Pretty bunny," Morrison commented.

"Indeed. Watch him." Donatti pressed a button by the windowsill. The rabbit stopped eating and began to hop about crazily. It seemed to leap higher each time its feet struck the floor. Its fur stood out spikily in all directions. It eyes were wild.

"Stop that! You're electrocuting him!"

Donatti released the button. "Far from it. There's a very low-yield charge in the floor. Watch the rabbit, Mr. Morrison!"

The rabbit was crouched about ten feet away from the dish of pellets. His nose wriggled. All at once he hopped away into a corner.

"If the rabbit gets a jolt often enough while he's eating," Donatti said, "he makes the association very quickly. Eating causes pain. Therefore, he won't eat. A few more shocks, and the rabbit will starve to death in front of his food. It's called aversion training."

Light dawned in Morrison's head.

"No, thanks." He started for the door.

"Wait, please, Mr. Morrison."

Morrison didn't pause. He grabbed the door knob . . . and felt it slip solidly through his hand. "Unlock this."

"Mr. Morrison, if you'll just sit down—"

"Unlock this door or I'll have the cops on you before you can say Marlboro Man."

"*Sit down.*" The voice was as cold as shaved ice.

Morrison looked at Donatti. His brown eyes were muddy

and frightening. My God, he thought, I'm locked in here with a psycho. He licked his lips. He wanted a cigarette more than he ever had in his life.

"Let me explain the treatment in more detail," Donatti said.

"You don't understand," Morrison said with counterfeit patience. "I don't want the treatment. I've decided against it."

"No, Mr. Morrison. *You're* the one who doesn't understand. You don't have any choice. When I told you the treatment had already begun, I was speaking the literal truth. I would have thought you'd be tipped to that by now."

"You're crazy," Morrison said wonderingly.

"No. Only a pragmatist. Let me tell you all about the treatment."

"Sure," Morrison said. "As long as you understand that as soon as I get out of here I'm going to buy five packs of cigarettes and smoke them all on the way to the police station." He suddenly realized he was biting his thumbnail, sucking on it, and made himself stop.

"As you wish. But I think you'll change your mind when you see the whole picture."

Morrison said nothing. He sat down again and folded his hands.

"For the first month of the treatment, our operatives will have you under constant supervision," Donatti said. "You'll be able to spot some of them. Not all. But they'll always be with you. *Always*. If they see you smoke a cigarette, I get a call."

"And I suppose you bring me here and do the old rabbit trick," Morrison said. He tried to sound cold and sarcastic, but he suddenly felt horribly frightened. This was a nightmare.

15

"Oh, no," Donatti said. "Your wife gets the rabbit trick, not you."

Morrison looked at him dumbly.

Donatti smiled. "You," he said, "get to watch."

After Donatti let him out, Morrison walked for over two hours in a complete daze. It was another fine day, but he didn't notice. The monstrousness of Donatti's smiling face blotted out all else.

"You see," he had said, "a pragmatic problem demands pragmatic solutions. You must realize we have your best interests at heart."

Quitters, Inc., according to Donatti, was a sort of foundation—a nonprofit organization begun by the man in the wall portrait. The gentleman had been extremely successful in several family businesses—including slot machines, massage parlors, numbers, and a brisk (although clandestine) trade between New York and Turkey. Mort "Three-Fingers" Minelli had been a heavy smoker—up in the three-pack-a-day range. The paper he was holding in the picture was a doctor's diagnosis: lung cancer. Mort had died in 1970, after endowing Quitters, Inc., with family funds.

"We try to keep as close to breaking even as possible," Donatti had said, "But we're more interested in helping our fellow man. And of course, it's a great tax angle."

The treatment was chillingly simple. A first offense and Cindy would be brought to what Donatti called "the rabbit room." A second offense, and Morrison would get the dose. On a third offense, both of them would be brought in together. A fourth offense would show grave cooperation problems and would require sterner measures. An operative would be sent to Alvin's school to work the boy over.

"Imagine," Donatti said, smiling, "how horrible it will be for the boy. He wouldn't understand it even if someone explained. He'll only know someone is hurting him because Daddy was bad. He'll be very frightened.''

"You bastard," Morrison said helplessly. He felt close to tears. "You dirty, filthy bastard."

"Don't misunderstand," Donatti said. He was smiling sympathetically. "I'm sure it won't happen. Forty percent of clients never have to be disciplined at all—and only ten percent have more than three falls from grace. Those are reassuring figures, aren't they?''

Morrison didn't find them reassuring. He found them terrifying.

"Of course, if you transgress a *fifth* time—"

"What do you mean?"

Donatti beamed. "The room for you and your wife, a second beating for your son, and a beating for your wife."

Morrison, driven beyond the point of rational consideration, lunged over the desk at Donatti. Donatti moved with amazing speed for a man who had apparently been completely relaxed. He shoved the chair backward and drove both of his feet over the desk and into Morrison's belly. Gagging and coughing, Morrison staggered backward.

"Sit down, Mr. Morrison," Donatti said benignly. "Let's talk this over like rational men."

When he could get his breath, Morrison did as he was told. Nightmares had to end sometime, didn't they?

Quitters, Inc., Donatti had explained further, operated on a ten-step punishment scale. Steps six, seven, and eight consisted of further trips to the rabbit room (and increased voltage) and more serious beatings. The ninth step would be the breaking of his son's arms.

"And the tenth?" Morrison asked, his mouth dry.

Donatti shook his head sadly. "Then we give up, Mr. Morrison. You become part of the unregenerate two percent."

17

"You really give up?"

"In a manner of speaking." He opened one of the desk drawers and laid a silenced .45 on the desk. He smiled into Morrison's eyes. "But even the unregenerate two percent never smoke again. We guarantee it."

The Friday Night Movie was *Bullitt,* one of Cindy's favorites, but after an hour of Morrison's mutterings and fidgetings, her concentration was broken.

"What's the matter with you?" she asked during station identification.

"Nothing . . . everything," he growled. "I'm giving up smoking."

She laughed. "Since when? Five minutes ago?"

"Since three o'clock this afternoon."

"You really haven't had a cigarette since then?"

"No," he said, and began to gnaw his thumbnail. It was ragged, down to the quick.

"That's wonderful! What ever made you decide to quit?"

"You," he said. "And . . . and Alvin."

Her eyes widened, and when the movie came back on, she didn't notice. Dick rarely mentioned their retarded son. She came over, looked at the empty ashtray by his right hand, and then into his eyes. "Are you really trying to quit, Dick?"

"Really." And if I go to the cops, he added mentally, the local goon squad will be around to rearrange your face, Cindy.

"I'm glad. Even if you don't make it, we both thank you for the thought, Dick."

"Oh, I think I'll make it," he said, thinking of the muddy, homicidal look that had come into Donatti's eyes when he kicked him in the stomach.

* * *

He slept badly that night, dozing in and out of sleep. Around three o'clock he woke up completely. His craving for a cigarette was like a low-grade fever. He went downstairs and to his study. The room was in the middle of the house. No windows. He slid open the top drawer of his desk and looked in, fascinated by the cigarette box. He looked around and licked his lips.

Constant supervision during the first month, Donatti had said. Eighteen hours a day during the next two—but he would never know *which* eighteen. During the fourth month, the month when most clients backslid, the "service" would return to twenty-four hours a day. Then twelve hours of broken surveillance each day for the rest of the year. After that? Random surveillance for the rest of the client's life.

For the rest of his life.

"We may audit you every other month," Donatti said. "Or every other day. Or constantly for one week two years from now. The point is, *you won't know.* If you smoke, you'll be gambling with loaded dice. Are they watching? Are they picking up my wife or sending a man after my son right now? Beautiful, isn't it? And if you do sneak a smoke, it'll taste awful. It will taste like your son's blood."

But they couldn't be watching now, in the dead of night, in his own study. The house was grave-quiet.

He looked at the cigarettes in the box for almost two minutes, unable to tear his gaze away. Then he went to the study door, peered out into the empty hall, and went back to look at the cigarettes some more. A horrible picture came: his life stretching before him and not a cigarette to be found. How in the name of God was he ever going to be able to make another tough presentation to a wary client, without that cigarette burning nonchalantly between his fingers as he approached the charts and layouts? How would he be able to endure Cindy's endless garden shows without a cigarette? How could he even get up in the morning and face the day without a cigarette to smoke as he drank his coffee and read the paper?

He cursed himself for getting into this. He cursed Donatti. And most of all, he cursed Jimmy McCann. How could he have done it? The son of a bitch had *known*. His hands trembled in their desire to get hold of Jimmy Judas McCann.

Stealthily, he glanced around the study again. He reached into the drawer and brought out a cigarette. He caressed it, fondled it. What was that old slogan? *So round, so firm, so fully packed.* Truer words had never been spoken. He put the cigarette in his mouth and then paused, cocking his head.

Had there been the slightest noise from the closet? A faint shifting? Surely not. But—

Another mental image—that rabbit hopping crazily in the grip of electricity. The thought of Cindy in that room—

He listened desperately and heard nothing. He told himself that all he had to do was go to the closet door and yank it open. But he was too afraid of what he might find. He went back to bed but didn't sleep for a long time.

In spite of how lousy he felt in the morning, breakfast tasted good. After a moment's hesitation, he followed his customary bowl of cornflakes with scrambled eggs. He was grumpily washing out the pan when Cindy came downstairs in her robe.

"Richard Morrison! You haven't eaten an egg for breakfast since Hector was a pup."

Morrison grunted. He considered *since Hector was a pup* to be one of Cindy's stupider sayings, on a par with *I should smile and kiss a pig.*

"Have you smoked yet?" she asked, pouring orange juice.

20

"No."

"You'll be back on them by noon," she proclaimed airily.

"Lot of goddamn help you are!" he rasped, rounding on her. "You and anyone else who doesn't smoke, you all think . . . ah, never mind."

He expected her to be angry, but she was looking at him with something like wonder. "You're really serious," she said. "You really are."

"You bet I am." *You'll never know* how *serious. I hope.*

"Poor baby," she said, going to him. "You look like death warmed over. But I'm very proud."

Morrison held her tightly.

Scenes from the life of Richard Morrison, October–November: Morrison and a crony from Larkin Studios at Jack Dempsey's bar. Crony offers a cigarette. Morrison grips his glass a little more tightly and says: *I'm quitting.* Crony laughs and says: *I give you a week.*

Morrison waiting for the morning train, looking over the top of the *Times* at a young man in a blue suit. He sees the young man almost every morning now, and sometimes at other places. At Onde's, where he is meeting a client. Looking at 45s in Sam Goody's, where Morrison is looking for a Sam Cooke album. Once in a foursome behind Morrison's group at the local golf course.

Morrison getting drunk at a party, wanting a cigarette — but not quite drunk enough to take one.

Morrison visiting his son, bringing him a large ball that squeaked when you squeezed it. His son's slobbering, delighted kiss. Somehow not as repulsive as before. Hugging his son tightly, realizing what Donatti and his colleagues had so cynically realized before him: love is the most pernicious drug of all. Let the romantics debate its existence. Pragmatists accept it and use it.

Morrison losing the physical compulsion to smoke little by little, but never quite losing the psychological craving, or the need to have something in his mouth—cough drops, Life Savers, a toothpick. Poor substitutes, all of them.

And finally, Morrison hung up in a colossal traffic jam in the Midtown Tunnel. Darkness. Horns blaring. Air stinking. Traffic hopelessly snarled. And suddenly, thumbing open the glove compartment and seeing the half-open pack of cigarettes in there. He looked at them for a moment, then snatched one and lit it with the dashboard lighter. If anything happens, it's Cindy's fault, he told himself defiantly. I told her to get rid of all the damn cigarettes.

The first drag made him cough smoke out furiously. The second made his eyes water. The third made him feel light-headed and swoony. It tastes awful, he thought.

And on the heels of that: My God, what am I doing?

Horns blatted impatiently behind him. Ahead, the traffic had begun to move again. He stubbed the cigarette out in the ashtray, opened both front windows, opened the vents, and then fanned the air helplessly like a kid who has just flushed his first butt down the john.

He joined the traffic flow jerkily and drove home.

"Cindy?" he called. "I'm home."

No answer.

"Cindy? Where are you, hon?"

The phone rang, and he pounced on it. "Hello? Cindy?"

"Hello, Mr. Morrison," Donatti said. He sounded pleasantly brisk and businesslike. "It seems we have a small business matter to attend to. Would five o'clock be convenient?"

"Have you got my wife?"

"Yes, indeed." Donatti chuckled indulgently.

"Look, let her go," Morrison babbled. "It won't happen again. It was a slip, just a slip, that's all. I only had three drags and for God's sake *it didn't even taste good*!''

"That's a shame. I'll count on you for five then, shall I?''

"Please,'' Morrison said, close to tears. "Please—''

He was speaking to a dead line.

At 5 P.M. the reception room was empty except for the secretary, who gave him a twinkly smile that ignored Morrison's pallor and disheveled appearance. "Mr. Donatti?'' she said into the intercom. "Mr. Morrison to see you.'' She nodded to Morrison. "Go right in.''

Donatti was waiting outside the unmarked room with a man who was wearing a SMILE sweatshirt and carrying a .38. He was built like an ape.

"Listen,'' Morrison said to Donatti. "We can work something out, can't we? I'll pay you. I'll—''

"Shaddap,'' the man in the SMILE sweatshirt said.

"It's good to see you,'' Donatti said. "Sorry it has to be under such adverse circumstances. Will you come with me? We'll make this as brief as possible. I can assure you your wife won't be hurt . . . this time.''

Morrison tensed himself to leap at Donatti.

"Come, come,'' Donatti said, looking annoyed. "If you do that, Junk here is going to pistol-whip you, and your wife is still going to get it. Now where's the percentage in that?''

"I hope you rot in hell,'' he told Donatti.

Donatti sighed. "If I had a nickel for every time someone expressed a similar sentiment, I could retire. Let it be a lesson to you, Mr. Morrison. When a romantic tries to do a good thing and fails, they give him a medal. When a pragmatist succeeds, they wish him in hell. Shall we go?''

Junk motioned with the pistol.

Morrison preceded them into the room. He felt numb.

23

The small green curtain had been pulled. Junk prodded him with the gun. This is what being a witness at the gas chamber must have been like, he thought.

He looked in. Cindy was there, looking around bewilderedly.

"Cindy!" Morrison called miserably. "Cindy, they—"

"She can't hear you," Donatti said. "One-way glass. Well, let's get it over with. It really was a very small slip. I believe thirty seconds should be enough. Junk?"

Junk pressed the button with one hand and kept the pistol jammed firmly into Morrison's back with the other.

It was the longest thirty seconds of his life.

When it was over, Donatti put a hand on Morrison's shoulder and said, "Are you going to throw up?"

"No," Morrison said weakly. His forehead was against the glass. His legs were jelly. "I don't think so." He turned around and saw that Junk was gone.

"Come with me," Donatti said.

"Where?" Morrison asked apathetically.

"I think you have a few things to explain, don't you?"

"How can I face her? How can I tell her that I . . . I . . ."

"I think you're going to be surprised," Donatti said.

The room was empty except for a sofa. Cindy was on it, sobbing helplessly.

"Cindy?" he said gently.

She looked up, her eyes magnified by tears. "Dick?" she whispered. "Dick? Oh . . . Oh God . . ." He held her tightly. "Two men," she said against his chest. "In the house and at first I thought they were burglars and then I thought they were going to rape me and then they took me someplace with a blindfold over my eyes and . . . and . . . oh it was *h-horrible*—"

"Shhh," he said. "Shhh."

"But why?" she asked, looking up at him. "Why would they—"

"Because of me," he said. "I have to tell you a story, Cindy—"

When he had finished, he was silent a moment and then said, "I suppose you hate me. I wouldn't blame you."

He was looking at the floor, and she took his face in both hands and turned it to hers. "No," she said. "I don't hate you."

He looked at her in mute surprise.

"It was worth it," she said. "God bless these people. They've let you out of prison."

"Do you mean that?"

"Yes," she said, and kissed him. "Can we go home now? I feel much better. Ever so much."

The phone rang one evening a week later, and when Morrison recognized Donatti's voice, he said. "Your boys have got it wrong. I haven't even been near a cigarette."

"We know that. We have a final matter to talk over. Can you stop by tomorrow afternoon?"

"Is it—"

"No, nothing serious. Bookkeeping really. By the way, congratulations on your promotion."

"How did you know about that?"

"We're keeping tabs," Donatti said noncommittally, and hung up.

When they entered the small room, Donatti said, "Don't look so nervous. No one's going to bite you. Step over here, please."

Morrison saw an ordinary bathroom scale. "Listen, I've gained a little weight, but—"

"Yes, seventy-three percent of our clients do. Step up, please."

Morrison did, and tipped the scales at one-seventy-four.

"Okay, fine. You can step off. How tall are you, Mr. Morrison?"

"Five-eleven."

"Okay, let's see." He pulled a small card laminated in plastic from his breast pocket. "Well, that's not too bad. I'm going to write you a prescription for some highly illegal diet pills. Use them sparingly and according to directions. And I'm going to set your maximum weight at . . . let's see . . ." He consulted the card again. "One-eighty-two, how does that sound? And since this is December first, I'll expect you the first of every month for a weigh-in. No problem if you can't make it, as long as you call in advance."

"And what happens if I go over one-eighty-two?"

Donatti smiled. "We'll send someone out to your house to cut off your wife's little finger," he said. "You can leave through this door, Mr. Morrison. Have a nice day."

Eight months later:

Morrison runs into the crony from the Larkin Studios at Dempsey's bar. Morrison is down to what Cindy proudly calls his fighting weight: one sixty-seven. He works out three times a week and looks as fit as a whipcord. The crony from Larkin, by comparison, looks like something the cat dragged in.

Crony: Lord, how'd you ever stop? I'm locked into this damn habit tighter than Tillie. The crony stubs his cigarette out with real revulsion and drains his scotch.

Morrison looks at him speculatively and then takes a small white business card out of his wallet. He puts it on the bar between them. You know, he says, these guys changed my life.

* * *

26

Twelve months later:
Morrison receives a bill in the mail. The bill says:

QUITTERS, INC.
237 East 46th Street
New York, N.Y. 10017

1 Treatment	$2500.00
Counselor (Victor Donatti)	$2500.00
Electricity	$ .50
TOTAL (Please pay this amount)	$5000.50

Those sons of bitches! he explodes. They charged me for the electricity they used to . . . to . . .
Just pay it, she says, and kisses him.

Twenty months later:
Quite by accident, Morrison and his wife meet the Jimmy McCanns at the Helen Hayes Theatre. Introductions are made all around. Jimmy looks as good, if not better than he did on that day in the airport terminal so long ago. Morrison has never met his wife. She is pretty in the radiant way plain girls sometimes have when they are very, very happy.

She offers her hand and Morrison shakes it. There is something odd about her grip, and halfway through the second act, he realizes what it was. The little finger on her right hand is missing.

You Can't Be Too Careful

·

Ruth Rendell

Londoner Ruth Rendell has won numerous awards for her crime fiction, including two Best Short Story Edgars from the Mystery Writers of America and two best novel awards (a Current Crime Silver Cup and a Gold Dagger) from the British Crime Writers Association. Whether she is writing about her series character, Inspector Wexford of the village of Kingsmarkham (Speaker of Mandarin, An Unkindness of Ravens), producing such polished nonseries suspense novels as Master of the Moor, or creating expert short stories (as can be found in The Fever Tree, The Girl Friend, and other collections), she is one of the genre's most respected talents. "You Can't Be Too Careful" is among the best—and most chilling—of her shorter works.

Della Galway went out with a man for the first (and almost the last) time on her nineteenth birthday. He parked his car, and as they were going into the restaurant she asked him if he had locked all the doors and the boot. When he turned back and said, yes, he'd better do that, she asked him why he didn't have a burglar-proof locking device on the steering wheel.

Her parents had brought her up to be cautious. When she left that happy home in that safe little provincial town, she took her parents' notions with her to London. At first she could only afford the rent of a single room. It upset her that the other tenants often came in late at night and left the front door on the latch. Although her room was at the top of the house and she had nothing worth stealing, she lay in bed sweating with fear. At work it was just the same. Nobody bothered about security measures. Della was always the last to leave, and sometimes she went back two or three times to check that all the office doors and the outer door were shut.

The personnel officer suggested she see a psychiatrist.

Della was very ambitious. She had an economics degree and a business studies diploma, and had come out top at the end of her secretarial course. She knew a psychiatrist would find something wrong with her—they had to earn their money like everyone else—and long sessions of treatment would follow, which wouldn't help her toward her goal, that of becoming the company's first woman director. They always held that sort of thing against you.

"That won't be necessary," she said in her brisk way. "It was the firm's property I was worried about. If they like to risk losing their valuable equipment, that's their look-out."

She stopped going back to check the doors—it didn't prey on her mind much as her own safety wasn't involved—and three weeks later two men broke in, stole all the electric typewriters, and damaged the computer beyond repair. It proved her right, but she didn't say so. The threat of the psychiatrist had frightened her so much that she never again aired her burglar obsession at work.

When she got a promotion and a salary raise, she decided to get a flat of her own. The landlady was a woman after her own heart. Mrs. Swanson liked Della from the first and explained to her, as to a kindred spirit, the security arrangements.

"This is a very nice neighborhood, Miss Galway, but

the crime rate in London is rising all the time, and I always say you can't be too careful.''

Della said she couldn't agree more.

"So I always keep this side gate bolted on the inside. The back door into this little yard must also be kept locked and bolted. The bathroom window looks out into the garden, you see, so I like the garden door and the bathroom door to be locked at night, too.''

"Very wise,'' said Della, noting that the window in the bed-sitting room had screws fixed to its sashes, which prevented its being opened more than six inches. "What did you say the rent was?''

"Twenty pounds a week.'' Mrs. Swanson was a landlady first, and a kindred spirit second, so when Della hesitated, she said, "It's a garden flat, completely self-contained and you've got your own phone. I shan't have any trouble in letting it. I've got someone else coming to view it at two.''

Della stopped hesitating. She moved in at the end of the week, having supplied Mrs. Swanson with references and assured her she was quiet, prudent as to locks and bolts, and not inclined to have "unauthorized'' people to stay overnight. By unauthorized people, Mrs. Swanson meant men. Since the episode over the car on her nineteenth birthday, Della had entered tentatively upon friendships with men, but no man had ever taken her out more than twice and none had ever got as far as to kiss her. She didn't know why this was, as she had always been polite and pleasant, insisting on paying her share, careful to carry her own coat, handbag, and parcels so as to give her escort no trouble, ever watchful of his wallet and keys, offering to have the theatre tickets in her own safe-keeping, and anxious not to keep him out too late. That one after another men dropped her worried her very little. No spark of sexual feeling had ever troubled her, and the idea of sharing her orderly, routine-driven life with a man—untidy, feckless, casual creatures as they all, with the exception of her father, seemed to be—was a daunting one. She meant to get to the top on her own. One day perhaps, when she was about thirty-five and with a high-powered lady executive's salary, then if some like-minded, quiet, and prudent man came along. . . . In the meantime, Mrs. Swanson had no need to worry.

Della was very happy with her flat. It was utterly quiet, a little sanctum tucked at the back of the house. She never heard a sound from her neighbors in the other parts of the house and they, of course, never heard a sound from her. She encountered them occasionally when crossing from her own front door to the front door of the house. They were mouselike people who scuttled off to their holes with no more than a nod and a "good evening." This was as it should be. The flat, too, was entirely as it should be.

The bed-sitter looked just like a living room by day, for the bed was let down from a curtained recess in the wall only at night. Its window overlooked the yard, which Della never used. She never unbolted the side gate or the back door or, needless to say, attempted to undo the screws and open the window more than six inches.

Every evening, when she had washed the dishes and wiped down every surface in the immaculate, well-fitted kitchen, had her bath, made her bedtime drink, and let the bed down from the wall, she went on her security rounds just as her father did at home. First, she unlocked and unbolted the back door and crossed the yard to check that the side gate was securely fastened. It always was, as no one ever touched it, but Della liked to make absolutely sure, and sometimes went back several times in case her eyes had deceived her. Then she bolted and locked the back door, the garden door, and the bathroom door. All these doors opened out of a small room, about ten feet square—Mrs. Swanson called it the garden room—which in its turn could be locked off by yet another door from the kitchen. Della locked it. She rather regretted she couldn't lock the door that led from the kitchen into the bed-sitting room, but, owing to some oversight on Mrs. Swanson's part, there was no lock on it. However, her own front door in the bed-sitter itself was locked, of course, on the Yale. Finally, before getting into bed, she bolted the front door.

Then she was safe. Though she sometimes got up once or twice more to make assurance trebly sure, she generally settled down at this point into blissful sleep, certain that even the most accomplished of burglars couldn't break in.

There was only one drawback—the rent.

"The flat," said Mrs. Swanson, "is really intended for two people. A married couple had it before you, and before that two ladies shared it."

"I couldn't share my bed," said Della with a shudder, "or, come to that, my room."

"If you found a nice friend to share, I wouldn't object to putting up a single bed in the garden room. Then your friend could come and go by the side gate, provided you were prepared to *promise* me it would always be bolted at night."

Della wasn't going to advertise for a flatmate. You couldn't be too careful. Yet she had to find someone if she was going to afford any new winter clothes, not to mention heating the place. It would have to be the right person, someone to fill all her own exacting requirements as well as satisfy Mrs. Swanson. . . .

"Ooh, it's lovely!" said Rosamund Vine. "It's so quiet and clean. And you've got a garden! You should see the dump I've been living in. It was overrun with mice."

"You don't get mice," said Della repressively, "unless you leave food about."

"I won't do that. I'll be ever so careful. I'll go halves with the rent and I'll have the key to the back door, shall I? That way I won't disturb you if I come in late at night."

"I hope you won't come in late at night," said Della. "Mrs. Swanson's very particular about that sort of thing."

"Don't worry." Rosamund sounded rather bitter. "I've nothing and no one to keep me out late. Anyway, the last bus passes the end of the road at a quarter of twelve."

Della pushed aside her misgivings, and Mrs. Swanson, interviewing Rosamund, appeared to have none. She made a point of explaining the safety precautions, to which Rosamund listened meekly and with earnest nods of her head. Della was glad this duty hadn't fallen on her, as she didn't want Rosamund to tell exaggerated tales about her at work. So much the better if she could put it all on Mrs. Swanson.

Rosamund Vine had been chosen with the care Della devoted to every choice she made. It had taken three weeks of observation and keeping her ears open to select her. It wouldn't do to find someone on too low a salary or, on the other hand, someone with too lofty a position in the company. She didn't like the idea of a spectacularly good-looking girl, for such led hectic lives, or too clever a girl, for such might involve her in tiresome arguments. An elegant girl would fill the cupboards with clothes and the bathroom with cosmetics. A gifted girl would bring in musical instruments or looms or paints or trunks full of books. Only Rosamund, of all the candidates, qualified. She was small and quiet and prettyish, a secretary (though not Della's secretary), the daughter of a clergyman who, by coincidence, had been at the same university at the same time as Della's father. Della, who had much the same attitude as Victorian employers had to their maids' "followers," noted that she had never heard her speak of a boyfriend or overheard any cloak-room gossip as to Rosamund's love life.

The two girls settled down happily together. They seldom went out in the evenings. Della always went to bed at eleven sharp and would have relegated Rosamund to her own room at this point but for one small difficulty. With Rosamund in the garden room—necessarily sitting on her bed as there was nowhere else to sit—it wasn't possible for Della to make her security rounds. Only once had she tried doing it with Rosamund looking on.

"Goodness," Rosamund had said, "this place is like Fort Knox. All those keys and bolts! What are you so scared of?"

"Mrs. Swanson likes to have the place locked up," said Della, but the next night she made hot drinks for the two of them and sent Rosamund to wait for her in the bed-sitter before creeping out into the yard for a secret check-up.

When she came back, Rosamund was examining her bedside table. "Why do you put everything in order like that, Della? Your book at right angles to the table and your cigarette packet at right angles to your book, and, look, your ashtray's exactly an inch from the lamp as if you measured it out."

"Because I'm a naturally tidy person."

"I do think it's funny your smoking. I never would have guessed you smoked till I came to live here. It doesn't sort of seem in character. And your glass of water. Do you want to drink water in the night?"

"Not always," Della said patiently. "But I might want to, and I shouldn't want to have to get up and fetch it, should I?"

Rosamund's questions didn't displease her. It showed that the girl wanted to learn the right way to do things. Della taught her that a room must be dusted every day, the fridge defrosted once a week, the table laid for breakfast before they went to bed, all the windows closed, and the catches fastened. She drew Rosamund out as to the places she had previously lived in with a view to contrasting past squalor with present comfort, and she received a shock when Rosamund made it plain that in some of those rooms, attics, converted garages, she had lived with a man. Della made no comment but froze slightly. And Rosamund, thank goodness, seemed to understand her disapproval and didn't go into details. But soon after that she began going out in the evenings.

Della didn't want to know where she was going or with whom. She had plenty to occupy her own evenings, what with the work she brought home, her housework, washing and ironing, her twice-weekly letter to her mother and father, and the commercial Spanish she was teaching herself from gramophone records. It was rather a relief not to have Rosamund fluttering about. Besides, she could do her security rounds in peace. Not, of course, that she could check up on the side gate till Rosamund came in. Necessarily, it had to remain unbolted, and the back door to which Rosamund had the key, unlocked. But always by ten to twelve at the latest she'd hear the side gate open and close and hear Rosamund pause to draw the bolts. Then her feet tiptoeing across the yard, then the back door unlocked, shut, locked. After that, Della could sleep in peace.

The first problem arose when Rosamund came in one night and didn't bolt the gate after her. Della listened carefully in the dark, but she was positive those bolts had not been drawn. Even if the back door was locked, it was unthinkable to leave that side gate on nothing all night but its flimsy latch. She put on her dressing gown and went through the kitchen into the garden room. Rosamund was already in bed, her clothes flung about on the coverlet. Della picked them up and folded them. She was coming back from the yard, having fastened those bolts, when Rosamund sat up and said, "What's the matter? Can't you sleep?"

"Mrs. Swanson," said Della with a light indulgent laugh, "wouldn't be able to sleep if she knew you'd left that side gate unbolted."

"Did I? Honestly, Della, I don't know what I'm doing half the time. I can't think of anyone but Chris. He's the most marvelous person and I do think he's just as mad about me as I am about him. I feel as if he's changed my whole life."

Della let her spend nearly all the following evening describing the marvelous Chris, how brilliant he was—though at present unable to get a job fitting his talents—how amusing, how highly educated—though so poor as to be reduced to borrowing a friend's room while that friend was away. She listened and smiled and made appropriate remarks, but she wondered when she had last been so bored. Every time she got up to try and play one of her Spanish records, Rosamund was off again on another facet of Chris's dazzling personality, until at last Della had to say she had a headache and would Rosamund mind leaving her on her own for a bit?

"Anyway, you'll see him tomorrow. I've asked him for a meal."

Unluckily, this happened to be the evening Della was going to supper with her aunt on the other side of London. They had evidently enjoyed themselves, judging by the mess in the kitchen, Della thought when she got home. There were few things she disliked more than wet dishes left to drain. Rosamund was asleep. Della crept out into the yard and checked that the bolts were fastened.

"I heard you wandering about ever so late," said Rosamund in the morning. "Were you upset about anything?"

"Certainly not. I simply found it rather hard to get to sleep because it was past my normal time."

"Aren't you funny?" said Rosamund, and she giggled.

The next night she missed the last bus.

Della had passed a pleasant evening, studying firstly the firm's annual report, then doing a Spanish exercise. By eleven she was in bed, reading the memoirs of a woman company chairman. Her bedside light went off at half-past and she lay in the dark waiting for the sound of the side gate.

Her clock had luminous hands, and when they passed ten to twelve she began to feel a nasty, tingly, jumping sensation all over her body. She put on the light, switched it off immediately. She didn't want Rosamund bursting in with all her silly questions and comments. But Rosamund didn't burst in, and the hands of the clock closed together on midnight. There was no doubt about it. The last bus had gone and Rosamund hadn't been on it.

Well, the silly girl needn't think she was going to stand this sort of thing. She'd bolt that side gate herself and Rosamund could stay out in the street all night. Of course, she might ring the front doorbell, she was silly and inconsiderate enough to do that, but it couldn't be helped. Della would far rather be awakened at one or two o'clock than lie there knowing that side gate was open for anyone to come in. She put on her dressing gown and made her way through the spotless kitchen to the garden room. Rosamund had hung a silly sort of curtain over the back door, not a curtain really but a rather dirty Indian bedspread. Della

37

lifted it distastefully—and then she realized. She couldn't bolt the side gate because the back door into the yard was locked and Rosamund had the key.

A practical person like herself wasn't going to be done that way. She'd go out by the front door, walk round to the side entrance and—but, no, that wouldn't work either. If she opened the gate and bolted it on the inside, she'd simply find herself bolted inside the yard. The only thing was to climb out of the window. She tried desperately to undo the window screws, but they had seized up from years of disuse and she couldn't shift them. Trembling now, she sat down on the edge of her bed and lit a cigarette. For the first time in her life she was in an insecure place by night, alone in a London flat, with nothing to separate her from hordes of rapacious burglars but a feeble back door lock that any tyro of a thief could pick open in five minutes.

How criminally careless of Mrs. Swanson not to have provided the door between the bed-sitter and the kitchen with a lock! There was no heavy piece of furniture she could place against the door. The phone was by her bed, of course. But if she heard a sound and dialed for the police, was there a chance of their getting there before she was murdered and the place ransacked?

What Mrs. Swanson *had* provided was one of the most fearsome-looking bread knives Della had ever seen. She fetched it from the kitchen and put it under her pillow. Its presence made her feel slightly safer, but suppose she didn't wake up when the man came in, suppose . . . ? That was ridiculous, she wouldn't sleep at all. Exhausted, shaken, feeling physically sick, she crawled under the bedclothes and, after concentrated thought, put the light out. Perhaps, if there was no light on, he would go past her, not know she was there, make his way into the main part of the house, and if by then she hadn't actually died of fright . . .

At twenty minutes past one, when she had reached the point of deciding to phone for a car to take her to a hotel, the side gate clicked and Rosamund entered the yard. Della fell back against the pillows with a relief so tremendous that she couldn't even bother to go out and check the bolts. So what if it wasn't bolted? The man would have to pass Rosamund first, kill her first. Della found she didn't care at all about what might happen to Rosamund, only about her own safety.

She sneaked out at half past six to put the knife back, and she was sullenly eating her breakfast, the flat immaculate, when Rosamund appeared at eight.

"I missed the last bus. I had to get a taxi."

"You could have phoned."

"Goodness, you sound just like my mother. It was bad enough having to get up and . . ." Rosamund blushed and put her hand over her mouth. "I mean, go *out* and get that taxi and. . . . Well, I wasn't all that late," she muttered.

Her little slip of the tongue hadn't been lost on Della. But she was too tired to make any rejoinder beyond saying that Mrs. Swanson would be very annoyed if she knew, and would Rosamund give her fair warning next time she intended to be late? Rosamund said when they met again that evening that she couldn't give her fair warning as she could never be sure herself. Della said no more. What, anyway, would be the use of knowing what time Rosamund was coming in when she couldn't bolt the gate?

Three mornings later her temper flared.

On two of the intervening nights Rosamund had missed the last bus. The funny thing was that she didn't look at all tired or jaded, while Della was worn out. For three hours on the previous night she had lain stiffly clutching the bread knife while the old house creaked about her and the side gate rattled in the wind.

"I don't know why you bother to come home at all."

"Won't you mind if I don't?"

"Not a bit. Do as you like."

Stealthily, before Rosamund left the flat by the front door, Della slipped out and bolted the gate. Rosamund, of course (being utterly imprudent), didn't check the gate before she locked the back door. Della fell into a heavy sleep at ten o'clock, to be awakened just after two by a thudding on the side gate followed by a frenzied ringing of the front doorbell.

"You locked me out!" Rosamund sobbed. "Even my mother never did that. I was locked out in the street and I'm frozen. What have I done to you that you treat me like that?"

"You said you weren't coming home."

"I wasn't going to, but we went out and Chris forgot his key. He's had to sleep at a friend's place. I wish I'd gone there, too!"

They were evidently two of a kind. Well suited, Della thought. Although it was nearly half past two in the morning this seemed the best moment to have things out. She addressed Rosamund in her precise, schoolmistressy voice.

"I think we'll have to make other arrangements, Rosamund. Your ways aren't my ways, and we don't really get on, do we? You can stay here till you find somewhere else, but I'd like to start looking round straightaway."

"But what have I *done*? I haven't made a noise or had my friends here. I haven't even used your phone, not once. Honestly, Della, I've done my best to keep the place clean and tidy, and it's nearly killed me!"

40

"I've explained what I mean. We're not the same kind of people."

"I'll go on Saturday. I'll go to my mother—it won't be any worse, God knows—and then maybe Chris and I . . ."

"You'd better go to bed now," Della said coldly, but she couldn't get any sleep herself. She was wondering how she had been such a bad judge of character, and wondering too what she was going to do about the rent. Find someone else, of course. An older woman perhaps, a widow or a middle-aged spinster. . . .

What she was determined not to do was reveal to Rosamund, at this late stage, her anxiety about the side gate. If anything remained to comfort her, it was the knowledge that Rosamund thought her strong, mature, and sensible. But not revealing it brought her an almost unbearable agony. For Rosamund seemed to think the very sight of her would be an embarrassment to Della. Each evening she was gone from the flat before Della got home, and each time she had gone out leaving the side gate unbolted and the back door locked. Della had no way of knowing whether she would come in on the last bus or get a taxi or be seen home in the small hours by Chris. She didn't know whether Chris lived near or far away, and now she wished she had listened more closely to Rosamund's confidences and asked a few questions of her own. Instead, she had only thought with a shudder how nasty it must be to have to sleep with a man, and had wondered if she would ever bring herself to face the prospect.

Each night she took the bread knife to bed with her, confirmed in her conviction that she wasn't being unreasonable when one of the mouselike people whom she met in the hall told her the house next door had been broken into and its old woman occupant knocked on the head. Rosamund came in once at one, once at half past two, and once she didn't come in at all. Della got great bags under

41

her eyes and her skin looked gray. She fell asleep over her desk at work, while a bright-eyed, vivacious Rosamund regaled her friends in the cloakroom about the joys of her relationship with Chris.

But now there was only one more night to go. . . .

Rosamund had left a note to say she wouldn't be home. She'd see Della on the following evening when she collected her cases to take them to her mother. But she'd left the side gate unbolted. Della seriously considered bolting it and then climbing back over it into the side entrance, but it was too high and smooth for her to climb and there wasn't a ladder. Nothing for it but to begin her vigil with the cigarettes, the glass of water, the phone, and the bread knife. It ought to have been easier, this last night, just because it was the last. Instead, it was worse than any of the others. She lay in the dark, thinking of the old woman next door, of the house that was precisely the same as the one next door, and of the intruder who now knew the best and simplest way in. She tried to think of something else, anything else, but the strongest instinct of all overrode all her feeble attempts to concentrate on tomorrow, on work, on ambition, on the freedom and peace of tomorrow, when that gate would be fastened for good, never again to be opened.

Rosamund had said she wouldn't be in. But you couldn't rely on a word she said. Della wasn't, therefore, surprised (though she was overwhelmingly relieved) to hear the gate click just before two. Sighing with a kind of ecstasy—for tomorrow had come—she listened for the sound of the bolts being drawn across. The sound didn't come. Well, that was a small thing. She'd fasten the bolts herself when Rosamund was in bed. She heard footsteps moving very softly, and then the back door was unlocked. Rosamund took a longer time than usual about unlocking it, but maybe she was tired or drunk or heaven knew what.

Silence.

Then the back door creaked and made rattling sounds as if Rosamund hadn't bothered to relock it. Wearily, Della hoisted herself out of bed and slipped her dressing gown round her. As she did so, the kitchen light came on. The light showed round the edges of the old door in a brilliant phosphorescent rectangle. That wasn't like Rosamund, who never went into the kitchen, who fell immediately into bed without even bothering to wash her face. A long shiver ran through Della. Her body taut but trembling, she listened. Footsteps were crossing the kitchen floor and the fridge door was opened. She heard the sounds of fumbling in cupboards, a drawer was opened, and silver rattled. She wanted to call out, "Rosamund, Rosamund, is that you?" but she had no voice. Her mouth was dry and her voice had gone. Something occurred to her that had never struck her before. It struck her with a great thrust of terror. How would she know, how had she ever known, whether it was Rosamund or another who entered the flat by the side gate and the frail back door?

Then there came a cough.

It was a slight cough, the sound of someone clearing his throat, but it was unmistakably *his* throat. There was a man in the kitchen.

Della forgot the phone. She remembered—though she had scarcely for a moment forgotten her—the old woman next door. Blind terror thrust her to her feet, plunged her hand under the pillow for the knife. She opened the kitchen door, and he was there, a tall man, young and strong, standing right there on the threshold with Mrs. Swanson's silver in one hand and Mrs. Swanson's heavy iron pan in the other. Della didn't hesitate. She struck hard with the knife, struck again and again until the bright blood flew across the white walls and the clean ironing and the table neatly laid for breakfast.

* * *

The policeman was very nice to Rosamund Vine. He called her by her christian name and gave her a cup of coffee. She drank the coffee, though she didn't really want it as she had had a cup at the hospital when they told her Chris was dead.

"Tell me about last night, will you, Rosamund?"

"I'd been out with my boyfriend—Chris—Chris Maitland. He'd forgotten his key and he hadn't anywhere to sleep, so I said to come back with me. He was going to leave early in the morning before she—before Della was up. We were going to be very careful about that. And we were terribly quiet. We crept in at about two."

"You didn't call out?"

"No, we thought she was asleep. That's why we didn't speak to each other, not even in whispers. But she must have heard us." Her voice broke a little. "I went straight to bed. Chris was hungry. I said if he was as quiet as a mouse he could get himself something from the fridge, and I told him where the knives and forks and plates were. The next thing I heard this ghastly scream and I ran out and—and Chris was. . . . There was blood everywhere. . . ."

The policeman waited until she was calmer.

"Why do you think she attacked him with a knife?" he asked.

"I don't know.

"I think you do, Rosamund."

"Perhaps I do." Rosamund looked down. "She didn't like me going out."

"Because she was afraid of being there alone?"

"Della Galway," said Rosamund, "wasn't afraid of anything. Mrs. Swanson was nervous about burglars, but Della wasn't. Everyone in the house knew about the woman next door getting coshed, and they were all nervous. Except Della. She didn't even mention it to me, and she must have known.''

"So she didn't think Chris was a burglar?''

"Of course she didn't.'' Rosamund started to cry. "She saw a man—my man. She couldn't get one of her own. Every time I tried to talk about him she went all cold and standoffish. She heard us come in last night and she understood and—and it sent her over the edge. It drove her crazy. I'd heard they wanted her to see a psychiatrist at work, and now I know why.''

The policeman shivered a little, in spite of his long experience. Fear of burglars he could understand, but this. . . . "She'll see one now,'' he said, and then he sent the weeping girl home to her mother.

People Who Kill

.

Loren D. Estleman

Loren D. Estleman is one of today's best practitioners of the so-called hard-boiled crime story. His novels featuring Detroit private eye Amos Walker—among them, The Glass Highway, Sugartown, Every Brilliant Eye—are hard-bitten, uncompromising studies of life and death on the mean streets of urban America. "People Who Kill," an Amos Walker story published here for the first time, is a somewhat different but no less gritty tale about those same mean streets. The versatile and prolific Estleman has also published three novels—the latest, Any Man's Death (1986)—about a former Mob hit man named Macklin, and a number of Westerns, one of which, Aces and Eights, won a Western Writers of America Spur as Best Novel of 1981.

"People who kill are different from you and me."

The guy doing the talking was a professor at the University of Detroit, one of the new breed with parlor hair pushed back behind his ears, a brown corduroy jacket, and a skinny tie like you see in early Dean Martin movies without Jerry Lewis. He had a gunfighter's droopy mustache that kept getting in his wine and a pair of those glasses that react to light in steel rims. He was a little drunk, but then so was everyone else in the party except me. I was working.

We were sitting at a big round table inside the red plush

candy box of a downtown club; the professor and his trim
wife and their guests, a former U.S. congressman and *his*
wife, a lean woman in her fifties with very blond hair and
no flesh on her face, and me. The former congressman, a
large, smiling bald man, was guest lecturing at the university. I was there to keep an eye on the string of matched
pearls his wife had wound around her skinny neck. My
specialty as a private investigator is tracing missing persons, but the guard work would look good on my résumé,
and anyway my bank account could use the transfusion.

The professor's trim wife laughed quietly. The laugh
fluttered at the hollow of her throat and her teeth showed
liquid white against her red lipstick. I was watching her
whenever I wasn't watching the other woman's pearls.
"How'd we get on the subject of killing?" asked the professor's wife.

"Sorry. I was just thinking about this fellow in tonight's
News, who shot and killed the kid breaking into his house.
The paper said the guy was popular in his neighborhood
and had no criminal record. But he's old enough to be a
veteran of World War II, and I'll lay you any odd that's
where he was trained to kill. There are two kinds of killers,
those who are born and those who undergo rigorous conditioning to overcome their natural inclination toward non-
violence. Which is why I'm saying that people who kill
aren't like you and me."

"I'm not so sure," put in the congressman's wife. "If
I ever found myself in this man's position, all alone late at
night with an intruder trying to get in, I wouldn't hesitate
to use a gun if I had one. The instinct for self-preservation
runs deep."

The congressman said, "You surprise me, Ellen. I spent
two terms fighting for stiffer gun laws."

The professor's smile was a paper cut over his glass.
"You might want to pull the trigger, but wanting to and

pulling it aren't the same. All that has been bred out of us. Assuming it was there to begin with."

"Well, I find the whole thing repugnant," said his wife. But her eyes glittered.

"Why are we arguing when we have an expert right here?" The congressman turned his beaming politician's face on me. "What about it, Amos? Are killers an aberration or part of the natural order?"

"Walker's an example on my side," said the professor. "He fought in Vietnam and has had to do with guns ever since."

His wife patted his hand. "Let him talk, Carl."

"I'm just the help."

"Don't be difficult," the congressman insisted. "With all respect to Carl, you're the only one here whose opinion counts in this case."

"I know of someone," I said, "but the story takes time."

"They don't lock up here until two," said the professor.

They were all watching me. I moved a shoulder and got started.

"He was crowding sixty when this happened, a chunky little old guy with a lot of rumpled white hair. They called him Whitey back on Jefferson where he hung out in his old black overcoat, but his real name was Walter and he'd been married and raised a girl. The wife died and the girl moved out and never came back. He was deaf in one ear, by the way, a thing that kept him out of the military during the war, so he had no combat training. He was a retired cabinetmaker living on a small pension in an apartment house on Michigan until it went condo, and then he relocated in a condemned hotel on Jefferson. It came down later to make room for the Renaissance Center. Dillinger had stayed there once when Illinois got too hot, but the place had to go so they could put up another hotel where no one stayed.

"Anyway, Whitcy checked out the rooms on the ground floor where he wouldn't have to climb any stairs, but derelicts and rats had claimed all those, and the only vacancies on the second were on the side facing the river and the wind from Windsor came cold as a ghost's breath through the broken panes. He settled finally for a room on the third with plywood over the window and empties insulating it on both sides. He had some blankets and a kerosene heater and there was a squirrel-chewed mattress on the floor, and as long as his monthly check kept coming care of General Delivery, he could afford to eat. A lot of old people with nice homes and relatives to look after them live worse.

"Whitey was a night person. Thirty years on the graveyard shift are hard to shake, and with no light to read by and nothing to read even if he had light, he started taking long walks after midnight, when the streets are safe only for poor people and muggers. His rounds usually took him behind furniture stores, where he rescued items he could use from the dumpsters: a chair with a broken rung, a table missing a leg, part of a bed frame—things he could carry up to his room and fix up for his own use, with worn-out tools he got from the same place, and sometimes sell back to the stores where he got them. This is how he spent his days when he wasn't sleeping. In four months of these nighttime scrounges, he was stopped only once, by a bored cop who wanted to know what he was doing carrying a rickety bookcase through the streets at one thirty in the morning. The cop was probably too bored to hear the answer, and let him go. Being old and poor in this town is as good as being invisible.

"When you make a habit of being out at that hour, you tend to see a lot worth keeping to yourself, and Whitey soon learned the wisdom of keeping his feet moving and his eyes straight ahead. He never walked faster than when he was crossing the mouth of an alley or cutting through a sheltered parking lot. Not seeing things requires special skill, because you not only have to not see something, but also *look* like you didn't see it in case someone sees you not seeing it. Am I making sense?'' I looked at the professor.

"A great deal,'' he said. "But then I don't teach English.''

I went on. "This night I'm talking about, Whitey dropped the ball. It was January, the wind chill was knocking around twenty below, and to avoid the icy air blasting between two buildings he ducked into an underground garage, carrying an end table with a wrinkled veneer, and found himself looking at four guys grunting and cursing between a pair of parked cars. One guy had another's arms pinned behind his back and the other two were putting it to the pinned guy with their fists and a galvanized pipe. Moonlight from the entrance replayed the whole thing in shadows on the concrete wall.

"Whitey couldn't just keep going without walking right past them, and not seeing something is difficult under those circumstances. He turned back the way he came, but forgot he was carrying the end table and hung up one of its legs on someone's bumper. He lost his grip and the table hit the floor with nothing near the racket a truck makes spilling off a haulaway trailer. Somebody yelled and Whitey took off running. Behind him the table made some more noise and someone cursed, but he didn't look back to see who had stumbled over it. He hit the street on the fly, galloped around the corner of the building the garage was under, clattered through an alley, vaulted a construction sawhorse, and half slid, half rolled down a hill being gouged out for another underground garage for guys like the ones chasing him to beat up other guys in. He landed running and didn't stop until his lungs tasted bloody in his throat. Remember that he was almost sixty and that he hadn't run more than half a block to catch a DSR bus since high school. When his heart slowed to twice its normal rate and he didn't hear footsteps behind him with his good ear, he wound his way back to his condemned hotel, hugging shadows and looking in every direction but up and down, contrary to his normal rules for survival. He stayed in his room all the next day and didn't go out the night after that. He didn't even leave to eat.

"He couldn't afford a daily paper and, of course, he didn't own a television set, so he had no way of knowing that the guy he had seen being worked over in the garage died the following morning at Detroit Receiving without regaining consciousness, or that the cops were questioning a local numbers chief that the dead guy had owed eight hundred dollars to. Seems the muscle that the chief had sent to remind him of his obligation had gotten a little too enthusiastic with the pipe. So about the time Whitey was figuring it was safe to venture out, the crew was busy canvasing the winos and bag ladies downtown for a line on the only witness to their murder.

"About dusk on his second day indoors, Whitey heard loud voices and put his eye to the crack between the plywood and his window frame in time to see the three guys entering the building. The pipe man was a big black with a lot of jaw and an arrest record for ADW going back to before the riots, but only one conviction. His name was Leon something. His partners were a dead-eyed, long-haired, nineteen-year-old white named Chick and another black about the same age everyone called Sugar Ray on account of the scar tissue over his eyes, only he didn't get that in the ring but from his old man, who he put in the hospital when he got too big to knock down. What the cops call a salt-and-pepper team. Chick was the only one who had a gun, Sugar Ray preferring his fists and Leon his pipe.

It was Chick who had been holding the victim that night in the garage.

"Another thing Whitey didn't know was that while the trio had succeeded in bribing and threatening his address out of Detroit's walking wounded, they still didn't know what room he was staying in. So Sugar Ray questioned the bums and degenerates on the ground floor, Chick got to work searching the building from the bottom up, and Leon climbed the stairs to the sixth floor and started working his way down with pipe in hand. Meanwhile, Whitey, thinking they were heading straight for his room, hid out in the vacant hole next door, hoping they'd think he was out and would go away. He crouched in a littered corner with his overcoat drawn over his head to shut out the cold and the noise of shouts and blows from downstairs.

"Chick was ten minutes kicking in doors on the first and second levels and pointing his gun at a lot of mold and cracked plaster. Whitey heard him mounting the squawking steps to his floor, heard more wood splintering as Chick zigzagged down the hall from room to room shattering locks that hadn't worked in years. Realizing his mistake, the old man backed into a closet and drew the door shut. When Chick got to Whitey's quarters he noticed the signs of occupancy and spent a little more time searching that one. He came up empty, but he'd seen the tools and the repaired furniture and must have remembered the abandoned table in the garage and known he was getting close. He poked his head through the empty doorway of the room opposite Whitey's, then strode kitty-corner to the next one down. That was the one Whitey was hiding in.

"He reared back and threw a heel at the lock, but the door had a broken latch and when it swung open he had to wrestle with his momentum to keep his face off the floor. Just then he caught a movement out of the corner of his right eye. He spun and fired. Glass collapsed and something made a shrill boinging noise, and he felt a blow to his ribs and his feet were snatched out from under him and he landed hard on his chest, almost letting go of the gun. He felt moist warmth under him and he must have known at that moment that he'd been shot.

"What he probably never knew was that the movement he'd fired at was his own reflection in the bathroom mirror to the right of the door, and that his bullet had struck the tiles behind the mirror at an angle, ricocheted, skidded off the adjacent wall, and struck him. In the process the soft-nosed slug had changed its shape a couple of times, and that, together with its wobbling trajectory, had made a hole in him the size of a baby's fist, through which his blood was pumping at the rate of about a quart every three minutes. There are five quarts of blood in the body of a full-grown man, and, well, you figure it out.

"Whitey, of course, had no idea what was going on. He thought he was the one being shot at, and since there seemed no good reason to stay where he was, he piled out through the closet door and, seeing two legs sticking out of the open bathroom door, leaped over them and out the exit. He had a survivor's instinct for not stopping to ask himself questions he had no time to answer.

"By this time, having found the other tenants too far gone on drugs and rotgut to remember who Whitey was, much less where, Sugar Ray had taken up guard duty at the foot of the stairs. He heard the shot and thinking that Chick had got his man, headed on up to view the remains. He was rounding the second flight when he met Whitey coming down the third.

"The old man did an about-face while Sugar Ray was still trying to piece together what this meant in terms of Chick, and bounded back the other way, intending to go up past the third floor. But then he heard heavy footsteps farther up and ran back down his own hallway instead.

Sugar Ray, assimilated now, was taking the flight three steps at a time with his fists balled.''

I stopped to light a cigarette and looked around at my audience. "I know what you're thinking. It would've been poetic if Sugar Ray and Leon the Pipe had met on that third-floor landing and seen to each other. But they weren't armed for that, and anyway Leon was stalled somewhere up above, probably trying to figure out at what level the shot had been fired.

"Getting back to Sugar Ray. He reached the hallway in time to see Whitey, the dark tail of his overcoat flying behind him, leap into the shadows at the far end. It was getting dark now. The slugger had been wondering if the other man had a gun, but the fact that he was running instead of shooting reassured him and he thundered down that echoing old corridor as fast as his long legs would take him. At the end he ran out of floor and plunged kiyoodling down through three stories of dark cold nothing.

"Whitey had stopped just short of the empty elevator shaft he knew was there and flattened himself against the wall while Sugar Ray hurtled past and down, landing on his feet with the grace of a born athlete and driving his knees into his chin hard enough to snap his neck like a dry stick. For a long time after that, no doctor thought he would live, but you can visit him now at the State Forensics Center in Ypsilanti, where they feed him liquids and turn him over from time to time to prevent bedsores.

"While Ray was crumpled up down there groaning among the empty bottles and other scraps of garbage the building's tenants had been throwing into the shaft for years, Whitey tried again for the stairs. But Sugar Ray's cries had reached Leon, and once again the old man heard his tread, this time on the flight immediately above. It was as if some invisible force wouldn't let him leave; he was the Flying Dutchman of the third floor. Not trusting the elevator trick to work a second time, and that having been pretty much an accident anyway, he ducked through the nearest open door.

"He didn't know what room he was in. It was getting hard to see and he'd lost his bearings. He closed the door and in turning tripped over something on the floor. He landed on top of whatever it was and rolled off in a panic, because in that instant he realized it was Chick's body. He'd made a complete circle and ended up in the room where he'd started.

"Chick wasn't moving, and whether he was dead yet isn't important to the story. The floor was slippery under Whitey's hand. When he realized why, he jerked it away and barked his wrist on something hard that moved when he struck it. He closed his hand around it, and he was holding Chick's gun.

"Leon was in the hall now. A pale yellow oval slid under the door and Whitey shrank back with a gasp, but it sprang away and he knew the man with the pipe was swinging a flashlight beam from side to side in front of him as he crept through the darkness on the balls of his feet, softly calling Chick's and Sugar Ray's names. Whitey held his breath until the sighing of the floorboards under Leon's weight grew faint. Then he moved as quickly as he could without making a noise that would carry down the hall.

"Once you've got your coat off it isn't easy to put it on a man who's dead or dying. The arms aren't where you need them to be and the sleeve linings keep snagging on buttons and things. But he got it on the motionless man finally and got up and backed into the shadows, gripping the butt of the gun growing warm and slippery in his hand. He had never held one before and he was surprised at how heavy it was. He had heard about safeties and he hoped there was nothing like that on this gun because he wouldn't know how to take it off. He did know about cocking it, which he did with both thumbs. Shards from the broken mirror crunched under the thin soles of his shoes, but he wasn't worried about making noise now. He kept backing until his shoulder blades touched the tiles. There he waited with his heart bounding off his breastbone.

"By now Leon had had time to reach the end of the hall, but no one knows if he trained his light on the bottom of the shaft and saw Sugar Ray. His failure to raise either of his partners must have put him on his guard in any case. To Whitey it seemed a good hour before the squeak of an occasional hinge told him the pipe man was making his way back in Whitey's direction one room at a time, poking the flash into each dark empty cell with his weapon probably raised. Whatever small sounds the old man had made putting his coat on Chick and getting ready had apparently died at the door, although to him they had seemed loud enough to bring half the underworld crashing in on him. He stood in the cold moldy dark sweating into his collar and shoes and listening to the air dragging in and out of his lungs. His eyes had adjusted to the faint city glow leaking through the ventilator louvers over the toilet and he could see Chick's inert bulk in his own black overcoat on the floor. If he hadn't been dead before, he certainly was now.

"A soft rubber sole kissed the sprung boards on the other side of the door, Whitey thought; but he had learned long ago not to trust his defective hearing. To calm himself he switched the gun from his right to his left hand and wiped his right palm down his thigh. Then he changed grips again and stopped breathing. The door to the hall was opening.

"It inched open as if pushed by the phantom beam that followed it into the room. The light nudged a smoky path through the blackness, prowled the area beyond the edge of the empty bathroom doorway, and attached itself to the dead man's feet sticking out over the threshold. Leon took his breath in sharply. Then the light touched the worn hem of Whitey's overcoat on the corpse and the intruder came in the rest of the way, the pipe dangling at the end of his right arm. Enough illumination came back up off the littered tile floor to expose a wolfish grin on Leon's face. The smell of spent cordite was still thick in the enclosed space, and he must have thought he was looking at Chick's handiwork. Which he was, but not in the way he thought.

" 'Chick?' he said, and lifted the beam to take in the rest of the room.

"Whitey fired then, twice into the center of the light that was blinding him. The reports thudded massively against the tiles, the recoil vibrating up his arm and through his body, shaking loose what shreds of mirror glass remained on the wall he was touching.

"Something clanged under the echoing of the shots. Whitey stood unmoving while the choking smoke curled and twisted toward the ventilator and out. When it cleared he was prepared to fire again because there was still light in the room, but then he saw it bending along the floor from the abandoned flash lying against Chick's leg. He was alone with the dead man.

"Now he moved, stepping over the body but almost falling when something rolled out from under his foot. He caught himself against the jamb and knew without looking that the object was Leon's pipe. He left it there but picked up the flash. The fresh bloodstains on the floor looked black in the light. Leon was wounded.

"Whitey followed the dribbling trial out of the room and up the hall toward the stairs. The flashlight beam reflected off a big dark puddle on the landing. He could smell it now, sharp and musty in the icy air. The traces meandered down two flights, at the bottom of which the clear outline of one of Leon's waffle-patterned soles where he had stepped in his own leakage pointed toward the second-floor hallway. The light found no stains on the last flight before the ground. In his shock and panic Leon had miscounted his flights.

"There was nothing keeping the old man from leaving the building. Instead he turned and followed the stains. The gun was part of his hand now.

"Debris and great peeling sheets of wallpaper made bizarre shadows before the flash. The doors of most of the rooms on that floor had been kicked in by Chick, but he ignored them. The trail continued down the hall.

"He found Leon sitting on the floor with his back against the closed elevator doors that made the corridor a dead end, whimpering with both hands buried in the gaping black hole above his belt. His bowels were torn, their stench foul enough to have texture. He screwed up his slick face against the light in his eyes and said something unintelligible in a pleading tone.

"Whitey didn't make him wait. He snapped off the flash and there was an instant of darkness before the flame from the muzzle splattered it. Leon's body arched, the back of his head striking the elevator doors with a reverberating boom, and then his torso sagged and his big chin settled into the hollow of his right shoulder. Whitey was still standing there holding the weapon when the cops came."

I took advantage of the silence to lay in an inch of red wine in my glass. The congressman's wife was the first to speak.

"Is that a true story?"

I nodded, wetting my tongue. "I spent three weeks tracking down derelicts who were in the building that night and collecting affidavits for the public defender who represented Whitey at his trial. The rest of it came from the old man himself."

"What happened to him?" asked the professor.

"He pulled a year for third-degree murder knocked down

from first. The coroner ruled death by misadventure on Chick, and Sugar Ray's testimony by closed-circuit television from his hospital room failed to incriminate Whitey, but the judge wouldn't go self-defense on Leon because the old man had his chance to flee after shooting him the first time. He's living in a convalescent home in Southfield now. The hearing in his other ear went finally, but he doesn't need it to fix furniture in the workshop for sale by the Salvation Army.''

"I think that's nice," said the professor's wife.

The Sweetest Man in the World

·

Donald E. Westlake

Donald E. Westlake is crime fiction's clown prince, justifiably renowned for such hilarious comic capers as The Fugitive Pigeon, God Save the Mark *(winner of the 1967 MWA Best Novel Edgar),* The Hot Rock, *and* Dancing Aztecs. *"The Sweetest Man in the World" is characteristically playful Westlake. But when he dons one of his pseudonyms—Richard Stark or Tucker Coe—there is a much darker and more serious side to the clown prince. His novels as Stark, featuring the amoral thief named Parker, are violent portraits of life on society's underbelly; and his series about disgraced ex-cop Mitch Tobin, written under the Coe name, are superb studies of a man trapped and almost destroyed by his own savage guilt.*

I adjusted my hair in the hall mirror before opening the door. My hair was gray, and piled neatly on top of my head. I smoothed my skirt, took a deep breath, and opened the door.

The man in the hallway was thirtyish, well dressed, quietly handsome, and carrying a briefcase. He was also somewhat taken aback to see me. He glanced again at the apartment number on the door, looked back at me, and said, "Excuse me, I'm looking for Miss Diane Wilson."

"Yes, of course," I said. "Do come in."

He gazed past me uncertainly, hesitating on the doorstep, saying, "Is she in?"

"I'm Diane Wilson," I said.

He blinked. "*You're* Diane Wilson?"

"Yes, I am."

"The Diane Wilson who worked for Mr. Edward Cunningham?"

"Yes, indeed." I made a sad face. "Such a tragic thing." I said. "He was the sweetest man in the world, Mr. Cunningham was."

He cleared his throat, and I could see him struggling to regain his composure. "I see," he said. "Well, uh—well, Miss Wilson, my name is Fraser, Kenneth Fraser. I represent Transcontinental Insurance Association."

"Oh, no," I said. "I have all the insurance I need, thank you."

"No, no," he said. "I beg your pardon, I'm not here to *sell* insurance. I'm an investigator for the company."

"Oh, they all say that," I said, "and then when they get inside they *do* want to sell something. I remember one young man from an encyclopedia company—he swore up and down he was just taking a survey, and he no sooner—"

"Miss Wilson," Fraser said determinedly, "I am *definitely* not a salesman. I am not here to discuss your insurance with you; I am here to discuss Mr. Cunningham's insurance."

"Oh, I wouldn't know anything about that," I said. "I simply handled the paperwork in Mr. Cunningham's real estate office. His private business affairs he took care of himself."

"Miss Wilson, I—" He stopped, and looked up and down the hallway. "Do we have to speak out here?" he asked.

"Well, I don't know that there's anything for us to talk about," I said. I admit I was enjoying this.

"Miss Wilson, there *is* something for us to talk about." He put down the briefcase and took out his wallet. "Here," he said. "Here's my identification."

I looked at the laminated card. It was very official and very complex and included Fraser's photograph, looking open-mouthed and stupid.

Fraser said, "I will *not* try to sell you insurance, nor will I ask you any details about Mr. Cunningham's handling of his private business affairs. That's a promise. Now, *may* I come in?"

It seemed time to stop playing games with him; after all, I didn't want him getting mad at me. He might go poking around too far, just out of spite. So I stepped back and said, "Very well then, young man, you may come in. But I'll hold you to that promise."

We went into the living room, and I motioned at the sofa, saying, "Do sit down."

"Thank you." But he didn't seem to like the sofa when he sat on it, possibly because of the clear plastic cover it had over it.

"My nieces come by from time to time," I said. "That's why I have those plastic covers on all the furniture. You know how children can be."

"Of course," he said. He looked around, and I think the entire living room depressed him, not just the plastic cover on the sofa.

Well, it was understandable. The living room was a natural consequence of Miss Diane Wilson's personality, with its plastic slipcovers, the doilies on all the tiny tables, the little plants in ceramic frogs, the windows with venetian blinds *and* curtains *and* drapes, the general air of over-crowded neatness. Something like the house Mrs. Muskrat has in all those children's stories.

I pretended not to notice his discomfort. I sat down on the chair that matched the sofa, adjusted my apron and skirt over my knees, and said, "Very well, Mr. Fraser. I'm ready to listen."

He opened his briefcase on his lap, looked at me over it, and said, "This may come as something of a shock to you, Miss Wilson. I don't know if you were aware of the extent of Mr. Cunningham's policy holdings with us."

"I already told you, Mr. Fraser, that I—"

"Yes, of course," he said hastily. "I wasn't asking, I was getting ready to tell you myself. Mr. Cunningham had three policies with us of various types, all of which automatically became due when he died."

"Bless his memory," I said.

"Yes. Naturally. At any rate, the total on these three policies comes to one hundred twenty-five thousand dollars."

"Gracious!"

"With double indemnity for accidental death, of course," he went on, "the total payable is two hundred fifty thousand dollars. That is, one quarter of a million dollars."

"Dear me!" I said. "I would never have guessed."

Fraser looked carefully at me. "And you are the sole beneficiary," he said.

I smiled blankly at him, as though waiting for him to go on, then permitted my expression to show that the import of his words was gradually coming home to me. Slowly I sank back into the chair. My hand went to my throat, to the bit of lace around the collar of my dress.

"Me?" I whispered. "Oh, Mr. Fraser, you must be joking!"

"Not a bit," he said. "Mr. Cunningham changed his

beneficiary just one month ago, switching from his wife to you.''

"I can't believe it," I whispered.

"Nevertheless, it is true. And since Mr. Cunningham did die an accidental death, burning up in his real estate office, and since such a large amount of money was involved, the routine is to send an investigator around, just to be sure everything's all right.''

"Oh," I said. I was allowing myself to recover. I said, "That's why you were so surprised when you saw me."

He smiled sheepishly. "Frankly," he said, "yes."

"You had expected to find some sexy young thing, didn't you? Someone Mr. Cunningham had been having an—a relationship with.''

"The thought had crossed my mind," he said, and made a boyish smile. "I do apologize," he said.

"Accepted," I said, and smiled back at him.

It was beautiful. He had come here with a strong preconception, and a belief based on that preconception that something was wrong. Knock the preconception away and he would be left with an embarrassed feeling of having made a fool of himself. From now on he would want nothing more than to be rid of this case, since it would serve only to remind him of his wrong guess and the foolish way he'd acted when I'd first opened the door.

As I had supposed he would, he began at once to speed things up, taking a pad and pen from his briefcase and saying, "Mr. Cunningham never told you he'd made you his beneficiary?''

"Oh, dear me, no. I only worked for the man three months."

"Yes, I know," he said. "It did seem odd to us."

"Oh, his poor wife," I said. "She may have neglected him but—"

"Neglected?"

"Well," I allowed myself this time to show a pretty confusion. "I shouldn't say anything against the woman," I went on. "I've never so much as laid eyes on her. But I do know that not once in the three months I worked there did she ever come in to see Mr. Cunningham, or even call him on the phone. Also, from some things he said—"

"What things, Miss Wilson?"

"I'd rather not say, Mr. Fraser. I don't know the woman, and Mr. Cunningham is dead. I don't believe we should sit here and talk about them behind their backs."

"Still, Miss Wilson, he did leave his insurance money to you."

"He was always the sweetest man," I said. "Just the sweetest man in the world. But why he would—" I spread my hands to show bewilderment.

Fraser said, "Do you suppose he had a fight with his wife? Such a bad one that he decided to change his beneficiary, looked around for somebody else, saw you, and that was that."

"He was always very good to me," I said. "In the short time I knew him I always found Mr. Cunningham a perfect gentleman and the most considerate of men."

"I'm sure you did," he said. He looked at the notes he'd been taking, and muttered to himself. "Well, that might explain it. It's nutty, but—" He shrugged.

Yes, of course he shrugged. Kick away the preconception, leave him drifting and bewildered for just a second, and then quickly suggest another hypothesis to him. He clutched at it like a drowning man. Mr. Cunningham had had a big fight with Mrs. Cunningham. Mr. Cunningham had changed his beneficiary out of hate or revenge, and had chosen Miss Diane Wilson, the dear middle-aged lady he'd recently hired as his secretary. As Mr. Fraser had so succinctly phrased it, it was nutty, but—

I said, "Well, I really don't know what to say. To tell the truth, Mr. Fraser, I'm overcome."

"That's understandable," he said. "A quarter of a million dollars doesn't come along every day."

"It isn't the amount," I said. "It's how it came to me. I have never been rich, Mr. Fraser, and because I never married I have always had to support myself. But I am a good secretary, a willing worker, and I have always handled my finances, if I say so myself, with wisdom and economy. A quarter of a million dollars is, as you say, a great deal of money, but I do not *need* a great deal of money. I would much rather have that sweet man Mr. Cunningham alive again than have all the money in the world."

"Of course." He nodded, and I could see he believed every word I had said.

I went further. "And particularly," I said, "to be given money that should certainly have gone to his wife. I just wouldn't have believed Mr. Cunningham capable of such a hateful or vindictive action."

"He probably would have changed it back later on," Fraser said. "After he had cooled down. He only made the change three weeks before—before he passed on."

"Bless his soul," I said.

"There's one final matter, Miss Wilson," he said, "and then I'll leave you alone."

"Anything at all, Mr. Fraser," I said.

"About Mr. Roche," he said. "Mr. Cunningham's former partner. He seems to have moved from his old address, and we can't find him. Would you have his current address?"

"Oh, no," I said. "Mr. Roche left the concern before I was hired. In fact, Mr. Cunningham hired me because, after Mr. Roche left, it was necessary to have a secretary in order to be sure there was always someone in the office.''

"I see," he said. "Well—" He put the pad and pen back into the briefcase and started to his feet, just as the doorbell rang.

"Excuse me," I said. I went out to the hallway and opened the door.

She came boiling in like a hurricane, pushing past me and shouting. "Where is she? Where is the hussy?''

I followed her into the living room, where Fraser was standing and gaping at her in some astonishment as she continued to shout and to demand to know where *she* was.

I said, "Madam, please. This happens to be my home.''

"Oh, does it?" She stood in front of me, hands on hips. "Well then, you can tell me where I'll find the Wilson woman.''

"Who?''

"Diane Wilson, the little tramp. I want to—''

I said, "I am Diane Wilson.''

She stood there, open-mouthed, gaping at me.

Fraser came over then, smiling a bit, saying, "Excuse me, Miss Wilson, I think I know what's happened.'' He turned to the new visitor and said, "You're Mrs. Cunningham, aren't you?''

Still open-mouthed, she managed to nod her head.

Fraser identified himself and said, "I made the same mistake you did—I came here expecting to find some vamp. But as you can see—'' And he gestured at me.

"Oh, I *am* sorry," Mrs. Cunningham said to me. She was a striking woman in her late thirties. "I called the insurance company, and when they told me Ed had changed all his policies over to you, I naturally thought—well—you know.''

"Oh, dear," I said. "I certainly hope you don't think—"

"Oh, not at all," Mrs. Cunningham said, and smiled a bit, and patted my hand. "I wouldn't think that of *you*," she said.

Fraser said, "Mrs. Cunningham, didn't your husband tell you he was changing the beneficiary?"

"He certainly didn't," she said with sudden anger. "And neither did that company of yours. They should have told me the minute Ed made that change."

Fraser developed an icy chill. "Madam," he said, "a client has the right to make anyone he chooses his beneficiary, and the company is under no obligation to inform anyone that—"

"Oh, that's all right," I said. "I don't need the money. I'm perfectly willing to share it with Mrs. Cunningham."

Fraser snapped around to me, saying, "Miss Wilson, you aren't under any obligation at all to this woman. The money is legally and rightfully yours." As planned, he was now one hundred percent on my side.

Now it was time to make him think more kindly of Mrs. Cunningham. I said, "But this poor woman has been treated shabbily, Mr. Fraser. Absolutely shabbily. She was married to Mr. Cunningham for—how many years?"

"Twelve," she said, "twelve years," and abruptly sat down on the sofa and began to sob.

"There, there," I said, patting her shoulder.

"What am I going to *do*?" she wailed. "I have no money, nothing. He left me nothing but debts! I can't even afford a decent burial for him!"

"We'll work it out," I assured her. "Don't you worry, we'll work it out." I looked at Fraser and said, "How long will it take to get the money?"

He said, "Well, we didn't discuss whether you want it

68

in installments or in a lump sum. Monthly payments are usually—''

''Oh, a lump sum,'' I said. ''There's so much to do right away, and then my older brother is a banker in California. *He'll* know what to do.''

''If you're sure—'' He was looking at Mrs. Cunningham, and didn't yet entirely trust her.

I said, ''Oh, I'm sure this poor woman won't try to cheat me, Mr. Fraser.''

Mrs. Cunningham cried, ''Oh, God!'' and wailed into her handkerchief.

''Besides,'' I said, ''I'll phone my brother and have him fly east at once. He can handle everything for me.''

''I suppose,'' he said, ''if we expedite things, we could have your money for you in a few days.''

''I'll have my brother call you,'' I said.

''Fine,'' he said. He hesitated, holding his briefcase. ''Mrs. Cunningham, are you coming along? Is there anywhere I can drop you?''

''Let the woman rest here awhile,'' I said. ''I'll make her some tea.''

''Very well.''

He left reluctantly. I walked him to the front door, where he said to me, quietly, ''Miss Wilson, do me a favor.''

''Of course, Mr. Fraser.''

''Promise me you won't sign anything until your brother gets here to advise you.''

''I promise,'' I said, sighing.

''Well,'' he said, ''one more item and I'm done.''

''Mr. Roche, you mean?''

''Right. I'll talk to him, if I can find him. Not that it's necessary.'' He smiled and said good-bye and walked away down the hall.

I closed the door, feeling glad he didn't think it necessary to talk to Roche. He would have found it somewhat difficult to talk to Roche, since Roche was in the process of being buried under the name of Edward Cunningham, his charred remains in the burned-out real estate office having been identified under that name by Mrs. Edward Cunningham.

Would Roche have actually pushed that charge of embezzlement he'd been shouting about? Well, the question was academic now, though three months ago it had seemed real enough to cause me to strangle the life out of him, real enough to cause me to set up this hasty and desperate— but, I think, rather ingenious—plan for getting myself out of the whole mess entirely. The only question had been whether or not our deep-freeze would preserve the body sufficiently over the three months of preparation, but the fire had settled that problem, too.

I went back into the living room. She got up from the sofa and said, "What's all this jazz about a brother in California?"

"Change of plans," I said. "I was too much the innocent, and you were too much the wronged woman. Without a brother, Fraser might have insisted on hanging around, helping me with the finances himself. And the *other* Miss Wilson is due back from Greece in two weeks."

"That's all well and good," she said. "But where is this brother going to come from? She doesn't have one, you know—the real Miss Wilson, I mean."

"I know." That had been one of the major reasons I'd hired Miss Wilson in the first place—aside from our general similarity of build—the fact that she *had* no relatives, making it absolutely safe to take over her apartment during my impersonation.

My wife said, "Well? What are you going to do for a brother?"

I took off the gray wig and scratched my head, feeling

great relief. "I'll be the brother," I said. "A startling resemblance between us."

She shook her head, grinning at me. "You are a one, Ed," she said. "You sure are a one."

"That's me," I said. "The sweetest man in the world."

Just for Kicks

·

Ed McBain

No one writes better police procedural novels than Ed
McBain (Evan Hunter), as he has proven over and over again
with his series—begun in 1956 with Cop Hater and contin-
uing to the present—about the men and women of the 87th
Precinct. The more than forty novels in this popular series,
and his many other criminous works published under the
names of Evan Hunter, Richard Marsten, Hunt Collins, and
Curt Cannon, earned him a richly deserved Grand Master
Award from MWA in 1986. McBain is also an accomplished
writer of short crime fiction. "Just for Kicks" is among the
best of his stories, as are those to be found in his collections,
The Jungle Kids and The McBain Brief.

It was sad about Charlie Franklin.

The saddest part, of course, was his apparent happiness.
To look at him you'd never guess he was filled with anything but wild, soaring joy. He was, after all, a handsome
man of thirty-four years, and a bachelor to boot. As art
director of Smith, Carruthers, Cole and Carney—a Madi-
son Avenue advertising agency—his salary, by the most
conservative estimate, probably fell somewhere between
forty and fifty thousand dollars a year, not to mention
Christmas bonuses and all the models he could date. He
had dated quite a few of them. Invariably they'd come to
see his apartment after an evening of fun and revelry. He

lived in the top two floors of a discreet brownstone on Seventieth Street, just off Park Avenue. The walls of his duplex were covered with many high-quality prints and several originals, including a pencil drawing that Picasso had made on a tablecloth and that had cost Charlie two thousand dollars the summer he was getting drunk on La Costa Brava. Since he still got drunk occasionally, his liquor cabinet was stocked with expensive whiskeys. His closets were packed with hand-tailored clothes. His kitchen shelves brimmed with fine china and rare gourmet treats.

But Charlie Franklin was a very sad man.

He tried to explain this to Ed Bell, the firm's copy chief, one midnight in the dead of January. The men had been working late on a particularly tough nut, a presentation for the Fabglo Lipstick account. It must be said here that Smith, Carruthers, Cole and Carney was a very high-type advertising agency, which had been known to drop backward accounts who were not forward-thinking. Its advertising consisted mainly of striking photographic layouts coupled with terse provocative copy, usually of the one-line-sell variety. Once, a world-famous airline refused to believe that the agency could explain radar guided flight in a single line of copy. Well, Smith, Carruthers, Cole and Carney promptly showed those backward-thinking cotton-pickers the door. That was the way they worked. Proud, you might say.

The men had been in the office all that night trying to conjure up a striking photographic layout, which they could then couple with their characteristically provocative hunk of one-line copy. They had finally vanquished the elusive beast. The photograph would show a statuesque blonde wearing nothing but Fabglo Lipstick. In concession to *The New York Times* and its genteel advertising department, the girl would be carrying a primitive war club, strategically and concealingly draped across her prow. At the maiden's feet would be a disorderly pile of unconscious cavemen. The copy would read "KNOCK THEM DEAD WITH FABGLO RED." The ad was a thing to stir imaginations and cause the heart to beat faster. It would also, they hoped, sell lipstick. So the men clapped each other on the back and went to Charlie's pad for an overdue nightcap. They couldn't go to Ed Bell's pad because Ed was a commuter who lived fifty miles away in a ten-room colonial, which you might not want to call a "pad" to begin with. So they went to Charlie's duplex.

It was while Charlie was pouring out liberal doses of Canadian Club that he said, "Are you pleased with it, Ed?"

Ed Bell was by nature a very cautious and nervous man, the type who starts at every sound. His enthusiasm that night, however, knew no bounds. "The ad, do you mean?" he said. "Charlie, I think we've got a skyrocket here. Let's just hope Fabglo doesn't throw water on the fuse before we get it on the launching platform."

"But does it please you?" Charlie asked.

"It gasses me," Ed said. "It's stimulating and thought-provoking. It's artistic and sophisticated." He paused. "It's also somewhat sexy. Why? Something bother you about it?"

"Well, I . . ."

"What's the matter, Charlie?"

"I don't know what it is, Ed. But . . . Well, I just don't seem to get a charge out of things."

Ed thought this over for a moment. "You've thrown out your line and got a nibble," he said. "Now bring the tuna aboard."

"I don't know how to put it more plainly, Ed. I just don't get a bang out of things."

"You mean your work? The agency?"

"No. I mean everything."

"Everything? Well now, you've started a landslide. So

74

let's dig some of the rocks away and try to find daylight. How long have you felt this way? You can confide in me."

"All my life," Charlie said.

"You mean . . . nothing's ever given you a charge? Nothing?"

"Nothing," Charlie said glumly.

"Girls?"

"Not even girls," Charlie said. "No matter what their size, shape, and frame of mind."

"Well now, Charlie," Ed said cautiously, "you've just dropped an H-bomb. Let's come out of the shelter and check our Geigers. Maybe the fallout isn't as bad as the blast. You don't like women, so okay. Any man can get around to feeling that way. But there are other things in life, Charlie."

"Like for instance?"

"Like for instance"—and here Ed held up his glass—"booze."

"I've tasted every liquor, wine, cordial, and beer on the market. Domestic, imported, and bathtub. I've had it straight, mixed, and in coffee, tea, and even milk. I've thrown a jigger of rye and a jigger of scotch into the same glass of beer and then drunk it. I mixed rum, gin, and bourbon in the blender with a slice of lime. I've even drunk hair tonic. No kicks, Ed. No bang."

"There are stronger things than whiskey," Ed said, his voice dropping to a conspiratorial whisper. He looked at Charlie expectantly. Charlie shook his head.

"I've tried marijuana, cocaine, heroin, morphine, dolophon, opium, and any drug you'd care to name. I've mixed heroin and cocaine in what is called a 'speedball.' I've smoked it, sniffed it, skin-popped it, and mainlined it. Once I soaked a stick of marijuana in a martini, dried it off, and then smoked it." He paused. Sadly, he said, "No bang."

"Mmmm," Ed said. "Well, let's take a walk in the woods and see if there's anything in the traps we set. How about music? Surely music pleases you."

"I began with the three B's," Charlie said, "same place everyone starts. Then I moved to the Russians. Tschaikovsky, Rimsky-Korsakov, Borodin, Moussorgsky, Balakirev, and Cui. No kicks. I tried Chabrier, Stravinsky, Hanson, Holst, and Ravel. No charge. I moved through every classical composer living or dead or aging or sick."

"What about popular stuff?"

"I went from jazz to swing to cool bop to hard bop to rock and roll. I've run the gamut from Bix Beiderbecke through Thelonius Monk to Sal Mineo. I've even bought children's records, for God's sake. Have you ever heard Tubby the Tuba?"

"No," Ed admitted.

"No bang," Charlie said. "I've even listened to madrigals and Gregorian chants. Folk music. Voodoo mumbo-jumbo."

"No bang?" Ed said.

"No bang."

"Well, how about art, man? That's your first love. Doesn't *that* excite you?"

"I've seen everything from the cave drawings up. I sure don't understand all of it—but I don't like any of it."

"Not even your Picasso tablecloth?" Ed asked, astonished.

"Not even that. I'm thinking of taking it down and sending it to the laundry."

"Well now, don't get nervous," Ed said nervously. "There are other things in life. Let's just send up a few trial rockets and see if we can leave a stain on the moon, okay? You've got theatres and . . ."

"Who wants to see sick plays about queer people and spinsters in Venice?"

". . . and movies . . ."

"Who wants travelogues in Cinemascope?"

". . . and books! Charlie, there are millions of books!"

"I'm reading now," Charlie said glumly. "It's my latest project, but it won't be any different, I know it. I started with *Beowulf*, and it was putrid. I've been working my way up through the centuries. Shakespeare was corny and Hemingway was trite. I'm reading the bestseller list stuff now, but I'm bored to tears. It's no use, Ed. There's just nothing in life that gives me any kicks. I even hated baseball and ice cream when I was a kid." He looked for a moment as if he would cry. "Aw, what's the use?" he asked plaintively. "Food is bland, and nature is dull. Men are uninteresting, and women are unexciting. I've seen it all and heard it all and tasted it all and felt it all, and it all stinks. There's nothing left."

"Well," Ed said morosely, "I wish I could help you, Charlie."

"You can't."

"Maybe I ought to run along home. Maybe you need sleep."

"What's the sense in sleeping?" Charlie said. "You only have to get up in the morning."

Ed put on his coat. "Don't let this throw you," he advised. "Look around for a hold, and then pin this to the mat."

Charlie smiled. "Sure," he said.

At the door, Ed shook hands with him and then paused, listening. "What's that?" he said.

Charlie listened, too. "Somebody getting home downstairs," he said.

"Man, how can you stand living in the city?" Ed said. "Aren't you afraid of burglars?"

"A burglar might be interesting."

Ed patted his arm. "Look, get some sleep, will you?" he said.

"There's a book I want to finish first."

"Oh? Something interesting?"

"So-so."

"What's the title?"

"Compulsion," Charlie said.

It would be unfair to say that this novel about two boys who commit a thrill murder first gave Charlie the idea of killing just for kicks. The book strongly condemned the act of the would-be supermen, and Charlie was hardly an impressionable juvenile-delinquent type. But in much the same way as the boys' minds were infatuated with the printed words of Nietzsche, so too was Charlie lured by *these* printed words.

In the studio the next day, posing a model for a perfume ad that read, "THE SWEET SMELL OF DANGER: EAU DE BOUQUET," Charlie obviously did not have his mind on his work. The model was an overflowing brunette clad in a pale diaphanous wrapper and clutching, for effect, a bunch of flowers. Oddly, people from every department in the agency kept dropping in on Charlie while he posed the girl. Oddly, all of the visitors were men, but they nonetheless had very pertinent questions to ask of the art director.

One fellow asked, "Should I use a 1-H or a 2-H pencil for these rough sketches, Charlie?"

Another asked, "How do you spell 'cat,' Charlie?"

An office boy entered agog and asked, "Is it all right to empty the wastebasket in your office, Mr. Franklin?"

Charlie seemed very tolerant of the interruptions. The brunette model, slightly chilled in the sheer wrapper, kept clutching the flowers for effect.

"Bend over a little, please," Charlie said, and the girl did so with amazingly abundant alacrity. The photographer, unwilling to believe the beauty he had seen inverted in the lens of his camera, pulled his head from beneath the black hood and blinked his eyes.

"That's nice," Charlie said, "Now hold it."

Charlie was thinking it might not be a bad idea to kill somebody, just to see if there'd be a thrill in it. The one thing, in fact, that didn't send him into the street in instant search of a victim was the possibility that even a murder might not provide any kicks. And what could he do then? Ride a Mongolian pony? Join the Russian Air Force? Climb a flagpole in Topeka? If this ultimate experience of taking another man's life failed to give him a bang, what on earth could he try next?

Where's your gumption, Charlie Franklin? he asked himself.

Be American, for God's sake! How will you know whether or not the thrill is there until you try it? Did you know, for example, that oysters with oatmeal provided no charge until you'd tried that delicate dish? Of course not! Did you know that Shostakovitch played backwards was as uninspiring as and far more cacophonous than Shostakovitch played forwards—until you'd tried it? How can you tell if there's going to be any fun in anything until you try it? Where's your native initiative? Where's your spark, Charlie boy?

You're right, he told himself silently. Aloud to the model, he said, "Dear, close the wrapper a little. You'll catch cold." But he didn't even look at her.

His mind was made up. He would kill somebody, just for kicks. If it worked out, fine. If not, so it didn't matter.

So he laid his plans.

If there was to be a killing, it would have to be a perfect one. Charlie was far too sensitive a man to even think of allowing himself to fall into the hands of the police. His victim, therefore, could not be his mother, although he admitted with wry psychiatric chucklings that she was his first choice. Nor could he pick a victim at random as the boys in the book had done. There were too many imponderables in such a plan of action. If there was some danger in choosing a victim whose personal habits were well known, there was a converse safety factor in knowing the chosen victim would perform in a way that could be predetermined.

Fondly, with loving care, he chose Ed Bell as the victim.

Ed was a bachelor who, like Charlie, lived alone. Unlike Charlie, Ed was a highly nervous man who had been unable to endure the uncertain and frightening clutter of New York City. Ed had voluntarily become a commuter who lived in northern Westchester on a six-acre tract of land upon which stood his old colonial house. Ed chose a colonial because he wanted to hear the rich squeak of old burnished timbers under his feet. He wanted to see antique exposed beams in the ceiling. Besides, an old house was cheaper than building a new one. He had named his place Bell's Toll, the title being an inverted pun, ha, on the price he paid daily in the city in order to enjoy his creaky retreat in the exurbs. But whatever price he was forced to pay in the rat race, Ed Bell had surely achieved aloneness.

His nearest crotchety neighbor, two acres away, was shielded from him by a magnificent stand of pines—"These stately American monarchs," the real estate agent had said—the very presence of which had increased the price of the acreage by several thousand dollars. The pines, monarchs that they were, provided a very formidable sight and sound barrier against the crotchety modern house on the right of Ed's colonial. To the left of Ed's house were four choice acres of his own land, twelve acres of undeveloped land, which was used as a garbage dumping area for the town, and then a factory, which made Christmas balls. The factory was owned by the town supervisor, which, Ed perhaps unjustly felt, accounted for its presence in a residential-zoned area. In any case, Ed knew complete solitude at night. Screened from the modern monstrosity, separated from the penetratingly sweet aroma of burning garbage by his own four acres, a long way away from the Christmas-ball makers, Ed felt like an island indeed. The country was essential to his peace of mind. He'd actually been frightened all the while he lived in New York. Lying alone in his narrow bed, he would listen to the sounds of traffic, starting at every backfire, listening to footsteps in the hallway of his apartment building, frightful lest some burglar or some drunken individual stumble into his apartment. In a highly pressurized business like Ed's, where a single line of copy spoke volumes, it was no wonder he was a nervous man.

But the country, Charlie assumed, had demolished all of Ed's fears and anxieties. Ed went to bed every night at ten o'clock—except on weekends, of course. On weekends, oh that gay dog went to local dramatic productions and church socials and all sorts of wild and gay revelries in northern Westchester. But during the week, he avoided all temptation. He would arrive in town at 7:16, drive from the station to his house in a Volkswagen, prepare his own dinner, read awhile, lock the doors and windows—a dreadful habit left over from his cautious, nervous city existence—and then go to sleep. By six the next morning, he would be ready to enter the rat race again, a rested and contented man.

Charlie planned to kill him while he slept. That was the only humane thing to do, and Charlie did not wish to be cruel to an old friend. He also knew exactly which weapon he would use, the only logical and practical weapon, it seemed to him: a crossbow.

He probably would have made his murder attempt sooner, but he had a little difficulty turning up a crossbow. He finally found one in a Third Avenue antique shop. When the proprietor asked him, "Going to hang it over the fireplace?" Charlie answered, "No, going to kill someone with it."

The proprietor laughed all over the place. "Better give you the arrows then, huh?" he said, holding his sides.

"One arrow will be enough," Charlie said, for that was all he planned to use. He had not shot spitballs from a rubberband with deadly accuracy as a boy for nothing.

So, carefully, he laid his plans. Unfortunately, the planning brought him no joy. But he prayed the actual murder would.

On a Wednesday in February, as Ed was leaving the office at five, Charlie approached him. "Are you going straight home tonight?" he asked.

"Yes," Ed said. "Why?"

"Thought you might stop at my place for a drink," Charlie said, not meaning the invitation at all, of course.

"Thanks, some other time, Charlie," Ed said. "I want to eat and hit the sack. I'm bushed."

"You'll probably have people dropping in all night long," Charlie said with probing shrewdness.

"No, I don't socialize during the week," Ed said. "You know that. I'll be in bed by eight-thirty. I don't like February anyway. It depresses me. I'd rather be in bed than sitting around. February's a rotten month, don't you think?"

"How do you mean?"

"I don't know. Spooky. Eerie. Sounds outside the house, wind blowing, brrrr, makes me nervous." He shuddered a little. "How's your problem coming, Charlie?"

"I'm working on it," Charlie said.

"Good. Lead it to the scaffold, and I'll hold the basket," Ed said.

"I'll try. Good night, Ed. Sleep tight."

"You said it," Ed said, and he left the office.

At eight o'clock that night, the crossbow on the front seat of the car, Charlie started the drive to northern Westchester. He hoped to be there by nine-thirty at the latest, at which time he would shoot an arrow into Ed Bell's heart. The police, in their wisdom, would conclude, after much thought, that an Indian had killed Ed. And while they combed the country's reservations, Charlie would sit back and enjoy—he hoped—the pleasure of what he'd done.

He reached Bell's Toll at nine-thirty. He parked the car near the stand of American monarchs, doused the lights, and then started up the driveway on foot. There was the smell of growing Westchester things in the air, and the smell of burning Westchester garbage. Carrying the crossbow, Charlie sniffed deeply of the air. He did not walk on the gravel. He walked soundlessly instead on the soft turf at the side of the drive. The big colonial house came into view. Not a light was burning. Ed, then, was already asleep. Charlie listened to the sound of the wind, and the sound of the shutters banging against the clapboard of the house. He had felt no joy of anticipation on the ride up, and he felt no joy now, no excitement. He wondered again if the murder would provide the thrill he was seeking. He refused to believe otherwise. There simply *had* to be some good things in life. At nine forty-five, using a chisel, he forced the front door.

He was familiar with the house, having been Ed's legitimate guest there on many occasions. His eyes, too, were already accustomed to the darkness. He moved swiftly toward the staircase leading to the bedrooms upstairs. He was not at all nervous. When the old burnished timbers squeaked richly under his feet, he paid them no mind. The door to the master bedroom was just ahead at the end of the hall. Charlie cocked the crossbow and walked toward it. He listened for a moment, and then eased the door open. He still felt no thrill of anticipation. Doubt again crossed his mind. *Would* this provide the charge, the kicks, the bang? The door creaked noisily on its Revolutionary War hinges. There was a moment's stillness, and then Ed sat upright in bed. Trained by years of interrupted city sleep, fearful of the February night noises, he stared into the darkness and his voice crackled briskly across the length of the room.

"Who is it!"

Charlie did not answer. He raised the crossbow and leveled it at the bed. Ed moved with amazing swiftness. There was a medley of sound in the next instant, Ed's shout, and then the noise of a drawer sliding open swiftly, and then another louder shocking noise.

And Charlie Franklin, for the first and last time, finally got a real bang out of life.

He got it when Ed yanked the pistol from the night-table drawer and shot him twice in the head.

Smuggler's Island

•

Bill Pronzini

In his twenty years as a professional writer, Bill Pronzini has published more than forty novels, two collections, three nonfiction books, and some three hundred short stories, articles, and book reviews; and has edited or co-edited over fifty anthologies in a variety of fields. He is a two-time winner of the Private Eye Writers of America Shamus, once for Best Novel of 1981 (Hoodwink) and once for Best Short Story of 1983 ("Cat's-Paw"); both of these feature his San Francisco–based "Nameless Detective." A nonseries story, "Smuggler's Island" is the tale of the deadly chain of events that follow a wealthy eccentric's purchase of a fog-shrouded island off the California coast.

The first I heard that somebody had bought Smuggler's Island was late on a cold, foggy morning in May. Handy Manners and Davey and I had just brought the *Jennie Too* into the Camaroon Bay wharf, loaded with the day's limit in salmon—silvers mostly, with a few big kings—and Handy had gone inside the processing shed at Bay Fisheries to call for the tally clerk and the portable scales. I was helping Davey hoist up the hatch covers, and I was thinking that he handled himself fine on the boat and what a shame it'd be if he decided eventually that he didn't want to go into commercial fishing as his livelihood. A man likes to see his only son take up his chosen profession. But

85

Davey was always talking about traveling around Europe, seeing some of the world, maybe finding a career he liked better than fishing. Well, he was only nineteen. Decisions don't come quick or easy at that age.

Anyhow, we were working on the hatch covers when I heard somebody call my name. I glanced up, and Pa and Abner Frawley were coming toward us from down-wharf, where the café was. I was a little surprised to see Pa out on a day like this; he usually stayed home with Jennie when it was overcast and windy because the fog and cold air aggravated his lumbago.

The two of them came up and stopped, Pa puffing on one of his home-carved meerschaum pipes. They were both seventy-two and long retired—Abner from a manager's job at the cannery a mile up the coast, Pa from running the general store in the village—and they'd been cronies for at least half their lives. But that was where all resemblance between them ended. Abner was short and round and white-haired, and always had a smile and a joke for everybody. Pa, on the other hand, was tall and thin and dour; if he'd smiled any more than four times in the forty-seven years since I was born I can't remember it. Abner had come up from San Francisco during the Depression, but Pa was a second-generation native of Camaroon Bay, his father having emigrated from Ireland during the short-lived potato boom in the early 1900s. He was a good man and a decent father, which was why I'd given him a room in our house when Ma died six years ago, but I'd never felt close to him.

He said to me, "Looks like a good catch, Verne."

"Pretty good," I said. "How come you're out in this weather?"

"Abner's idea. He dragged me out of the house."

I looked at Abner. His eyes were bright, the way they always got when he had a choice bit of news or gossip to tell. He said, "Fella from Los Angeles went and bought Smuggler's Island. Can you beat that?"

"Bought it?" I said. "You mean outright?"

"Yep. Paid the county a hundred thousand cash."

"How'd you hear about it?"

"Jack Kewin, over to the real estate office."

"Who's the fellow who bought it?"

"Name's Roger Vauclain," Abner said. "Jack don't know any more about him. Did the buying through an agent."

Davey said, "Wonder what he wants with it?"

"Maybe he's got ideas of hunting treasure," Abner said and winked at him. "Maybe he heard about what's hidden in those caves."

Pa gave him a look. "Old fool," he said.

Davey grinned, and I smiled a little and turned to look to where Smuggler's Island sat wreathed in fog half a mile straight out across the choppy harbor. It wasn't much to look at, from a distance or up close. Just one big oblong chunk of eroded rock about an acre and a half in size, surrounded by a lot of little islets. It had a few stunted trees and shrubs, and a long headland where gulls built their nests, and a sheltered cove on the lee shore where you could put in a small boat. That was about all there was to it—except for those caves Abner had spoken of.

They were located near the lee cove and you could only get into them at low tide. Some said caves honeycombed the whole underbelly of the island, but those of us who'd ignored warnings from our parents as kids and gone exploring in them knew that this wasn't so. There were three caves and two of them had branches that led deep into the rock, but all of the tunnels were dead ends.

This business of treasure being hidden in one of those caves was just so much nonsense, of course—sort of a local legend that nobody took seriously. What the treasure was supposed to be was two million dollars in greenbacks that had been hidden by a rackets courier during Prohibition, when he'd been chased to the island by a team of Revenue agents. There was also supposed to be fifty cases of high-grade moonshine secreted there.

The bootlegging part of it had a good deal of truth though. This section of the northern California coast was a hotbed of illegal liquor traffic in the days of the Volstead Act, and the scene of several confrontations between smugglers and Revenue agents; half a dozen men on both sides had been killed, or had turned up missing and been presumed dead. The way the bootleggers worked was to bring ships down from Canada outfitted as distilleries—big stills in their holds, bottling equipment, labels for a dozen different kinds of Canadian whiskey—and anchor them twenty-five miles offshore. Then local fishermen and imported hirelings would go out in their boats and carry the liquor to places along the shore, where trucks would be waiting to pick it up and transport it down to San Francisco or east into Nevada. Smuggler's Island was supposed to have been a short-term storage point for whiskey that couldn't be trucked out right away, which may or may not have been a true fact. At any rate, that was how the island got its name.

Just as I turned back to Pa and Abner, Handy came out of the processing shed with the tally clerk and the scales. He was a big, thick-necked man, Handy, with red hair and a temper to match; he was also one of the best mates around and knew as much about salmon trolling and diesel engines as anybody in Camaroon Bay. He'd been working for me eight years, but he wouldn't be much longer. He was saving up to buy a boat of his own and only needed another thousand or so to swing the down payment.

Abner told him right away about this Roger Vauclain

buying Smuggler's Island. Handy grunted and said, "Anybody that'd want those rocks out there has to have rocks in his head."

"Who do you imagine he is?" Davey asked.

"One of those damn-fool rich people probably," Pa said. "Buy something for no good reason except that it's there and they want it."

"But why Smuggler's Island in particular?"

"Got a fancy name, that's why. Now he can say to his friends, why look here, I own a place up north called Smuggler's Island, supposed to have treasure hidden on it."

I said, "Well, whoever he is and whyever he bought it, we'll find out eventually. Right now we've got a catch to unload."

"Sure is a puzzler though, ain't it, Verne?" Abner said.

"It is that," I admitted. "It's a puzzler, all right."

If you live in a small town or village, you know how it is when something happens that has no immediate explanation. Rumors start flying, based on few or no facts, and every time one of them is retold to somebody else it gets exaggerated. Nothing much goes on in a place like Camaroon Bay anyhow—conversation is pretty much limited to the weather and the actions of tourists and how the salmon are running or how the crabs seem to be thinning out a little more every year. So this Roger Vauclain buying Smuggler's Island got a lot more lip service paid to it than it would have someplace else.

Jack Kewin didn't find out much about Vauclain, just that he was some kind of wealthy resident of southern California. But that was enough for the speculations and the rumors to build on. During the next week I heard from different people that Vauclain was a real estate speculator who was going to construct a small private club on the island; that he was a retired bootlegger who'd worked the coast during Prohibition and had bought the island for nostalgic reasons; that he was a front man for a movie company that was going to film a big spectacular in Camaroon Bay and blow up the island in the final scene. None of these rumors made much sense, but that didn't stop people from spreading them and half believing in them.

Then, one night while we were eating supper Abner came knocking at the front door of our house on the hill above the village. Davey went and let him in, and he sat down at the table next to Pa. One look at him was enough to tell us that he'd come with news.

"Just been talking to Lloyd Simms," he said as Jennie poured him a cup of coffee. "Who do you reckon just made a reservation at the Camaroon Inn?"

"Who?" I asked.

"Roger Vauclain himself. Lloyd talked to him on the phone less than an hour ago; says he sounded pretty hard-nosed. Booked a single room for a week, be here on Thursday."

"Only a single room?" Jennie said. "Why, I'm disappointed, Abner. I expected he'd be traveling with an entourage." She's a practical woman and when it comes to things she considers nonsense, like all the hoopla over Vauclain and Smuggler's Island, her sense of humor sharpens into sarcasm.

"Might be others coming up later," Abner said seriously.

Davey said, "Week's a long time for a rich man to spend in a place like Camaroon Bay. I wonder what he figures to do all that time?"

"Tend to his island, probably," I said.

"Tend to it?" Pa said. "Tend to what? You can walk over the whole thing in two hours."

"Well, there's always the caves, Pa."

He snorted. "Grown man'd have to be a fool to go wandering in those caves. Tide comes in while he's inside, he'll drown for sure."

"What time's he due in on Thursday?" Davey asked Abner.

"Around noon, Lloyd says. Reckon we'll find out then what he's planning to do with the island."

"Not planning to do anything with it, I tell you," Pa said. "Just wants to *own* it."

"We'll see," Abner said. "We'll see."

Thursday was clear and warm, and it should have been a good day for salmon; but maybe the run had started to peter out, because it took us until almost noon to make the limit. It was after two o'clock before we got the catch unloaded and weighed in at Bay Fisheries. Davey had some errands to run and Handy had logged enough extra time, so I took the *Jennie Too* over to the commercial slips myself and stayed aboard her to hose down the decks. When I was through with that, I set about replacing the port outrigger line because it had started to weaken and we'd been having trouble with it.

I was doing that when a tall man came down the ramp from the quay and stood just off the bow, watching me. I didn't pay much attention to him; tourists stop by to rubberneck now and then, and if you encourage them they sometimes hang around so you can't get any work done. But then this fellow slapped a hand against his leg, as if he were annoyed, and called out in a loud voice, "Hey, you there. Fisherman."

I looked at him then, frowning. I'd heard that tone before: sharp, full of self-granted authority. Some city people are like that; to them, anybody who lives in a rural village is a low-class hick. I didn't like it and I let him see that in my face. "You talking to me?"

"Who else would I be talking to?"

I didn't say anything. He was in his forties, smooth-looking, and dressed in white ducks and a crisp blue windbreaker. If nothing else, his eyes were enough to make you dislike him immediately; they were hard and unfriendly and said that he was used to getting his own way.

He said, "Where can I rent a boat?"

"What kind of boat? To go sport fishing?"

"No, not to go sport fishing. A small cruiser."

"There ain't any cruisers for rent here."

He made a disgusted sound, as if he'd expected that. "A big outboard then," he said. "Something seaworthy."

"It's not a good idea to take a small boat out of the harbor," I said. "The ocean along here is pretty rough—"

"I don't want advice," he said. "I want a boat big enough to get me out to Smuggler's Island and back. Now who do I see about it?"

"Smuggler's Island?" I looked at him more closely. "Your name happen to be Roger Vauclain, by any chance?"

"That's right. You heard about me buying the island, I suppose. Along with everybody else in this place."

"News gets around," I said mildly.

"About that boat," he said.

"Talk to Ed Hawkins at Bay Marine on the wharf. He'll find something for you."

Vauclain gave me a curt nod and started to turn away.

I said, "Mind if I ask *you* a question now?"

He turned back. "What is it?"

"People don't go buying islands very often," I said, "particularly one like Smuggler's. I'd be interested to know your plans for it."

"You and every other damned person in Camaroon Bay."

92

I held my temper. "I was just asking. You don't have to give me an answer."

He was silent for a moment. Then he said, "What the hell, it's no secret. I've always wanted to live on an island, and that one out there is the only one around I can afford."

I stared at him. "You mean you're going to *build* on it?"

"That surprises you, does it?"

"It does," I said. "There's nothing on Smuggler's Island but rocks and a few trees and a couple of thousand nesting gulls. It's fogbound most of the time, and even when it's not the wind blows at thirty knots or better."

"I like fog and wind and ocean," Vauclain said. "I like isolation. I don't like people much. That satisfy you?"

I shrugged. "To each his own."

"Exactly," he said, and went away up the ramp.

I worked on the *Jennie Too* another hour, then I went over to the Wharf Café for a cup of coffee and a piece of pie. When I came inside I saw Pa, Abner, and Handy sitting at one of the copper-topped tables. I walked over to them.

They already knew that Vauclain had arrived in Camaroon Bay. Handy was saying, "Hell, he's about as friendly as a shark. I was over to Ed Hawkin's place shooting the breeze when he came in and demanded Ed get him a boat. Threw his weight around for fifteen minutes until Ed agreed to rent him his own Chris-Craft. Then he paid for the rental in cash, slammed two fifties on Ed's desk like they were singles and Ed was a beggar."

I sat down. "He's an eccentric, all right," I said. "I talked to him for a few minutes myself about an hour ago."

"Eccentric?" Abner said, and snorted. "That's just a

93

name they give to people who never learned manners or good sense.''

Pa said to me. "He tell you what he's fixing to do with Smuggler's Island, Verne?''

"He did, yep.''

"Told Abner too, over to the inn.'' Pa shook his head, glowering, and lighted a pipe. "Craziest damned thing I ever heard. Build a house on that mess of rock, live out there. Crazy, that's all.''

"That's a fact,'' Handy said. "I'd give him more credit if he was planning to hunt for that bootlegger's treasure.''

"Well, I'm sure not going to relish having him for a neighbor,'' Abner said. "Don't guess anybody else will either.''

None of us disagreed with that. A man likes to be able to get along with his neighbors, rich or poor. Getting along with Vauclain, it seemed, was going to be a chore for everybody.

In the next couple of days Vauclain didn't do much to improve his standing with the residents of Camaroon Bay. He snapped at merchants and waitresses, ignored anybody who tried to strike up a conversation with him, and complained twice to Lloyd Simms about the service at the inn. The only good thing about him, most people were saying, was that he spent the better part of his days on Smuggler's Island—doing what, nobody knew exactly—and his nights locked in his room. Might have been he was drawing up plans there for the house he intended to build on the island.

Rumor now had it that Vauclain was an architect, one of those independents who'd built up a reputation, like Frank Lloyd Wright in the old days, and who only worked for private individuals and companies. This was probably true since it originated with Jack Kewin; he'd spent a little time with Vauclain and wasn't one to spread unfounded gossip. According to Jack, Vauclain had learned that the island was for sale more than six months ago and had been up twice before by helicopter from San Francisco to get an aerial view of it.

That was the way things stood on Sunday morning when Jennie and I left for church at 10:00. Afterward we had lunch at a place up the coast, and then, because the weather was cool but still clear, we went for a drive through the redwood country. It was almost 5:00 when we got back home.

Pa was in bed—his lumbago was bothering him, he said—and Davey was gone somewhere. I went into our bedroom to change out of my suit. While I was in there the telephone rang, and Jennie called out that it was for me.

When I picked up the receiver, Lloyd Simms's voice said, "Sorry to bother you, Verne, but if you're not busy I need a favor."

"I'm not busy, Lloyd. What is it?"

"Well, it's Roger Vauclain. He went out to the island this morning like usual, and he was supposed to be back at three to take a telephone call. Told me to make sure I was around then, the call was important—you know the way he talks. The call came in right on schedule, but Vauclain didn't. He's still not back, and the party calling him has been ringing me up every half hour, demanding I get hold of him. Something about a bid that has to be delivered first thing tomorrow morning."

"You want me to go out to the island, Lloyd?"

"If you wouldn't mind," he said. "I don't much care about Vauclain, the way he's been acting, but this caller is driving me up a wall. And it could be something's the matter with Vauclain's boat; can't get it started or something. Seems kind of funny he didn't come back when he said he would."

I hesitated. I didn't much want to take the time to go out to Smuggler's Island; but then if there was a chance Vauclain was in trouble, I couldn't very well refuse to help.

"All right," I said. "I'll see what I can do."

We rang off, and I explained to Jennie where I was going and why. Then I drove down to the basin where the pleasure-boat slips were and took the tarp off Davey's sixteen-foot Sportliner inboard. I'd bought it for him on his sixteenth birthday, when I figured he was old enough to handle a small boat of his own, but I used it as much as he did. We're not so well off that we can afford to keep more than one pleasure craft.

The engine started right up for a change—usually you have to choke it several times on cool days—and I took her out of the slips and into the harbor. The sun was hidden by overcast now and the wind was up, building small whitecaps, running fogbanks in from the ocean but shredding them before they reached the shore. I followed the south jetty out past the breakwater and into open sea. The water was choppier there, the color of gunmetal, and the wind was pretty cold; I pulled the collar of my jacket up and put on my gloves to keep my hands from numbing on the wheel.

When I neared the island I swung around to the north shore and into the lee cove. Ed Hawkins's Chris-Craft was tied up there, all right, bow and stern lines made fast to outcroppings on a long, natural stone dock. I took the Sportliner in behind it, climbed out onto the bare rock, and made her fast. On my right, waves broke over and into the mouths of three caves, hissing long fans of spray. Gulls wheeled screeching above the headland; farther in, scrub oak and cypress danced like bobbers in the wind. It all made you feel as though you were standing on the edge of the world.

There was no sign of Vauclain anywhere at the cove, so I went up through a tangle of artichoke plants toward the center of the island. The area there was rocky but mostly flat, dotted with undergrowth and patches of sandy earth. I stopped beside a gnarled cypress and scanned from left to right. Nothing but emptiness. Then I walked out toward the headland, hunched over against the pull of the wind. But I didn't find him there either.

A sudden thought came to me as I started back and the hairs prickled on my neck. What if he'd gone into the caves and been trapped there when the tide began to flood? If that was what had happened, it was too late for me to do anything—but I started to run anyway, my eyes on the ground so I wouldn't trip over a bush or a rock.

I was almost back to the cove, coming at a different angle than before, when I saw him.

It was so unexpected that I pulled up short and almost lost my footing on loose rock. The pit of my stomach went hollow. He was lying on his back in a bed of artichokes, one arm flung out and the other wrapped across his chest. There was blood under his arm, and blood spread across the front of his windbreaker. One long look was all I needed to tell me he'd been shot and that he was dead.

Shock and an eerie sense of unreality kept me standing there another few seconds. My thoughts were jumbled; you don't think too clearly when you stumble on a dead man, a murdered man. And it *was* murder, I knew that well enough. There was no gun anywhere near the body, and no way it could have been an accident.

Then I turned, shivering, and ran down to the cove and took the Sportliner away from there at full throttle to call for the country sheriff.

Vauclain's death was the biggest event that had happened in Camaroon Bay in forty years, and Sunday night and Monday nobody talked about anything else. As soon as word got around that I was the one who'd discovered the body, the doorbell and the telephone didn't stop ringing—friends and neighbors, newspaper people, investigators. The only place I had any peace was on the *Jennie Too* Monday morning, and not much there because Davey and Handy wouldn't let the subject alone while we fished.

By late that afternoon the authorities had questioned just about everyone in the area. It didn't appear they'd found out anything though. Vauclain had been alone when he'd left for the island early Sunday; Abner had been down at the slips then and swore to the fact. A couple of tourists had rented boats from Ed Hawkins during the day, since the weather was pretty good, and a lot of locals were out in the harbor on pleasure craft. But whoever it was who had gone to Smuggler's Island after Vauclain, he hadn't been noticed.

As to a motive for the shooting, there were all sorts of wild speculations. Vauclain had wronged somebody in Los Angeles and that person had followed him here to take revenge. He'd treated a local citizen badly enough to trigger a murderous rage. He'd got in bad with organized crime and a contract had been put out on him. And the most farfetched theory of all: He'd actually uncovered some sort of treasure on Smuggler's Island and somebody'd learned about it and killed him for it. But the simple truth was, nobody had *any* idea why Vauclain was murdered. If the Sheriff's department had found any clues on the island or anywhere else, they weren't talking—but they weren't making any arrests either.

There was a lot of excitement, all right. Only underneath it all people were nervous and a little scared. A killer seemed to be loose in Camaroon Bay, and if he'd murdered once, who was to say he wouldn't do it again? A mystery is all well and good when it's happening someplace else, but when it's right on your doorstep you can't help but feel threatened and apprehensive.

I'd had about all the pestering I could stand by four o'clock, so I got into the car and drove up the coast to Shelter Cove. That gave me an hour's worth of freedom. But no sooner did I get back to Camaroon Bay, with the intention of going home and locking myself in my basement workshop, than a sheriff's cruiser pulled up behind me at a stop sign and its horn started honking. I sighed and pulled over to the curb.

It was Harry Swenson, one of the deputies who'd questioned me the day before, after I'd reported finding Vauclain's body. We knew each other well enough to be on a first-name basis. He said, "Verne, the sheriff asked me to talk to you again, see if there's anything you might have overlooked yesterday. You mind?"

"No, I don't mind," I said tiredly.

We went into the inn and took a table at the back of the dining room. A couple of people stared at us, and I could see Lloyd Simms hovering around out by the front desk. I wondered how long it would be before I'd stop being the center of attention every time I went someplace in the village.

Over coffee, I repeated everything that had happened Sunday afternoon. Harry checked what I said with the notes he'd taken; then he shook his head and closed the notebook.

"Didn't really expect you to remember anything else," he said, "but we had to make sure. Truth is, Verne, we're up against it on this thing. Damnedest case I ever saw."

"Guess that means you haven't found out anything positive."

"Not much. If we could figure a motive, we might be

able to get a handle on it from that. But we just can't find one.''

I decided to give voice to one of my own theories. "What about robbery, Harry?" I asked. "Seems I heard Vauclain was carrying a lot of cash with him and throwing it around pretty freely.''

"We thought of that first thing," he said. "No good, though. His wallet was on the body, and there was three hundred dollars in it and a couple of blank checks.''

I frowned down at my coffee. "I don't like to say this, but you don't suppose it could be one of these thrill killings we're always reading about?''

"Man, I hope not. That's the worst kind of homicide there is.''

We were silent for a minute or so. Then I said, "You find anything at all on the island? Any clues?''

He hesitated. "Well," he said finally, "I probably shouldn't discuss it—but then, you're not the sort to break a confidence. We did find one thing near the body. Might not mean anything, but it's not the kind of item you'd expect to come across out there.''

"What is it?''

"A cake of white beeswax," he said.

"Beeswax?''

"Right. Small cake of it. Suggest anything to you?''

"No," I said. "No, nothing.''

"Not to us either. Aside from that, we haven't got a thing. Like I said, we're up against it. Unless we get a break in the next couple of days, I'm afraid the whole business will end up in the Unsolved file— That's unofficial, now.''

"Sure," I said.

Harry finished his coffee. "I'd better get moving," he said. "Thanks for your time, Verne.''

I nodded, and he stood up and walked out across the

dining room. As soon as he was gone, Lloyd came over and wanted to know what we'd been talking about. But I'd begun to feel oddly nervous all of a sudden, and there was something tickling at the edge of my mind. I cut him off short, saying, "Let me be, will you, Lloyd? Just let me be for a minute."

When he drifted off, looking hurt, I sat there and rotated my cup on the table. Beeswax, I thought. I'd told Harry that it didn't suggest anything to me, and yet it did, vaguely. Beeswax. White beeswax . . .

It came to me then—and along with it a couple of other things, little things, like missing figures in an arithmetic problem. I went cold all over, as if somebody had opened a window and let the wind inside the room. I told myself I was wrong, that it couldn't be. But I wasn't wrong. It made me sick inside, but I wasn't wrong.

I knew who had murdered Roger Vauclain.

When I came into the house I saw him sitting out on the sun deck, just sitting there motionless with his hands flat on his knees, staring out to sea. Or out to where Smuggler's Island sat, shining hard and ugly in the glare of the dying sun.

I didn't go out there right away. First I went into the other rooms to see if anybody else was home, but nobody was. Then, when I couldn't put it off any longer, I got myself ready to face it and walked onto the deck.

He glanced at me as I leaned back against the railing. I hadn't seen much of him since finding the body, or paid much attention to him when I had; but now I saw that his eyes looked different. They didn't blink. They looked at me, they looked past me, but they didn't blink.

"Why'd you do it, Pa?" I said. "Why'd you kill Vauclain?"

I don't know what I expected his reaction to be. But

101

there wasn't any reaction. He wasn't startled, he wasn't frightened, he wasn't anything. He just looked away from me again and sat there like a man who has expected to hear such words for a long time.

I kept waiting for him to say something, to move, to blink his eyes. For one full minute and half of another, he did nothing. Then he sighed, soft and tired, and he said, "I knew somebody'd find out this time." His voice was steady, calm. "I'm sorry it had to be you, Verne."

"So am I."

"How'd you know?"

"You left a cake of white beeswax out there," I said. "Fell out of your pocket when you pulled the gun, I guess. You're just the only person around here who'd be likely to have white beeswax in his pocket, Pa, because you're the only person who hand-carves his own meerschaum pipes. Took me a time to remember that you use wax like that to seal the bowls and give them a luster finish."

He didn't say anything.

"Couple of other things, too," I said. "You were in bed yesterday when Jennie and I got home. It was a clear day, no early fog, nothing to aggravate your lumbago. Unless you'd been out someplace where you weren't protected from the wind—someplace like in a boat on open water. Then there was Davey's Sportliner starting right up for me. Almost never does that on cool days unless it's been run recently, and the only person besides Davey and me who has a key is you."

He nodded. "It's usually the little things," he said. "I always figured it'd be some little thing that'd finally do it."

"Pa," I said, "why'd you kill him?'

"He had to go and buy the island. Then he had to decide to build a house on it. I couldn't let him do that. I went out there to talk to him, try to get him to change his mind.

102

Took my revolver along, but only just in case; wasn't in-tending to use it. Only he wouldn't listen to me. Called me an old fool and worse, and then he give me a shove. He was dead before I knew it, seems like.''

"What'd him building a house have to do with you?''

"He'd have brought men and equipment out there, wouldn't he? They'd have dug up everything, wouldn't they? They'd have sure dug up the Revenue man.''

I thought he was rambling. "Pa . . .''

"You got a right to know about that, too,'' he said. He blinked then, four times fast. "In 1929 a fella named Frank Eberle and me went to work for the bootleggers. Hauling whiskey. We'd go out maybe once a month in Frank's boat, me acting as shotgun, and we'd bring in a load of 'shine—mostly to Shelter Cove, but sometimes we'd be told to drop it off on Smuggler's for a day or two. It was easy money, and your ma and me needed it, what with you happening along; and what the hell, Frank always said, we were only helping to give the people what they wanted.

"But then one night in 1932 it all went bust. We brought a shipment to the island and just after we started unloading it this man run out of the trees waving a gun and yelling that we were under arrest. A Revenue agent, been lying up there in ambush. Lying alone because he didn't figure to have much trouble, I reckon—and I found out later the government people had bigger fish to fry up to Shelter Cove that night.

"Soon as the agent showed himself, Frank panicked and started to run. Agent put a shot over his head, and before I could think on it I cut loose with the rifle I always carried. I killed him, Verne, I shot that man dead.''

He paused, his face twisting with memory. I wanted to say something—but what was there to say?

Pa said, "Frank and me buried him on the island, under

a couple of rocks on the center flat. Then we got out of there. I quit the bootleggers right away, but Frank, he kept on with it and got himself killed in a big shoot-out up by Eureka just before Repeal. I knew they were going to get me too someday. Only time kept passing and somehow it never happened, and I almost had myself believing it never would. Then this Vauclain came along. You see now why I couldn't let him build his house?''

"Pa," I said thickly, ''it's been forty-five years since all that happened. All anybody'd have dug up was bones. Maybe there's something there to identify the Revenue agent, but there couldn't be anything that'd point to you.''

"Yes, there could," he said. "Just like there was something this time—the beeswax and all. There'd have been something, all right, and they'd have come for me.''

He stopped talking then, like a machine that had been turned off, and swiveled his head away and just sat staring again. There in the sun, I still felt cold. He believed what he'd just said; he honestly believed it.

I knew now why he'd been so dour and moody for most of my life, why he almost never smiled, why he'd never let me get close to him. And I knew something else, too: I wasn't going to tell the sheriff any of this. He was my father and he was seventy-two years old; and I'd see to it that he didn't hurt anybody else. But the main reason was, if I let it happen that they really did come for him he wouldn't last a month. In an awful kind of way the only thing that'd been holding him together all these years was his certainty they *would* come someday.

Besides, it didn't matter anyway. He hadn't actually got away with anything. He hadn't committed one unpunished murder, or now two unpunished murders, because there is no such thing. There's just no such thing as the perfect crime.

I walked over and took the chair beside him, and together we sat quiet and looked out at Smuggler's Island. Only I didn't see it very well because my eyes were full of tears.

Wild Mustard

·

Marcia Muller

*Marcia Muller's San Francisco–based Sharon McCone, who
made her debut in* Edwin of the Iron Shoes *(1977), was
crime fiction's first fully realized, realistically portrayed fe-
male private detective. McCone's popularity has risen steadily since that time as a result of five additional novels and
such short stories as the sensitive and forcefully drawn "Wild
Mustard." Muller has also published three novels featuring
Santa Barbara museum curator Elena Oliverez, and begun
yet another series with* The Cavalier in White *(1986), this
one featuring Joanna Stark, a detective who specializes in
cases involving art theft and forgery.*

The first time I saw the old Japanese woman, I was having
brunch at the restaurant above the ruins of San Francisco's
Sutro Baths. The woman squatted on the slope, halfway
between its cypress-covered top and the flooded ruins of
the old bathhouse. She was uprooting vegetation and stuffing it into a green plastic sack.

"I wonder what she's picking," I said to my friend Greg.

He glanced out the window, raising one dark-blond eye-
brow, his homicide cop's eye assessing the scene. "Probably something edible that grows wild. She looks poor; it's
a good way to save grocery money."

Indeed the woman did look like the indigent old ladies
one sometimes saw in Japantown; she wore a shapeless

jacket and trousers, and her feet were clad in sneakers. A gray scarf wound around her head.

"Have you ever been down there?" I asked Greg, motioning at the ruins. The once-elegant baths had been destroyed by fire. All that remained now were crumbling foundations, half submerged in water. Seagulls swam on its glossy surface and, beyond, the surf tossed against the rocks.

"No. You?"

"No. I've always meant to, but the path is steep and I never have the right shoes when I come here."

Greg smiled teasingly. "Sharon, you'd let your private eye's instinct be suppressed for lack of hiking boots?"

I shrugged. "Maybe I'm not really that interested."

"Maybe not."

Greg often teased me about my sleuthing instinct, but in reality I suspected he was proud of my profession. An investigator for All Souls Cooperative, the legal services plan, I had dealt with a full range of cases—from murder to the mystery of a redwood hot tub that didn't hold water. A couple of the murders I'd solved had been in Greg's bailiwick, and this had given rise to both rivalry and romance.

In the months that passed, my interest in the old Japanese woman was piqued. Every Sunday that we went there—and we went there often because the restaurant was a favorite—the woman was scouring the slope, foraging for . . . what?

One Sunday in early spring, Greg and I sat in our window booth, watching the woman climb slowly down the dirt path. To complement the season, she had changed her gray headscarf for bright yellow. The slope swarmed with people, enjoying the release from the winter rains. On the far barren side where no vegetation had taken hold, an abandoned truck leaned at a precarious angle at the bottom of the cliff near the baths. People scrambled down, inspected the old truck, then went to walk on the concrete foundations or disappeared into a nearby cave.

When the waitress brought our check, I said, "I've watched long enough; let's go down there and explore."

Greg grinned, reaching in his pocket for change. "But you don't have the right shoes."

"Face it, I'll never have the right shoes. Let's go. We can ask the old woman what she's picking."

He stood up. "I'm glad you finally decided to investigate her. She might be up to something sinister."

"Don't be silly."

He ignored me. "Yeah, the private eye side of you has finally won out. Or is it your Indian blood? Tracking instinct, papoose?"

I glared at him, deciding that for that comment he deserved to pay the check. My one-eighth Shoshone ancestry—which for some reason had emerged to make me a black-haired throwback in a family of Scotch-Irish towheads—had prompted Greg's dubbing me "papoose." It was a nickname I did not favor.

We left the restaurant and passed through the chain link fence to the path. A strong wind whipped my long hair about my head, and I stopped to tie it back. The path wound in switchbacks past huge gnarled geranium plants and through a thicket. On the other side of it, the woman squatted, pulling up what looked like weeds. When I approached she smiled at me, a gold tooth flashing.

"Hello," I said. "We've been watching you and wondered what you were picking."

"Many good things grow here. This month it is the wild mustard." She held up a spring. I took it, sniffing its pungency.

"You should try it," she added. "It is good for you."

108

"Maybe I will." I slipped the yellow flower through my buttonhole and turned to Greg.

"Fat chance," he said. "When do you ever eat anything healthy?"

"Only when you force me."

"I have to. Otherwise it would be Hershey bars day in and day out."

"So what? I'm not in bad shape." It was true; even on this steep slope I wasn't winded.

Greg smiled, his eyes moving appreciatively over me. "No, you're not."

We continued down toward the ruins, past a sign that advised us:

CAUTION!
CLIFF AND SURF AREA
EXTREMELY DANGEROUS
PEOPLE HAVE BEEN SWEPT
FROM THE ROCKS AND DROWNED

I stopped, balancing with my hand on Greg's arm, and removed my shoes. "Better footsore than swept away."

We approached the abandoned truck, following the same impulse that had drawn other climbers. Its blue paint was rusted and there had been a fire in the engine compartment. Everything, including the seats and steering wheel, had been stripped.

"Somebody even tried to take the front axle," a voice beside me said, "but the fire had fused the bolts."

I turned to face a friendly looking, sunbrowned youth of about fifteen. He wore dirty jeans and a torn T-shirt.

"Yeah," another voice added. This boy was about the same age; a wispy attempt at a mustache sprouted on his upper lip. "There's hardly anything left, and it's only been here a few weeks."

109

"Vandalism," Greg said.

"That's it." The first boy nodded. "People hang around here and drink. Late at night they get bored." He motioned at a group of unsavory-looking men who were sitting on the edge of the baths with a couple of six-packs.

"Destruction's a very popular sport these days." Greg watched the men for a moment with a professional eye, then touched my elbow. We skirted the ruins and went toward the cave. I stopped at its entrance and listened to the roar of the surf.

"Come on," Greg said.

I followed him inside, feet sinking into coarse sand that quickly became packed mud. The cave was really a tunnel, about eight feet high. Through crevices in the wall on the ocean side I saw spray flung high from the rolling waves at the foot of the cliff. It would be fatal to be swept down through those jagged rocks.

Greg reached the other end. I hurried as fast as my bare feet would permit and stood next to him. The precipitous drop to the sea made me clutch at his arm. Above us, rocks towered.

"I guess if you were a good climber you could go up, and then back to the road," I said.

"Maybe, but I wouldn't chance it. Like the sign says . . ."

"Right." I turned, suddenly apprehensive. At the mouth of the tunnel, two of the disreputable men stood, beer cans in hand. "Let's go, Greg."

If he noticed the edge to my voice, he didn't comment. We walked in silence through the tunnel. The men vanished. When we emerged into the sunlight, they were back with the others, opening fresh beers. The boys we had spoken with earlier were perched on the abandoned truck, and they waved at us as we started up the path.

* * *

110

And so, through the spring, we continued to go to our favorite restaurant on Sundays, always waiting for a window booth. The old Japanese woman exchanged her yellow headscarf for a red one. The abandoned truck remained nose down toward the baths, provoking much criticism of the Park Service. People walked their dogs on the slope. Children balanced precariously on the ruins, in spite of the warning sign. The men lolled about and drank beer. The teenaged boys came every week and often were joined by friends at the truck.

Then, one Sunday, the old woman failed to show.

"Where is she?" I asked Greg, glancing at my watch for the third time.

"Maybe she's picked everything there is to pick down there."

"Nonsense. There's always something to pick. We've watched her for almost a year. That old couple is down there walking their German Shepherd. The teenagers are here. That young couple we talked to last week is over by the tunnel. Where's the old Japanese woman?"

"She could be sick. There's a lot of flu going around. Hell, she might have died. She wasn't all that young."

The words made me lose my appetite for my chocolate cream pie. "Maybe we should check on her."

Greg sighed. "Sharon, save your sleuthing for paying clients. Don't make everything into a mystery."

Greg had often accused me of allowing what he referred to as my "woman's intuition" to rule my logic—something I hated even more than references to my "tracking instinct." I knew it was no such thing; I merely gave free rein to the hunches that every good investigator follows. It was not a subject I cared to argue at the moment, however, so I let it drop.

But the next morning—Monday—I sat in the converted closet that served as my office at All Souls, still puzzling over the woman's absence. A file on a particularly boring tenants' dispute lay open on the desk in front of me. Finally I shut it and clattered down the hall of the big brown Victorian toward the front door.

"I'll be back in a couple of hours," I told Ted, the secretary.

He nodded, his fingers never pausing as he plied his new Selectric. I gave the typewriter a resentful glance. It, to my mind, was an extravagance, and the money it was costing could have been better spent on salaries. All Souls, which charged clients on a sliding fee scale according to their incomes, paid so low that several of the attorneys were compensated by living in free rooms on the second floor. I lived in a studio apartment in the Mission District. It seemed to get smaller every day.

Grumbling to myself, I went out to my car and headed for the restaurant above the Sutro Baths.

"The old woman who gathers wild mustard on the cliff," I said to the cashier, "was she here yesterday?"

He paused. "I think so. Yesterday was Sunday. She's always here on Sunday. I noticed her about eight, when we opened up. She always comes early and stays until about two."

But she had been gone at eleven. "Do you know her? Do you know where she lives?"

He looked curiously at me. "No, I don't."

I thanked him and went out. Feeling foolish, I stood beside the Great Highway for a moment, then started down the dirt path, toward where the wild mustard grew. Halfway there I met the two teenagers. Why weren't they in school? Dropouts, I guessed.

They started by, avoiding my eyes like kids will do. I stopped them. "Hey, you were here yesterday, right?"

The mustached one nodded.

"Did you see the old Japanese woman who picks the weeds?"

He frowned. "Don't remember her."

"When did you get here?"

"Oh, late. Really late. There was this party Saturday night."

"I don't remember seeing her either," the other one said, "but maybe she'd already gone by the time we got here."

I thanked them and headed down toward the ruins.

A little farther on, in the dense thicket through which the path wound, something caught my eye and I came to an abrupt stop. A neat pile of green plastic bags lay there, and on top of them was a pair of scuffed black shoes. Obviously she had come here on the bus, wearing her street shoes, and had only switched to sneakers for her work. Why would she leave without changing her shoes?

I hurried through the thicket toward the patch of wild mustard.

There, deep in the weeds, its color blending with their foliage, was another bag. I opened it. It was a quarter full of wilting mustard greens. She hadn't had much time to forage, not much time at all.

Seriously worried now, I rushed up to the Great Highway. From the phone booth inside the restaurant, I dialed Greg's direct line at the SFPD. Busy. I retrieved my dime and called All Souls.

"Any calls?"

Ted's typewriter rattled in the background. "No, but Hank wants to talk to you."

Hank Zahn, my boss. With a sinking heart, I remembered the conference we had had scheduled for half an hour ago. He came on the line.

"Where the hell are you?"

"Uh, in a phone booth."

"What I mean is, why aren't you here?"

"I can explain—"

"I should have known."

"What?"

"Greg warned me you'd be off investigating something."

"Greg? When did you talk to him?"

"Fifteen minutes ago. He wants you to call. It's important."

"Thanks!"

"Wait a minute—"

I hung up and dialed Greg again. He answered, sounding rushed. Without preamble, I explained what I'd found in the wild mustard patch.

"That's why I called you." His voice was unusually gentle. "We got word this morning."

"What word?" My stomach knotted.

"An identification on a body that washed up near Devil's Slide yesterday evening. Apparently she went in at low tide, or she would have been swept much farther to sea."

I was silent.

"Sharon?"

"Yes, I'm here."

"You know how it is out there. The signs warn against climbing. The current is bad."

But I'd never, in almost a year, seen the old Japanese woman near the sea. She was always up on the slope, where her weeds grew. "When was low tide, Greg?"

"Yesterday? Around eight in the morning."

Around the time the restaurant cashier had noticed her, and several hours before the teenagers had arrived. And in between? What had happened out there?

I hung up and stood at the top of the slope, pondering. What should I look for? What could I possibly find?

I didn't know, but I felt certain the old woman had not

114

gone into the sea by accident. She had scaled those cliffs with the best of them.

I started down, noting the shoes and the bags in the thicket, marching resolutely past the wild mustard toward the abandoned truck. I walked all around it, examining its exterior and interior, but it gave me no clues. Then I started toward the tunnel in the cliff.

The area, so crowded on Sundays, was sparsely populated now. San Franciscans were going about their usual business, and visitors from the tour buses parked at nearby Cliff House were leery of climbing down here. The teenagers were the only other people in sight. They stood by the mouth of the tunnel, watching me. Something in their postures told me they were afraid. I quickened my steps.

The boys inclined their heads toward one another. Then they whirled and ran into the mouth of the tunnel.

I went after them. Again, I had the wrong shoes. I kicked them off and ran through the coarse sand. The boys were halfway down the tunnel.

One of them paused, frantically surveying a rift in the wall. I prayed he wouldn't go that way, into the boiling waves below.

He turned and ran after his companion. They disappeared at the end of the tunnel.

I hit the hard-packed dirt and increased my pace. Near the end, I slowed and approached more cautiously. At first I thought the boys had vanished, but then I looked down. They crouched on a ledge below. Their faces were scared and young, so young.

I stopped where they could see me and made a calming motion. "Come on back up," I said. "I won't hurt you."

The mustached one shook his head.

"Look, there's no place you can go. You can't swim in that surf."

Simultaneously they glanced down. They looked back at me and both shook their heads.

I took a step forward. "Whatever happened, it couldn't have—" Suddenly I felt the ground crumble. My foot slipped and I pitched forward. I fell to one knee, my arms frantically searching for a support.

"Oh, God!" the mustached boy cried. "Not you, too!" He stood up, swaying, his arms outstretched.

I kept sliding. The boy reached up and caught me by the arm. He staggered back toward the edge and we both fell to the hard rocky ground. For a moment, we both lay there panting. When I finally sat up, I saw we were inches from the sheer drop to the surf.

The boy sat up, too, his scared eyes on me. His companion was flattened against the cliff wall.

"It's okay," I said shakily.

"I thought you'd fall just like the old woman," the boy beside me said.

"It was an accident, wasn't it?"

He nodded. "We didn't mean for her to fall."

"Were you teasing her?"

"Yeah. We always did, for fun. But this time we went too far. We took her purse. She chased us."

"Through the tunnel, to here."

"Yes."

"And then she slipped."

The other boy moved away from the wall. "Honest, we didn't mean for it to happen. It was just that she was so old. She slipped."

"We watched her fall," his companion said. "We couldn't do anything."

"What did you do with the purse?"

"Threw it in after her. There were only two dollars in it. Two lousy dollars." His voice held a note of wonder.

116

"Can you imagine, chasing us all the way down here for two bucks?"

I stood up carefully, grasping the rock for support. "Okay," I said. "Let's get out of here."

They looked at each other and then down at the surf.

"Come on. We'll talk some more. I know you didn't mean for her to die. And you saved my life."

They scrambled up, keeping their distance from me. Their faces were pale under their tans, their eyes afraid. They were so young. To them, products of the credit-card age, fighting to the death for two dollars was inconceivable. And the Japanese woman had been so old. For her, eking out a living with the wild mustard, two dollars had probably meant the difference between life and death.

I wondered if they'd ever understand.

Tex

•

John Jakes

Before he began writing his enormously popular American Bicentennial Series and such blockbuster bestsellers as North and South *and* Love and War, *John Jakes was a regular contributor of books and stories in several genres: fantasy, science fiction, Western, historical, and mystery/suspense. His crime fiction includes such novels as* A Night for Treason, The Devil Has Four Faces, *and* Johnny Havoc, *and such short stories as this grimly realistic account of what happens after an odd young soldier known as Tex is dishonorably discharged from the army.*

He walked out through the gates of Fort Sheridan with his dishonorable discharge in his pocket. Once free, he stopped along the edge of the highway, set down the plaid cardboard suitcase that contained some khaki underwear and a Gillette razor, and lit a cigarette. A fin-tailed powder-blue El Dorado came roaring down the highway, and slowed a little, as a blond girl with sunglasses and a silk scarf tied around her flying hair gave him an appraising glance. The car shot on by, going south toward Chicago. He raised his head and watched the car dwindle out of sight. He had not noticed the girl, but the direction she was driving made an impression on his mind. He ought to go back. It was a long way, but he ought to go back.

Fixing this idea firmly in his mind and concentrating on

it, he crossed the highway to the electric railway station. The hour was shortly past noon of a gray, somewhat chilly day. Long gray clouds were blowing down from Wisconsin and Canada.

In ten minutes the train of two green cars came along, and he boarded it. He got off in the small suburban town of Lake Bluff, because he spotted a Chevrolet agency as the train came to a stop. He crossed the same highway that ran by the army post and went into the agency, a blond boy with huge shoulders, only twenty-one years old by the calendar. Forty minutes later he drove out of the agency in a new two-door sedan, maroon in color. The automobile smelled fresh, of leather and metal. He headed west on Highway 176, humming a little tune. After several minutes he realized he could no longer avoid the thought that was badgering him. He had no reason to go south, all the long way back to Texas. No one was waiting for him there. Nothing was waiting for him. So when he came to the four-lane span of U.S. 41, the Skokie Highway, he turned north toward the Wisconsin line, admitting defeat. After a quarter of a mile he saw a car stalled by the side of the road, and as he slowed down, he saw the trouble, a flat left rear tire. A well-dressed woman was standing by the rear wheel, twisting a pair of white gloves in confusion. He pulled off onto the bumpy shoulder and climbed out.

"Can I help you?" he asked.

"Oh . . . if you would . . ." The woman seemed close to tears.

He studied the situation. The car had evidently swerved a bit when the flat tire forced it off the road, and the right rear wheel had dropped six inches over a ditch edge on the shoulder. He took off his coat, asked the woman to put the car in neutral when he gave the word, and stepped down into the foot-deep gully. He braced both hands on the bumper, called, "Put her in neutral," waited a moment

119

and then heaved. A muscle vibrated in his temple. The car rocked backward a fraction; he grunted softly and heaved, and it went up and over the lip with a tiny crash of pebbles. He clambered up again and wiped the back of his hand across his forehead.

He drew the ignition key and opened the trunk, saying, "You got a jack?"

The woman said she didn't know, although he had the trunk open and the woman was looking inside and the jack was in plain view. "Here we go," he said softly, and went to work. In ten minutes he had the spare on, and he handed the keys back to the woman, who still sniffled and rubbed at her eyes. She began to work at the clasp of her handbag.

"Please let me pay . . ."

"No, that's all right," he called, already behind the wheel of his own car. In the rear vision mirror he saw the woman drive onto the highway behind him. He lit another cigarette and began to hum again. After a while he managed to convince himself that the state of Wisconsin might be something pretty interesting to see.

At the end of three miles he felt thirsty. Nope, he said to himself. He drove past one roadhouse, and half a mile later, another. As soon as he started thinking about liquor, he began to notice the dismal gray clouds, and all of a sudden the discharge—which he had forgotten for a while— slipped into his mind again. His defenses crumbled. He saw gas pumps up ahead, and a sign that read, as he drew closer, *Billy's Cabins, Café, Dine and Dance*. He swung the wheel with a feeling of defeat and the tires crackled on gravel. He looked at his watch. Lord, it was already quarter to seven. No wonder it was so dark.

He went toward the café door. There were no other cars parked outside, and the dirty windows of the café were closed up with green blinds on which he could see the blisters of paint. He walked inside and blinked a moment, for the light was poor. The only illumination came from a large lamp sitting on the back bar. The place had a few tables of flimsy wood, with chairs upended on top, and a space for dancing and a pinball machine lit up with drawings of girls in bathing suits. It was called the Yacht Club.

No one was at the bar. He pulled up onto a stool. He could feel it coming now. He had been nuts to think it could be any different. Why, he'd even expected Billy's to be a comfortable little spot. He didn't really have a concrete notion of what he had expected it to be, but he knew definitely what he hadn't wanted it to be, and this was it.

"Hey!" he called.

A door in one corner led into a small room, which also had tables. Out of his line of vision a pair of feet scraped on the floor.

The bar was old-fashioned, with a large mirror. He stared at the rows of bottles with their silver pour spouts and looked away. The end portion of the back bar was a writhing confusion of plaster of Paris statuettes, no more than three alike: stallions, kewpies, coolies, blackamoors. There was also a wire rack of postcards featuring cartoons about vacations and outhouses. The lamp that threw the only light stood among the knickknacks. It was plaster of Paris, too, larger than the others. It represented a Chinese girl, and the bulb came out of the top of her head. The light filtered through a bright red shade. The Chinese girl was dressed in a purple gown and held a gold mirror in front of her face. Her right leg was crossed over her left in a sort of figure 4, and in the triangle of the figure 4 somebody had stuck a card, now dirty and brown, marked $4.95. The bar looked cheap and nightmarish. He wanted to get out, but then the proprietor came out of the other room and he felt embarrassed, so he stayed.

The proprietor was a woman, with a doughy face. She must have weighed three hundred pounds, and she wore a dirty pink dress. He could not tell if she was pregnant or just fat. A large plaster, which looked like a Dr. Scholl's, was stuck on her gray-looking neck. The plaster matched the color of her dress. He felt revolted. He wanted to run away, but he was pretty certain now this was the kind of place he belonged in. The woman came to a stop under a sign that hung on the top of the bar and read *Kwitcherbelliakin*.

Still, he wasn't completely sure.

"Yessir," said the woman.

What would it be? Only one, he said to himself.

"Bottle of Schlitz."

She opened a silvered cooler, uncapped the brown bottle, and set it on the bar. She also set out a tumbler and a black plastic ashtray, and he bought a nickel bag of Chesty potato chips. He opened the bag but did not touch the beer. He ate a chip and stared at the brown and gold Schlitz label. The woman went to the other end of the bar, sat down on a stool, and began to read a comic book.

Reluctantly he filled the tumbler with beer, watched the head rise, and drank part of it. He waited carefully to feel the effect. None. He swiveled his head and looked at the deserted room. The floor looked unwashed. From outside came the steady, certain hiss of tires, as the traffic roared north and south. He drank more beer, feeling now that he would probably have another after this one.

Things began to slip back into his memory, answering his own question to himself of how he had gotten here. He recalled the farm in Texas, and the taste of dust always in his mouth. He saw his father and his mother, dusty people, the man in overalls bleached nearly white, with the buttons no longer a shiny brass color, the woman in a dress that had once been a color but was now gray. They always read the Bible at night, and he remembered how his father had whipped him with a belt, using the buckle end, when he came home from town one night when he was about twelve, and said he wished he could taste whiskey. He had meant no harm. He had been curious about the signs displayed in the windows of only certain places, and he had just wanted to taste it. But sitting in Billy's and staring at the way the lamplight threw shadows on the Chinese girl, he could feel the tang of the buckle on his flesh.

One thing he had always had, strength. The huge shoulders. He never wanted to lick the other kids in grade school, but he could do it if it was necessary, as it sometimes was. Then high school, and though he had a tough time with his subjects, he learned football. They couldn't stop him when he was on the line. He remembered how the man in the linen suit had driven out to the farm, his senior year, and pulled up in a late model Oldsmobile and talked his father into letting him accept a scholarship to the state university.

There he learned to drink for the first time, and heavily. And when he got drunk he wanted to fight. He failed three courses his first semester, and without letting his folks know, left school, and enlisted in the army, rootless. Once he had written home, but the letter had come back unanswered, so he wrote to a friend of the family who told him his mother and father had been killed in a highway accident while on the way to the state fair. In the army he played football, and they wanted him to box, but he wouldn't, because he had to be sober when he boxed, and then he didn't like to fight, or thought he didn't. He only fought when he got drunk.

The first bad time was in a bar in El Paso, and two other soldiers who had been in the place said he had walked up to three Air Corps lieutenants who were drinking martinis.

"You don't like me," the other soldiers said he said.

"Shove, dogface," they said one of the lieutenants said.

He remembered nothing. He never remembered, once he got heavily drunk. He had been drunk, they told him, and had broken the arm of one of the lieutenants before the MPs dragged him away. He got in bad trouble for that one, because one of the Air Corps lieutenants had a father who was a brigadier general in Washington.

In between the big fights, there were all the small ones in bars and barracks when he took on just one man at a time. The second big fight was in a bar in Tijuana, when a Mexican stumbled and spilled tequila on him. It was six Mexicans against him, and when he woke up in the base hospital, he had two knife wounds in his side, but his buddies laughingly (and truthfully) said he had damn near killed every Mexican in the place. He got sick when he heard this, because he thought he didn't really want to fight.

The third time, two months ago, he had been in a bar in Highwood, near Fort Sheridan, and three master sergeants had been making loud remarks about his outfit. He didn't remember that either, of course, but learned the story afterward. One of the master sergeants died of a broken neck, and another, they said, would be crippled for life.

Sitting in Billy's, he remembered the whole road. Even the interview with the doctor who wasn't a regular doctor, Major Nevins. Even at this very moment he could not make sense out of the questions, though he remembered some of them:

"Did you ever feel you hated your parents, subconsciously, because of the way they restricted you?"

He said he didn't know what subconsciously meant.

Dr. Nevins, who had a mustache and talked like an Easterner, smiled patiently. "Well, did you ever think that about your parents and not want to admit it to yourself?"

"I guess so."

"Can't you remember?"

"Well, I guess I did think that. I always wished they wouldn't read the Bible so much."

And then about drinking:

"Why do you drink?"

"I like to."

"Why do you like to?"

"Well, I didn't like to at first, when I went to college, but after I got in trouble, fighting, I just couldn't stand to think about what I'd done, so I'd take a drink."

"You drink to keep from remembering what you did the last time you got drunk."

"I guess so."

"You're too strong, do you know that?"

"I guess I am strong, all right."

"If you were a weakling, it wouldn't make any difference. But you've got shoulders like a bull. You broke Master Sergeant Preebie's neck with one twist."

"I don't remember that."

Because he had gotten drunk and killed the master sergeant, but couldn't remember, they had to discharge him. Dr. Nevins wanted him to go to a hospital, but he didn't want to, and Nevins said he couldn't force it because on the surface it was just drunkenness causing the trouble, and the inquiry board called the killing accidental, even though they had to discharge him, of course, for it. Now, sitting in Billy's, with the traffic all heading someplace out on the highway, he wondered whether he should have gone to the hospital.

"Let me have another beer," he said.

The woman put down her comic book and got the beer. He felt a little lift now.

So that was where he had been. Now, where could he go?

Well, he knew, all right. He couldn't keep a job, not remembering he'd killed the sergeant, who was really a pretty good guy. He'd have to keep on drinking. He couldn't even be decent, or have a home. Maybe become a crook. Outside of the army they put you in prison for killing someone. All of a sudden, he knew that he would probably one day be executed for killing someone. It was only a question of time. That's all. Just a question of time.

Now that he had finally admitted it, finally told himself the truth, things seemed a little easier. At least he didn't have any wild ideas about pulling out. He just couldn't escape it. That was the way it was. He didn't feel like fighting any more. But it was a matter of time.

The door opened and a man came in. He was not over five feet three, and wore a yellow T-shirt and a greasy hat. He had a small, pointed face. The fat woman said, "Hello there, Mr. Tod. Haven't seen you for a week."

"I'm always around," said Mr. Tod. "Gimme a bottle of Miller's."

He drank again. He'd kill someone again, sure. It must be in the cards. He was never meant to do anything else, and though he didn't exactly understand why it had to work out so, he accepted it now. No use fighting it. No use prolonging it. It was just a matter of time.

He drank two more beers, and slowly felt the edge of reality going dull. His watch showed eight-thirty. The door opened and a girl came in. He stared at his glass, hearing her take a stool near him, and the fat woman said, "Hi, June."

"Hi," the girl said disgustedly. A car without a muffler gunned away, close outside. He turned his head slowly, curious, to look at the girl. She had brown hair and was very thin. She was wearing blue jeans and a man's white shirt, open at the throat and with sleeves rolled up. She had a narrow face and small breasts. She wasn't pretty at all. On the other side of her he could see Mr. Tod still sitting.

"Bourbon and water, will you?" June said to the fat woman.

"You sure got your dander up," said the fat woman. She poured the drink from one of the bottles.

"Oh, it's that Jim."

"Was that his car outside just now?"

"Yes."

The fat woman heaved a snort. "What did he do, throw you out?"

"No, sir! I *got* out. I'm through with him, he ain't worth my time. Stubborn. I wanted to go to the drive-in, but no," she mimicked acidly, "he wanted to go to his old stock car races. I got fed up. I told him to let me off."

"He always was stubborn," the fat woman agreed. June took a sip of her drink, shuddered, and glanced sidewise toward him.

"Oh, there's plenty more."

He licked his lips. Well, why not?

He waited until the fat woman went into the next room on an errand. Mr. Tod walked over and began to play the pinball machine. The lights flickered across the ceiling, buzzers stuttered like machine guns, and bells pinged. He picked up his beer glass and walked toward the girl. He sat down next to her.

"Kin I buy you one?"

"When I finish this one." She smiled. Her lipstick was a crooked, thin red line. Up close he could see she had hardly any lips at all, and had painted the lipstick up over flat skin.

"You from Sheridan?" the girl asked.

He nodded. "I got discharged today."

"Oh, you did! Where you from? Down South?"

"Texas."

"I'll bet they call you Tex."

"Yes, they do."

"Well, my name's June." She smiled again, making no pretenses.

After a moment he said, "Like to go for a ride? My car's outside."

"That maroon Chevy? That new one?"

"Bought it this afternoon."

"Oo!" She clapped her hands, then seized his arm. Her hand felt hot. "Listen, honey. Let me go to the little girl's room and fix my face and I'll meet you in the car. How about it?"

"Fine," he said, not meaning it.

He watched her vanish out a side door, and noticed how thin her rump was beneath the jeans. Then he remembered what he'd been thinking about when she walked in. Couldn't forget it for long. He looked around. Mr. Tod still worked the pinball machine. Outside the traffic roared, all going someplace. He shook his head. No go. In a year, or maybe ten, or maybe twenty, he'd kill somebody good and that would be all. It was just a matter of time. He felt like he wanted to lie down and have a nice long sleep, where he could forget it all. He didn't want to live all those years out.

The fat woman with the plaster on her neck came back. He started for the door, thinking of the girl. They could go for a ride. She ought to know some dark side road. It was just a matter of time anyway, now or ten years from now, what difference did it make, except that he was tired and knew the score.

He walked back to the bar, his mind made up, past Mr. Tod. He brushed Mr. Tod's shoulder but the man did not look around. He put his hands on the bar, feeling the wood, feeling worse and yet better. The woman had started to read another comic book, and she looked up. He said to her, "I want to buy a fifth of whiskey."

The Vanishing Men

·

Edward D. Hoch

Edward D. Hoch is widely considered to be the modern master of the criminous short story, having published well over six hundred in his thirty-year career. Further testimony to his expertise is the fact that for the past several years he has been editor of the distinguished annual, Year's Best Mystery & Suspense Stories. *Of the many series characters he has created, perhaps the most popular and enduring is Captain Leopold, head of the Violent Crimes Squad in a large upstate New York city. One of Leopold's cases, the oft-anthologized "The Oblong Room," won an MWA Edgar for Best Short Story of 1967. In "The Vanishing Men," he is also called on to solve a seemingly insolublecrime, three disappearances that just couldn't have happened. . . .*

Captain Leopold had known Jennings Blake for more than twenty years—ever since Leopold returned to the city and took the position with what was now the Violent Crimes Squad. Blake had represented Leopold during his divorce proceedings long ago, and their paths had crossed often in the courtroom during the years that followed.

On the sunny June morning when Jennings Blake came to visit Leopold in his little office on the second floor of Police Headquarters, they had not seen each other in more than a year. The lawyer had grown stouter and grayer, though Leopold could hardly mention these symptoms of middle age from which he himself suffered.

Instead he said, "I haven't seen you in court lately, Jennings. Letting the younger fellows handle the tough ones?"

The lawyer smiled, as if remembering and relishing their friendly rivalry of earlier years. "The ones I handle never get to court, Captain."

"You haven't changed a bit." Leopold leaned back, relaxing. Jennings Blake was like an old familiar friend, although they rarely saw each other socially. Even on a warm June day he still wore his traditional dark blue suit, the coat neatly buttoned over white shirt and tie. He'd dressed exactly the same when he handled Leopold's divorce twenty years ago. "What can I do for you today, counselor?"

"There's an odd sort of estate case I'm working on. Two important witnesses have vanished in the past week, and that bothers me."

"Have you reported it to Missing Persons?"

Blake shook his head. "They're both from out of town and I haven't reported it till now because I wasn't certain they'd really vanished. The whole thing is so bizarre—"

"Any reason to suspect violence?"

"Why do you ask?"

"You came to Violent Crimes rather than Missing Persons, so it's a natural question."

"I came here because I know you, Captain. But yes, there could be violence."

Leopold pulled a yellow legal pad across the desk and picked up a pencil. "Their names?"

"Sam Wellington and Rick O'Brian. They're merchant seamen. I brought them here to testify in a probate hearing later this week."

"Suppose you start at the beginning," Leopold suggested.

"Very well." The lawyer shifted a bit awkwardly in his chair. "Do you know what a nuncupative will is?"

"No idea," Leopold admitted.

"In this state and many others, the law allows members of the armed forces or mariners at sea to make an unwritten or nuncupative will under certain circumstances. The provision of such an oral will must be clearly established by at least two witnesses before it can be admitted to probate."

Leopold frowned. "You mean circumstances like a soldier going into battle or a seaman on a sinking ship?"

"Actually the law is not quite that strict. As long as the testator served in the armed forces during a declared or undeclared war, and was in a combat zone or on his way to a combat zone, a nuncupative will is valid in this state. And in the case of a merchant seaman, he can even be on board a ship tied up at a dock when he makes his oral will. The intent of the law, of course, is to recognize the imminent dangers constantly threatening members of the armed forces in wartime or mariners at sea at any time."

"And your case involves merchant seamen?"

"Correct. William Tree was a member of the merchant marine, the first mate on the cargo ship *Nancy Star*, registered in Panama but owned by an American firm. The ship encountered violent weather in the Caribbean last October. When some cargo on deck came loose, William Tree went out with some other men to secure it. Before he went, he told two witnesses—Wellington and O'Brian—that if anything happened to him he wanted everything he owned to go to his fiancée, Nicole Scanlon."

"Your client."

"My client, exactly. William Tree vanished from the deck of the ship, apparently swept overboard by a wave, although no one actually saw it happen. In any event, he was gone from the ship and was declared officially dead despite the absence of a body. *Lost at sea* is the quaint old term for it. Now we come to the crucial part. Two days before William Tree was lost at sea, his father died of a heart attack here in the city. Perhaps you've heard of Tree Enterprises."

"The newspaper publisher." The picture was emerging in Leopold's mind. Jennings Blake was in this because there was a great deal of money involved.

"Exactly. William Tree died without knowing of his father's death. The father had never approved of his maritime career, but nevertheless he left his estate in equal shares to his two sons—William and Paul. The estate, including the elder Tree's share in Tree Enterprises, amounts to about two million dollars."

"So if you can probate your oral will, your client receives about one million dollars. If you can't, brother Paul gets everything."

"Exactly. He would inherit William's share as next of kin. Their mother died some years ago and there are no other siblings."

"Now tell me about your two witnesses."

"Nicole was contacted by them last winter, a few months after William Tree's death. When she heard their story of the oral will, she came to me. There was some delay in the court hearing because of the necessity to establish the fact of William's death, but now it's scheduled for Thursday and I've brought in Wellington and O'Brian to testify. Only they've both disappeared."

"How?"

"Wellington was staying at the Holiday Inn. Last Saturday evening I went there to take a preliminary statement

132

from him. At one point I excused myself to use the bathroom. When I came back he was gone. There was a large damp spot on the rug by his chair, as if something had been spilled.''

''Was the door bolted on the inside?''

''No, he hadn't bolted or chained it after I arrived. He could have walked out, and that's what I supposed did happen. Until the second one.''

''Rick O'Brian?'' Leopold asked, consulting his notes.

Jennings Blake nodded. ''We met last evening at the outdoor café down at the Plaza. I stepped away from the table for a moment to get a pack of cigarettes and when I looked back he was gone. He was wearing a bright red jacket and should have been easy to spot, even in a crowd. But he was nowhere. I asked people at nearby tables, but no one noticed him leave.''

''How long was your back turned to the table?''

''Only the length of time it takes to drop some coins in the slot and pull the plunger for the cigarettes. Maybe ten seconds. He *couldn't* have gotten out of my range of vision that quickly. Besides, there was something else.''

''What?''

''Water spilled on his chair, as if a drink had overturned.''

''Just like Wellington.''

''Exactly.''

Leopold shrugged. ''Coincidence.''

''But where did they *go*, Captain? I brought them here, they were willing to testify, and then they simply vanished. With Wellington I figured he ran off to get drunk somewhere, but now that they've both vanished I think it's something more. I think someone's trying to keep them from testifying on Thursday.''

''The brother, Paul Tree?''

"I don't know. But something might have happened to them."

"How do you explain the water?"

The lawyer looked uncomfortable. "Someone might want us to connect these happenings with William Tree's death at sea—the wave that washed him away."

"You think Tree's not really dead? Or that he's come back from the dead?" Leopold was grinning now. Somehow he couldn't take it all as seriously as the lawyer did. "Do you have a picture of this fellow Tree?"

'I've only seen the newspaper photos of him. But I honestly don't—"

They were interrupted by Policewoman Connie Trent, who appeared at the door. "Could I see you for a moment, Captain?"

"Certainly. Excuse me, Jennings."

Connie's desk was in the squad room, just a few feet from Leopold's door. He joined her there and glanced at the note she held in her hand. "The desk sergeant downstairs just found this. He doesn't know who left it."

The typed message was brief and to the point: *Captain Leopold—Stay away from the lawyer Jennings Blake. The Tree affair does not concern the police.*

"Threatening letters to the police?" Leopold snorted. "Now I've seen everything! Ask Fletcher to check it for prints."

He turned and walked back into his office, and that was when he began to take the case seriously.

Jennings Blake had disappeared.

The office was empty.

And there was a large damp spot on the carpet by his chair.

Leopold's first reaction was to hurry into the squad room, looking for the missing man. But there were only the familiar detectives plus a few police officers filling out arrest reports. On a bench near the door a handcuffed burglary suspect sat smoking a cigarette.

"Connie, did you see what became of Jennings Blake?"

"Isn't he in your office?"

"No."

Fletcher's glassed-in cubicle was near the front of the squad room, by the room's only exit, and Leopold asked him next. Fletcher scratched his head and scowled. "The lawyer that came to see you, Captain? He didn't come by here. I been keeping my eye on our prisoner there, and I'd have noticed him if he walked by."

Leopold asked the rest of the detectives and police officers in the squad room. He even asked the burglary suspect. Their answers were all the same. They'd seen nothing of Jennings Blake. He hadn't come out through the squad room. Two more policemen came in with a box of stolen merchandise they'd recovered, and the place was suddenly busy. Leopold signaled Fletcher and Connie to join him in his office. "What is it, Captain?" Fletcher asked, glancing around. "Where's Blake?"

"Damned if I know. He just—vanished!"

Connie pointed. "He must have gone out the window."

It was true that both windows in the room were open about six inches at the bottom, providing a bit of breeze that was the office's only air conditioning. "He couldn't fit through that space," Leopold said. "And these damn windows are hard to raise and lower. Do you think he pushed it up, climbed out on the ledge, and sat there struggling to pull it down again?"

He demonstrated by pushing the window up with effort, and stuck his head out. They were only on the second floor, overlooking the parking lot, but the line of cars parked directly below the windows would have made for a hard landing. None of the hoods showed the dent or scrape that would have resulted from someone dropping onto one of them, nor were there any handy ropes dangling from the building. The building's fire escape was far out of reach, around the corner.

Leopold pulled his head back in. "No, Jennings couldn't have gone out this way."

"Then where is he?" Connie wanted to know.

Leopold walked to the door and stood there. The squad room was busy and noisy again, but there was still no Jennings Blake. If he left Leopold's office during the few seconds Leopold was at Connie's desk, he'd have had to walk past a dozen people without being seen. The other way, to the right of the office door, there was only an alcove with the coffee machine and filing cabinets. Not even a place to hide, and certainly no exit.

"I don't know," Leopold admitted. "I don't know what happened to him. Either he's playing some bizarre practical joke or—"

"Or what?"

"Or three men have now vanished under unusual circumstances. Look, Connie, get on the phone to Blake's office and home. Don't alarm them, but find out if he's turned up at either place. Leave a message for him to call here. Fletcher, take the note from Connie's desk and dust it for prints." He bent to the worn carpeting and tried to moisten his fingers with the spilled liquid. "Seems to be water, all right," he decided after touching a moist finger to his tongue. "There's no taste at all."

"But where did it come from?" Connie asked.

"I don't know. Maybe the same place that Jennings Blake went to."

It was after noon before they established with some certainty that Blake had indeed vanished. His wife was frantic and his secretary befuddled. After Fletcher confirmed there were no fingerprints on the note except the desk sergeant's and Connie's, Leopold drove out to visit Mrs. Blake.

Her first name was Ama and he'd met her once or twice at the large political gatherings that are commonplace around election time. She was a woman of fifty or so, still attractive but beginning to show the signs of age. "I can't believe he just disappeared."

"I can't believe it either," Leopold said, "and I was there."

"He's never done anything like this before."

"Never played a little practical joke? Never hidden from you in the house?"

"Never."

"Did he say anything to you about the estate case he's working on? The Tree estate?"

"We never discussed business at home. There are so many other things to talk about."

Leopold was deciding he didn't much care for Ama Blake. He wondered if her husband might have had the same feelings. Still, it would be easy enough for a lawyer to arrange a divorce without having to disappear. "Did he have any trouble with other partners in the firm?"

"I told you he never discussed it. Why are you here asking foolish questions when you should be out finding him?"

Leopold had to agree. "Don't worry, Mrs. Blake," he assured her as he left. "We'll find Jennings." But at that point he wouldn't have wanted to guess whether it would be dead or alive.

Blake's secretary gave him the address of his client, Nicole Scanlon, and Leopold reached her apartment in mid-afternoon. His reception was much friendlier than at the Blake household. Nicole was a dark-haired beauty, still in her twenties, who'd be on any man's mind while he was at sea.

"First of all, Inspector—"

"Captain," Leopold corrected.

"—Captain. I want it understood that when I became engaged to Bill I never had any idea he came from a wealthy family. He was the first mate on a ship and that was all I knew. He mentioned taking me to meet his father some time when he was in port, but we hadn't done it yet."

"It hardly matters when you discovered about the money," Leopold pointed out, feeling quite at home in the overstuffed armchair opposite her. The furniture was expensive and new, and he wondered if Tree had bought it with family money. "The fact remains that you knew it by the time his two shipmates contacted you."

"Well, yes," she admitted reluctantly.

"Wellington and O'Brian. What can you tell me about them?"

"I understand they're missing, too."

"Who told you?"

"Mr. Blake phoned me last night to see if either man had contacted me. It seems they both disappeared while they were with him."

Leopold nodded. "And now Jennings himself has disappeared."

"I can't understand that at all."

"Neither can I, and he vanished from my office." Leopold ran over the sequence of events for her. "I'm wondering if that note could have been left by either of the two missing witnesses. Did Wellington or O'Brian ever suggest you give them a cut of the estate in return for their testimony about the oral will?"

"Certainly not! I've never even met the men, or corresponded with them. They phoned me during the winter when they returned to port, and from there on I turned the entire matter over to Jennings Blake. He felt it was best that I didn't meet them until the probate hearing, to avoid just that sort of suspicion.''

"I had to suggest the possibility. There's a great deal of money involved here. When is the last time you spoke to the brother, Paul Tree?''

"Not recently. I never even met him while Bill was alive.'' He could see the anger building within her. "But if you're looking for some sort of dirty work, you certainly should talk to Paul. He's the only one who profits if that oral will is never probated.''

"I was thinking the same thing. Has he threatened you in any way?''

"Some months back, after I hired a lawyer and announced my intention of claiming a share of the estate, he came here one evening to see me and offered me ten thousand dollars as an out-of-court settlement. Mr. Blake advised me to turn it down.''

"Had Blake interviewed the two witnesses before last weekend?''

"Only by telephone. They were at sea much of the time. He had letters from each of them, but in an estate this size he said it would be necessary to produce the men in court. Oral wills are very much subject to the probate judge's interpretation of the law, and there's debate over whether the law should receive a strict or a liberal construction.''

"You sound like a lawyer yourself.''

She smiled. "It's all those hours listening to Mr. Blake go over the case.''

He left her at the door and went downstairs to his car. So far he'd learned very little about the Tree estate and nothing at all about the vanishing of Jennings Blake.

When Leopold returned to headquarters, Fletcher was gone from his office and a young patrolman he didn't know was chatting with Connie Trent at her desk. The officer wore his cap far back on his curly black hair, and his arms were handsomely tanned beneath the short-sleeved white shirt of his summer uniform. The name plate beneath his badge said *Rodgers,* and after he'd left, Leopold asked Connie. "Is Rodgers your latest conquest?"

She blushed prettily and busied herself with some reports. "I hardly know him. He's one of the new recruits. I could be his older sister."

"Sure. Or his mother." Before she could explode at that he quickly asked, "Anything on Blake?"

"Nothing. The judge is willing to postpone Thursday's probate hearing if he doesn't turn up. Did you talk to his wife?"

He nodded. "And to his client. I learned nothing from either of them. Did you check the motels where Wellington and O'Brian were registered?"

"Sure did. They were both there and they both disappeared without checking out. The bills went to Blake's office anyway, so that didn't matter. No one seems to think there was anything too unusual."

"So we only have Jennings Blake's word for it," Leopold mused.

"You think he made up the whole story?"

"Well, there's a client and an estate, but after that the whole business seems a bit vague. The idea of someone, ghost or human, entering my office and taking Blake away by force is even more fantastic than if he vanished willingly."

Connie stood up. "Let me get us some coffee and we'll talk about it."

The machine outside his office was working for a change. When she came in he was crouched on the floor behind his desk. "Can you see me?"

She was laughing so hard she almost spilled the coffee.

"Of course I can see you! What do you think you're doing?"

"I was wondering if Blake could have been hiding behind my desk when I looked in the first time."

"Not a chance."

"He's slimmer than I am."

"Still no chance, Captain. And if he hid behind the door you'd have seen his silhouette through the frosted glass."

Leopold got up and brushed off his knees. "So he really did leave this room, and it had to be either through the door or through the windows."

"Unless you've got a secret panel you never told us about."

He took a sip of coffee. "If he left by the door someone would have seen him. And if he left by the window, how did he manage to pull it down again, and to land on those cars below without injuring himself? And why would he do it in the first place?"

"Maybe you should have bars on your windows, Captain."

"What for? To keep lawyers from jumping out?"

"To keep *you* from trying it! I don't want to come in here and find you out on that ledge trying to shut the window after you."

"Don't worry."

He sent Connie back to her desk and sat there brooding for a time. He stared at the walls and the floor and the ceiling, and finally he got up and went out.

It was time to call on Paul Tree.

The surviving brother had his office on the top floor of the Tree Enterprises building, commanding a view to the south over the Sound that was truly breathtaking. "My office looks out on a parking lot," Leopold said sadly.

Paul Tree remained seated behind his desk. He barely

glanced at the windows. He was a man in his early thirties, though he had the mannerisms of someone much older. "I really don't understand the reason for your visit, Captain. You say no crime has been committed?"

"Three men seem to have vanished, including the attorney Jennings Blake, but we have no solid evidence of a crime as yet."

"If this is about my father's estate—"

"It is."

"It's that woman again," he said with some exasperation. "She's after my brother's share and she doesn't care how she gets it."

"You mean Nicole Scanlon?"

"Of course. She hired those two merchant seamen to make up that phony story, but when it gets down to delivering them in a court of law she can't produce."

"If anything's happened to them, you'd be a prime suspect," Leopold pointed out.

"All that's happened is that they got smart and went back to sea."

"And Jennings Blake?"

"I don't believe he's missing."

"I can tell you he is."

Paul Tree glanced at his watch. "Say, it's after five. I'm going home now."

"I thought newspapermen worked all night."

"Not this one. All those long hours got my father was an early grave."

"Tell me about your brother."

"What's there to tell? He ran away to sea and he was lost there."

"It's like something out of the last century."

"Yes, isn't it? Now you really must excuse me, Captain."

"If he spent so much time at sea how'd he manage to meet and become engaged to Nicole Scanlon?"

"You'd have to ask her that. Frankly, I'm not even too sure there was an engagement. Knowing my brother, he probably shacked up with her when he was in town."

"Has there been any hint that William might not have been killed at sea?"

"What?" Paul Tree seemed to lose his composure for the first time. "What do you mean?"

"I told you three men have disappeared. Water or wet spots were found at the site of each disappearance. Someone seems to be hinting that William has come back from the sea for these people."

"My God! Do you believe in ghosts, Captain?"

"Not in this case," Leopold answered, quite seriously. "I touched a bit of the water to my tongue and it had no taste at all. Your brother's ghost would surely have been dripping salt water, not fresh water."

"Well, fine, you've deduced it's not a ghost!"

"But I haven't deduced that it's not William. A ship might have picked him up, and perhaps now he's revenging himself on his two shipmates who left him to die."

"Did they do that?"

"I don't know," Leopold admitted. "They're not available for questioning. I have a case without any corpses at all. I not only don't know who did it—I don't even know what's been done, and to whom!"

"Well, I'm sure William wouldn't be walking around alive without contacting me. The courts are convinced he's dead and so am I."

"Nicole Scanlon says you tried to buy her off. Is that true?"

"I offered her some money. That's all she's after. My price just wasn't high enough."

"All right," Leopold said. "This whole thing may be

some sort of extortion scheme. If anyone contacts you for money, I want you to call me at once.''

''I surely will.''

Leopold was on his way back downtown when a call came in for him on the radio. A body had been found in the trunk of a stolen car at the airport parking lot. It appeared to be someone connected with the Blake affair.

Driving to the airport with his siren on, Leopold wondered if the body might be that of Jennings Blake himself. But when he arrived, pushing his way through a ring of curious spectators, he found Fletcher standing over the body of a man he'd never seen before.

''We found these in his pocket, Captain, but no wallet or identification.''

Leopold looked over the crumpled pack of cigarettes and a lighter that had *Nancy Star* stenciled on the side of it. There was also a tiny address book with a few names in it. The only local one was Jennings Blake, with his office phone number written after the name.

''How'd he die?'' Leopold asked.

''Shot once in the back of the head.''

''All right. It's probably Sam Wellington or Rick O'Brian, one of Blake's two witnesses, but I'm not taking any chances. Pick up Nicole Scanlon and ask her if she can identify the body.''

Fletcher scowled. ''If it's not Wellington or O'Brian, who could it be?''

''William Tree, if he came back from the dead.''

It was a good idea, the sort that would have made a bit of sense in such a crazy case, but it wasn't to be. Nicole Scanlon quickly doused it by saying the dead man looked nothing like her fiancé. ''See? Here's a picture of him, taken on his final voyage.''

Leopold inspected the snapshot from her wallet and had

to agree. "Then it's either Wellington or O'Brian. Any idea which?" The man in the picture, standing against the railing of a ship at sea, looked enough like Paul Tree to be his brother. A life preserver on the railing carried the name *Nancy Star*.

"No idea," she replied. "I told you I never met either man."

"That's right," Leopold agreed.

"Paul Tree would stop at nothing to keep me from getting that money."

"You think he killed this man?"

"That's your problem. But if it's either of my two witnesses, the oral will can't be probated."

"Not unless a new witness is found. William Tree might have made his statement before other crewmen as well."

"That's possible." She shivered a little. "Let's get out of here. I only hope you don't have me down tomorrow to identify another body."

"The second witness?"

"Or Jennings Blake."

It was a bad night and the morning was no better.

The newspapers had got wind of Blake's disappearance and there were reporters at Headquarters wanting to see and photograph Leopold's office. He often marveled at the power of the press, and wondered if there might be some way to use them in the present case. Thinking about it, looking at the morgue shot of the murdered man's face on his desk, he was interrupted by a call from Ama Blake.

"Do you mean someone as important as my husband can vanish from your office and never be seen again?" she asked, her voice crackling over the wire.

"I'm sure we'll see Jennings again," Leopold responded. "I'm doing everything I can to find him. Just be calm."

She hung up the phone, not bothering to say good-bye.

Leopold went out to the coffee machine and noticed that the cop named Rodgers was back at Connie's desk. Was he off duty, or maybe waiting to testify in a court case? If he continued to hang around, Leopold would have to speak to him. A date with Connie, if that's what he wanted, could be arranged over the telephone after working hours.

Leopold sat staring at his muddy coffee. Suddenly he knew how Jennings Blake had disappeared.

More important, he knew why.

Leopold was sitting in his car behind the building when he saw the blue Ford pull into the parking place in the next row. He could tell by the license number that it was a rented vehicle, and it took him only an instant to recognize the man he'd been waiting for.

"Hello, Jennings," he called out just as the lawyer reached the back door of the building.

Jennings Blake whirled at the sound of his name. "Leopold! I—what in hell are you doing here?"

"Waiting for you. After all, you did leave quite suddenly yesterday morning."

"I can explain all that."

"I know you can, but everything's changed now. We're talking about murder now—the murder of a merchant seaman named Sam Wellington."

Jennings Blake moistened his lips. "The noon papers said you hadn't identified him."

"It could only have been Wellington if I've got it figured right."

"How's that?"

"I've got two theories," Leopold said. "Let's see which one you buy. The first is this: you made up that whole story about the two witnesses disappearing. They never disappeared the way you said. They were kidnaped by Paul

Tree, with your help, and then murdered. You made up the vanishing story and then worked it in my office so I'd believe it. That theory makes you an accessory to murder, counselor."

The color had drained from his face as Leopold spoke. "It was nothing like that! I'm not involved in anything crooked. My God, I never knew anyone was going to be killed!"

"All right. Then let's go upstairs and I'll tell you my second theory."

"I was just—"

"I know where you were going, and I know why. I'll just go along."

Nicole Scanlon opened her apartment door and smiled when she saw Jennings. Her smile froze when she caught sight of Leopold, but he shouldered the door open before she could change her mind about letting them in. "Let's talk about it," Leopold said.

"About what?"

"The man you killed, Nicole."

"I didn't—"

"Let's all sit down and take it from the beginning. This is the way I figure it happened. William Tree was a fellow you knew, Nicole. Maybe you were engaged to him and maybe you weren't. It doesn't really matter, though I'm inclined to believe the latter was the case."

"I'm not going to—"

Leopold held up his hand. "Calm down. I haven't arrested you yet, and before I do I'll give you all the necessary warnings. In any event, William Tree—your friend Bill—was swept overboard during a storm and lost at sea. That much is true. Some months later one of his shipmates came to you with a scheme. He'd heard about the legality of oral wills for merchant seamen, and he knew you were Tree's girlfriend. He also knew from the newspapers that

Tree's wealthy father had died two days ahead of him. So he proposed that he and a shipmate become the necessary two witnesses to Tree's nuncupative will, leaving everything to you. In return for their fraudulent testimony, you would split the estate with them.''

She was staring at the floor, avoiding contact with Jennings Blake's eyes, as Leopold hurried on. "You hired Jennings to represent you, and then there was an unexpected turn of events. Jennings, hobbled by a somewhat shrewish wife, fell in love with you.''

"Now look here!'' the lawyer objected.

"I got the idea from something in my office this morning—a young cop trying to score with a policewoman. I remembered, Nicole, that you were home in midafternoon, apparently without a job, and that you had new, expensive furniture here. I could have been wrong, but the signs indicated you might have a wealthy male friend. Jennings fitted the picture, especially when I remembered your telling of all the hours he spent going over the case with you.''

Nicole blushed and remained silent. Jennings Blake was on his feet. "This has gone far enough, Leopold!''

"Sit down—I'm only beginning. All was going well last weekend till one of the witnesses, Sam Wellington, got cold feet when it came to actually signing a false document. While you were in the bathroom, Jennings, he got so nervous he spilled his drink and decided to scram. That was our first vanishing man. Naturally, you told Nicole and she hurried to her partner in fraud, Rick O'Brian. Since it was all his idea in the first place, he was anxious to rescue his plan.''

"Why Rick's idea rather than Wellington's?'' the lawyer asked, calming down a bit.

"If I believed your story, that's the way it had to be. The first disappearance had no real impossibility to it, and was easily explained without the events that followed. O'Brian's disappearance was an attempt to cloud the issue and make you, Jennings, think there was some sinister force at work.''

''How did O'Brian vanish from the table at that outdoor restaurant?''

''By the simplest trick in the world. You told me he was wearing a bright red jacket. He stood up, removed his jacket, bundled it under his arm, and walked away. When you turned around from the cigarette machine you were looking for a red jacket in the crowd and you didn't see one. Rick O'Brian had vanished, carefully spilling some water first to further connect his disappearance with the first one.''

''And what was this supposed to accomplish?'' Nicole asked.

''With both men gone so mysteriously, you could shift suspicion to William's brother, Paul. It would give you time to find Wellington and persuade him to play along—or else replace him with another so-called witness from among the crew. As it turned out, Wellington couldn't be persuaded. Maybe he even tried a touch of blackmail. In any event, you and O'Brian killed him.''

''Can you prove that in court?'' Jennings Blake challenged. Again he was on his feet, as if addressing a jury, defending the woman he loved.

''She lied to me about not being able to identify the body, Jennings. She said she'd never met either witness, and only talked to them on the phone. But she had a snapshot of William Tree taken on his final voyage. She didn't get it from you because you told me you'd seen nothing but a newspaper photo of him. She didn't get it from Tree because he never returned from the voyage. So she had to get it from one of the two witnesses, either in person or through the mail. Why lie about it, unless she was doing

149

something dishonest with them? And if she was involved in the fraud, it stands to reason she was involved in the murder.''

"That's a lie!" Nicole screamed. "I wasn't even there when Rick killed him!"

That was when the bedroom door opened and a man in a bright red jacket stepped out. He was holding a revolver and bringing it up fast.

"Well, the vanishing Mr. O'Brian!" Leopold said, and shot him in the shoulder.

It was Connie Trent who put the question to him first, back in his office at Headquarters. "That's fine, Captain, you've told us how you captured O'Brian and got a confession out of Nicole. But you haven't told us the most important part. How did Jennings Blake vanish from this room?"

"And why?" Fletcher added. "Since he wasn't involved in the fraud or the murder, what was his motive?"

"He had two motives really," Leopold responded, taking the last question first. "One was simply to bring me into a case that didn't yet have a violent crime. He told me he figured with me nosing around it would scare them off."

"He knew Nicole was involved?"

"He feared it. He suspected fraud after both witnesses disappeared so mysteriously—which brings us to his second motive for vanishing. He thought he knew how O'Brian had disappeared—by removing his jacket—but he had to test it out. So he came to my office yesterday morning and vanished the same way."

"By removing his jacket?"

Leopold nodded. "He was wearing a dark blue suit with a white shirt and tie. Take off the jacket and tie, and what do you have? A policeman's summer uniform.

He was wearing a badge and gun under his coat, to heighten the illusion, and he even had a policeman's peaked cap under his coat, pressed against his side. That was why I noticed him moving a bit awkwardly in that chair. He also had a little plastic bag of water, to complete the illusion.''

"But what happened to his coat and tie?''

"He bundled them up and shoved them out through the partly open window. The whole thing took mere seconds. Then he walked out of the office while I was reading that note at your desk. Connie—a note he'd dropped off on his way in. He figured you'd call me out to read it.''

"But what if I hadn't? Or what if we'd spotted the jacket when we looked out the window?''

"He dropped it between the cars and retrieved it on his way out—but you've got to realize it wouldn't have mattered if we caught him or prevented him from working his act. He wasn't committing a crime—only playing a little joke. He wanted to see if it would work. It did, beautifully, because there are often cops walking through the squad room that none of us know.'' He glanced at Connie as he said this, and she got his message. "We see the uniform, not the face. Without his suit coat, Jennings Blake vanished as easily as Rick O'Brian.''

"But why did he stay missing if it was only a joke?''

"Because it confirmed that his witnesses could have vanished voluntarily—and that made him suspect fraud. Any sort of fraud automatically involved Nicole, whom he loved. He decided to stay missing because he didn't want to go home to his wife. Because he still hoped to be with Nicole. That was why I knew he'd go to her apartment today when he read in the paper of Wellington's murder. I had them run a morgue shot on page one of the noon edition, and then I just went to her building and waited for him.''

"You made him reappear almost as cleverly as he disappeared," Connie commented.

Leopold smiled. "He taught me a good trick. I must try it myself some night when the Chief is camped out there waiting to see me."

"What about Nicole? Do you think she was in on the murder with O'Brian?"

"Connie, I guess we'll have to let a jury answer that one."

The Dettweiler Solution

•

Lawrence Block

*A suspense novelist of the front rank, Lawrence Block has an impressive credit list of nonseries novels (*Ariel, The Deadly Honeymoon*) and no less than three successful series—the adventures of spy Evan Tanner (*Me Tanner, You Jane*), burglar Bernie Rhodenbarr (*The Burglar in the Closet, Burglars Can't Be Choosers*), and tough ex-cop and part-time private eye Matt Scudder (*Eight Million Ways to Die*, which won a Private Eye Writers of America Shamus as Best Novel of 1982, and the recent* When the Sacred Gin Mill Closes*). One of his Matt Scudder short stories, "By the Dawn's Early Light," was the recipient of an MWA Edgar in 1985. "The Dettweiler Solution," a nonseries story, is Block at the top of his form.*

Sometimes you just can't win for losing. Business was so bad over at Dettweiler Bros. Fine Fashions for Men that Seth Dettweiler went on back to the store one Thursday night and poured out a five-gallon can of lead-free gasoline where he figured as it would do the most good. He lit a fresh Philip Morris King Size and balanced it on the edge of the counter so as it would burn for a couple of minutes and then get unbalanced enough to drop into the pool of gasoline. Then he got into an Oldsmobile that was about five days clear of a repossession notice and drove on home.

You couldn't have had a better fire dropping napalm on

a paper mill. Time it was done you could sift those ashes and not find so much as a collar button. It was far and away the most spectacularly total fire Schuyler County had ever seen, so much so that Maybrook Fidelity Insurance would have been a little tentative about settling a claim under ordinary circumstances. But the way things stood, there wasn't the slightest suspicion of arson, because what kind of a dimwitted hulk goes and burns down his business establishment a full week after his fire insurance has lapsed?

No fooling.

See, it was Seth's brother Porter who took care of paying bills and such, and a little over a month ago the fire insurance payment had been due, and Porter looked at the bill and at the bank balance and back and forth for a while, and then he put the bill in a drawer. Two weeks later there was a reminder notice, and two weeks after that there was a notice that the grace period had expired and the insurance was no longer in force, and then a week after that there was one pluperfect hell of a bonfire.

Seth and Porter had always got on pretty good. (They took after each other quite a bit, folks said. Especially Porter.) Seth was forty-two years of age, and he had that long Dettweiler face topping a jutting Van Dine jaw. (Their mother was a Van Dine hailing from just the other side of Oak Falls.) Porter was thirty-nine, equipped with the same style face and jaw. They both had black hair that lay flat on their heads like shoe polish put on in slapdash fashion. Seth had more hair left than Porter, in spite of being the older brother by three years. I could describe them in greater detail, right down to scars and warts and sundry distinguishing marks, but it's my guess that you'd enjoy reading all that about as much as I'd enjoy writing it, which is to say less than somewhat. So let's get on with it.

I was saying they got on pretty good, rarely raising their voices one to the other, rarely disagreeing seriously about anything much. Now the fire didn't entirely change the habits of a lifetime, but you couldn't honestly say that it did anything to improve their relationship. You'd have to allow that it caused a definite strain.

"What I can't understand," Seth said, "is how anybody who is fool enough to let fire insurance lapse can be an even greater fool by not telling his brother about it. That in a nutshell is what I can't understand."

"What beats *me*," Porter said, "is how the same person who has the nerve to fire a place of business for the insurance also does so without consulting his partner, especially when his partner just happens to be his brother."

"Allus I was trying to do," said Seth, "was save you from the criminal culpability of being an accessory before, to, and after the fact, plus figuring you might be too chicken-hearted to go along with it."

"Allus *I* was trying to do," said Porter, "was save you from worrying about financial matters you would be powerless to contend with, plus figuring it would just be an occasion for me to hear further from you on the subject of those bow ties."

"Well, you did buy one powerful lot of bow ties."

"I knew it."

"Something like a Pullman car full of bow ties, and it's not like every man and boy in Schuyler County's been getting this mad passion for bow ties of late."

"I just knew it."

"I wasn't the one brought up the subject, but since you went and mentioned those bow ties—"

"Maybe I should of mentioned the spats," Porter said.

"Oh, I don't want to hear about spats."

"No more than I wanted to hear about bow ties. Did we sell one single damn pair of spats?"

"We did."

"We did?"

"Feller bought one about fifteen months back. Had Maryland plates on his car, as I recall. Said he always wanted spats and didn't know they still made 'em.''

"Well, selling one pair out of a gross isn't too bad.''

"Now you leave off," Seth said.

"And you leave off of bow ties?''

"I guess.''

"Anyway, the bow ties and the spats all burned up in the same damn fire,'' Porter said.

"You know what they say about ill winds,'' Seth said. "I guess there's a particle of truth in it, what they say.''

While it didn't do the Dettweiler brothers much good to discuss spats and bow ties, it didn't solve their problems to leave off mentioning spats and bow ties. By the time they finished their conversation, all they were back to was square one, and the view from that spot wasn't the world's best.

The only solution was bankruptcy, and it didn't look to be all that much of a solution.

"I don't mind going bankrupt," one of the brothers said. (I think it was Seth. Makes no nevermind, actually. Seth, Porter, it's all the same who said it.) "I don't mind going bankrupt, but I sure do hate the thought of being broke.''

"Me too," said the other brother. (Porter, probably.)

"I've thought about bankruptcy from time to time.''

"Me too.''

"But there's a time and a place for bankruptcy.''

"Well, the place is all right. No better place for bankruptcy than Schuyler County.''

"That's true enough," said Seth. (Unless it was Porter.) "But this is surely not the time. Time to go bankrupt is in good times when you got a lot of money on hand. Only the damnedest kind of fool goes bankrupt when he's stony broke busted and there's a depression going on.''

156

What they were both thinking on during this conversation was a fellow name of Joe Bob Rathburton who was in the construction business over to the other end of Schuyler County. I myself don't know of a man in this part of the state with enough intelligence to bail out a leaky rowboat who doesn't respect Joe Bob Rathburton to hell and back as a man with good business sense. It was about two years ago that Joe Bob went bankrupt and he did it the right way. First of all he did it coming off the best year's worth of business he'd ever done in his life. Then what he did was he paid off the car and the house and the boat and put them all in his wife's name. (His wife was Mabel Washburn, but no relation to the Washburns who have the Schuyler County First National Bank. That's another family entirely.)

Once that was done, Joe Bob took out every loan and raised every dollar he possibly could, and he turned all that capital into green folding cash and sealed it in quart Mason jars, which he buried out back of an old pear tree that's sixty-plus years old and still bears fruit like crazy. And then he declared bankruptcy and sat back in his Mission rocker with a beer and a cigar and a real big-tooth smile.

"If I could think of anything worth doing," Porter Dettweiler said one night, "why, I guess I'd just go ahead and do it."

"Can't argue with that," Seth said.

"But I can't," Porter said.

"Nor I either."

"You might pass that old jug over here for a moment."

"Soon as I pour a tad for myself, if you've no objection."

"None whatsoever," said Porter.

They were over at Porter's place on the evening when this particular conversation occurred. They had taken to spending most of their evenings at Porter's on account of Seth had a wife at home, plus a daughter named Rachel who'd been working at the Ben Franklin store ever since dropping out of the junior college over at Monroe Center. Seth didn't have but the one daughter. Porter had two sons and a daughter, but they were all living with Porter's ex-wife, who had divorced him two years back and moved clear to Georgia. They were living in Valdosta now, as far as Porter knew. Least that was where he sent the check every month.

"Alimony jail," said Porter.

"How's that?"

"What I said was alimony jail. Where you go when you quit paying on your alimony."

"They got a special jug set aside for men don't pay their alimony?"

"Just an expression. I guess they put you into whatever jug's the handiest. All I got to do is quit sendin' Gert her checks and let her have them cart me away. Get my three meals a day and a roof over my head and the whole world could quit nagging me night and day for money I haven't got."

"You could never stand it. Bein' in a jail day in and day out, night in and night out."

"I know it," Porter said unhappily. "There anything left in that there jug, on the subject of jugs?"

"Some. Anyway, you haven't paid Gert a penny in how long? Three months?"

"Call it five."

"And she ain't throwed you in jail yet. Least you haven't got her close to hand so's she can talk money to you."

"Linda Mae givin' you trouble?"

"She did. Keeps a civil tongue since I beat up on her the last time."

"Lord knew what he was doin'," Porter said, "makin'

158

men stronger than women. You ever give any thought to what life would be like if wives could beat up on their husbands instead of the other way around?"

"Now I don't even want to think about that," Seth said.

You'll notice nobody was mentioning spats or bow ties. Even with the jug of corn getting discernibly lighter every time it passed from one set of hands to the other, these two subjects did not come up. Neither did anyone speak of the shortsightedness of failing to keep up fire insurance or the myopia of incincrating a building without ascertaining that such insurance was in force. Tempers had cooled with the ashes of Dettweiler Bros. Fine Fashions for Men, and once again Seth and Porter were on the best of terms.

Which just makes what happened thereafter all the more tragic.

"What I think I got," Porter said, "is no way to turn."

(This wasn't the same evening, but if you put the two evenings side by side under a microscope you'd be hard pressed to tell them apart each from the other. They were at Porter's little house over alongside the tracks of the old spur off the Wyandotte & Southern, which I couldn't tell you the last time there was a train on that spur, and they had their feet up and their shoes off, and there was a jug of corn in the picture. Most of their evenings had come to take on this particular shade.)

"Couldn't get work if I wanted to," Porter said, "which I don't and if I did I couldn't make enough to matter, and my debts is up to my ears and rising steady."

"It doesn't look to be gettin' better," Seth said. "On the other hand, how can it get worse?"

"I keep thinking the same."

"And?"

"And it keeps getting worse."

"I guess you know what you're talkin' about," Seth

said. He scratched his bulldog chin, which hadn't been in the same room with a razor in more than a day or two. "What I been thinkin' about," he said, "is killin' myself."

"You been thinking of that?"

"Sure have."

"I think on it from time to time myself," Porter admitted. "Mostly nights when I can't sleep. It can be a powerful comfort around about three in the morning. You think of all the different ways and the next thing you know you're asleep. Beats the stuffing out of counting sheep jumping fences. You seen one sheep you seen 'em all is always been my thoughts on the subject, whereas there's any number of ways of doing away with yourself."

"I'd take a certain satisfaction in it," Seth said, more or less warming to the subject. "What I'd leave is this note tellin' Linda Mae how her and Rachel'll be taken care of with the insurance, just to get the bitch's hopes up, and then she can find out for her own self that I cashed in that insurance back in January to make the payment on the Oldsmobile. You know it's pure uncut hell gettin' along without an automobile now."

"You don't have to tell me."

"Just put a rope around my neck," said Seth, smothering a hiccup, "and my damn troubles'll be over."

"And mine in the bargain,' Porter said.

"By you doin' your own self in?"

"Be no need," Porter said, "if you did *yourself* in."

"How you figure that?"

"What I figure is a hundred thousand dollars," Porter said. "Lord love a duck, if I had a hundred thousand dollars I could declare bankruptcy and live like a king!"

Seth looked at him, got up, walked over to him and took the jug away from him. He took a swig and socked the cork in place, but kept hold of the jug.

"Brother," he said, "I just guess you've had enough of this here."

"What makes you say that, brother?"

"Me killin' myself and you gettin' rich, you don't make sense. What you think you're talkin' about, anyhow?"

"Insurance," Porter said. "Insurance, that's what I think I'm talking about. Insurance."

Porter explained the whole thing. It seems there was this life insurance policy their father had taken out on them when they weren't but boys. Face amount of a hundred thousand dollars, double indemnity for accidental death. It was payable to him while they were alive, but upon his death the beneficiary changed. If Porter was to die, the money went to Seth. And vice versa.

"And you knew about this all along?"

"Sure did," Porter said.

"And never cashed it in? Not the policy on me and not the policy on you?"

"Couldn't cash 'em in," Porter said. "I guess I woulda if I coulda, but I couldn't so I didn't."

"And you didn't let these here policies lapse?" Seth said. "On account of occasionally a person can be just the least bit absentminded and forget about keeping a policy in force. That's been known to happen," Seth said, looking off to one side, "in matters relating to fire insurance, for example, and I just thought to mention it."

(I have the feeling he wasn't the only one to worry on that score. You may have had similar thoughts yourself, figuring you know how the story's going to end, what with the insurance not valid and all. Set your mind at rest. If that was the way it had happened, I'd never be taking the trouble to write it up for you. I got to select stories with some satisfaction in them if I'm going to stand a chance of selling them to the magazine, and I hope you don't figure

I'm sitting here poking away at this typewriter for the sheer physical pleasure of it. If I just want to exercise my fingers, I'll send them walking through the Yellow Pages if it's all the same to you.)

"Couldn't let 'em lapse," Porter said. "They're all paid up. What you call twenty-payment life, meaning you pay it in for twenty years and then you got it free and clear. And the way pa did it, you can't borrow on it or nothing. All you can do is wait and see who dies."

"Well, I'll be."

"Except we don't have to wait to see who dies."

"Why, I guess not. I just guess a man can take matters into his own hands if he's of a mind to."

"He surely can," Porter said.

"Man wants to kill himself, that's what he can go and do."

"No law against it," Porter said.

Now you know and I know that that last is not strictly true. There's a definite no-question law against suicide in our state, and most likely in yours as well. It's harder to make it stand up than a calf with four broken legs, however, and I don't recall that anyone hereabouts was ever prosecuted for it, or likely will be. It does make you wonder some what they had in mind writing that particular law into the books.

"I'll just have another taste of that there corn," Porter said, "and why don't you have a pull on the jug your own self? You have any idea just when you might go and do it?"

"I'm studying on it," Seth said.

"There's a lot to be said for doing something soon as a man's mind's made up on the subject. Not to be hurrying you or anything of the sort, but they say that he who hesitates is last." Porter scratched his chin. "Or some such," he said.

"I just might do it tonight."

"By God," Porter said.

"Get the damn thing over with. Glory Hallelujah and my troubles is over."

"And so is mine," said Porter.

"You'll be in the money then," said Seth, "and I'll be in the boneyard, and both of us is free and clear. You can just buy me a decent funeral and then go bankrupt in style."

"Give you Johnny Millbourne's number-one funeral," Porter promised. "Brass-bound casket and all. I mean, price is no object if I'm going bankrupt anyway. Let old Johnny swing for the money."

"You a damn good man, brother."

"You the best man in the world, brother."

The jug passed back and forth a couple more times. At one point Seth announced that he was ready, and he was halfway out the door before he recollected that his car had been repossessed, which interfered with his plans to drive it off a cliff. He came back in and sat down again and had another drink on the strength of it all, and then suddenly he sat forward and stared hard at Porter.

"This policy thing," he said.

"What about it?"

"It's on both of us, is what you said."

"If I said it then must be it's the truth."

"Well then," Seth said, and sat back, arms folded on his chest.

"Well then what?"

"Well then if *you* was to kill yourself, then *I'd* get the money and *you'd* get the funeral."

"I don't see what you're getting at," Porter said slowly.

"Seems to me either one of us can go and do it," Seth said. "And here's the two of us just takin' it for granted that I'm to be the one to go and do it, and I think we should think on that a little more thoroughly."

"Why, being as you're older, Seth."

"What's that to do with anything?"

"Why, you got less years to give up."

"Still be givin' up all that's left. Older or younger don't cut no ice."

Porter thought about it. "After all," he said, "it was your idea."

"That don't cut ice neither. I could mention I got a wife and child."

"I could mention I got a wife and three children."

"Ex-wife."

"All the same."

"Let's face it," Seth said. "Gert and your three don't add up to anything and neither do Linda Mae and Rachel."

"Got to agree," Porter said.

"So."

"One thing. You being the one who put us in this mess, what with firing the store, it just seems you might be the one to get us out of it."

"You bein' the one let the insurance lapse through your own stupidity, you could get us out of this mess through insurance, thus evenin' things up again."

"Now talkin' about stupidity—"

"Yes, talkin' about stupidity—"

"Spats!"

"Bow ties, damn you! *Bow ties!*"

You might have known it would come to that.

Now I've told you Seth and Porter generally got along pretty well and here's further evidence of it. Confronted by such a stalemate, a good many people would have wrote off the whole affair and decided not to take the suicide route at all. But not even spats and bow ties could deflect Seth and Porter from the road they'd figured out as the most logical to pursue.

164

So what they did, one of them tossed a coin, and the other one called it while it was in the air, and they let it hit the floor and roll, and I don't recollect whether it was heads or tails, or who tossed and who called—what's significant is that Seth won.

"Well, now," Seth said. "I feel I been reprieved. Just let me have that coin. I want to keep it for a luck charm."

"Two out of three."

"We already said once is as good as a million," Seth said, "so you just forget that two-out-of-three business. You got a week like we agreed, but if I was you I'd get it over soon as I could."

"I got a week," Porter said.

"You'll get the brass-bound casket and everything, and you can have Minnie Lucy Boxwood sing at your funeral if you want. Expense don't matter at all. What's your favorite song?"

"I suppose 'Your Cheatin' Heart.' "

"Minnie Lucy does that real pretty."

"I guess she does."

"Now you be sure and make it accidental," Seth said. "Two hundred thousand dollars goes just about twice as far as one hundred thousand dollars. Won't cost you a thing to make it accidental, just like we talked about it. What I would do is borrow Fritz Chenoweth's half-ton pickup and go up on the old Harburton Road where it takes that curve. Have yourself a belly full of corn and just keep goin' straight when the road doesn't. Lord knows I almost did that myself enough times without tryin'. Had two wheels over the edge less'n a month ago."

"That close?"

"That close."

"I'll be doggone," Porter said.

* * *

Thing is, Seth went on home after he failed to convince Porter to do it right away, and that was when things began to fall into the muck. Because Porter started thinking things over. I have a hunch it would have worked about the same way if Porter had won the flip, with Seth thinking things over. They were a whole lot alike, those two. Like two peas in a pod.

What occurred to Porter was would Seth have gone through with it if he lost, and what Porter decided was that he wouldn't. Not that there was any way for him to prove it one way or the other, but when you can't prove something you generally tend to decide on believing in what you want to believe, and Porter Dettweiler was no exception. Seth, he decided, would not have killed himself and didn't never have no intention of killing himself, which meant that for Porter to go through with killing his own self amounted to nothing more than damned foolishness.

Now it's hard to say just when he figured out what to do, but it was in the next two days, because on the third day he went over and borrowed that pickup off Fritz Chenoweth. "I got the back all loaded down with a couple sacks of concrete mix and a keg of nails and I don't know what all," Fritz said. "You want to unload it back of my smaller barn if you need the room."

"Oh, that's all right," Porter told him. "I guess I'll just leave it loaded and be grateful for the traction."

"Well, you keep it overnight if you have a mind," Fritz said.

"I just might do that," Porter said, and he went over to Seth's house. "Let's you and me go for a ride," he told Seth. "Something we was talking about the other night, and I went and got me a new slant on it, which the two of us ought to discuss before things go wrong altogether."

"Be right with you," Seth said, "soon as I finish this sandwich."

"Oh, just bring it along."

"I guess," said Seth.

No sooner was the pickup truck backed down and out of the driveway than Porter said, "Now will you just have a look over there, brother."

"How's that?" said Seth, and turned his head obligingly to the right, whereupon Porter gave him a good lick upside the head with a monkey wrench he'd brought along expressly for that purpose. He got him right where you have a soft spot if you're a little baby. (You also have a soft spot there if someone gets you just right with a monkey wrench.) Seth made a little sound that amounted to no more than letting his breath out, and then he went out like an icebox light when you have closed the door on it.

Now as to whether or not Seth was dead at this point I could not honestly tell you, unless I were to make up an answer knowing how slim is the likelihood of anyone presuming to contradict me. But the plain fact is that he might have been dead and he might not and even Seth could not have told you, being at the very least stone-unconscious all the time.

What Porter did was drive up the old Harburton Road, I guess figuring that he might as well stick to as much of the original plan as possible. There's a particular place where the road does a reasonably convincing imitation of a fishhook, and that spot's been described as Schuyler County's best natural brake on the population explosion since they stamped out the typhoid. A whole lot of folks fail to make that curve every year, most of them young ones with plenty of breeding years left in them. Now and then there's a movement to put up a guard rail, but the ecology people are against it so it never gets anywheres.

If you miss that curve, the next land you touch is a good five hundred feet closer to sea level.

So Porter pulls over to the side of the road and then he

gets out of the car and maneuvers Seth (or Seth's body, whichever the case may have been) so as he's behind the wheel. Then he stands alongside the car working the gas pedal with one hand and the steering wheel with the other and putting the fool truck in gear and doing this and that and the other thing so he can run the truck up to the edge and over, and thinking hard every minute about those two hundred thousand pretty green dollars that are destined to make his bankruptcy considerably easier to contend with.

Well, I told you right off that sometimes you can't win for losing, which was the case for Porter and Seth both, and another way of putting it is to say that when everything goes wrong there's nothing goes right. Here's what happened. Porter slipped on a piece of loose gravel while he was pushing, and the truck had to go on its own, and where it went was halfway and no farther, with its back wheel hung up on a hunk of tree limb or some such and its two front wheels hanging out over nothing and its motor stalled out deader'n a smoked fish.

Porter said himself a whole mess of bad words. Then he wasted considerable time shoving the back of that truck, forgetting it was in gear and not about to budge. Then he remembered and said a few more bad words and put the thing in neutral, which involved a long reach across Seth to get to the floor shift and a lot of coordination to manipulate it and the clutch pedal at the same time. Then Porter got out of the truck and gave the door a slam, and just about then a beat-up old Chevy with Indiana plates pulls up and this fellow leaps out screaming that he's got a tow rope and he'll pull the truck to safety.

You can't hardly blame Porter for the rest of it. He wasn't the type to be great at contingency planning anyhow, and who could allow for something like this? What he did, he gave this great sob and just plain hurled himself at the back of that truck, it being in neutral now, and the truck went sailing like a kite in a tornado, and Porter, well, what he did was follow right along after it. It wasn't part of his plan, but he just had himself too much momentum to manage any last-minute change of direction.

According to the fellow from Indiana, who it turned out was a veterinarian from Bloomington, Porter fell far enough to get off a couple of genuinely rank words on the way down. Last words or not, you sure wouldn't go and engrave them on any tombstone.

Speaking of which, he has the last word in tombstones, Vermont granite and all, and his brother Seth has one just like it. They had a double-barreled funeral, the best Johnny Millbourne had to offer, and they each of them reposed in a brass-bound casket, the top-of-the-line model. Minnie Lucy Boxwood sang "Your Cheatin' Heart," which was Porter's favorite song, plus she sang Seth's favorite, which was "Old Buttermilk Sky," plus she also sang free gratis "My Buddy" as a testament to brotherly love.

And Linda Mae and Rachel got themselves two hundred thousand dollars from the insurance company, which is what Gert and her kids in Valdosta, Georgia, also got. And Seth and Porter have an end to their miseries, which was all they really wanted before they got their heads turned around at the idea of all that money.

The only thing funnier than how things don't work out is how they do.

The Unholy Three

•

William Campbell Gault

William Campbell Gault began writing for the pulps in 1936 and turned to novels in 1952 with Don't Cry for Me, *which won an MWA Best First Novel Edgar. Since then he has published more than twenty-five additional mystery and suspense novels, the most recent being* The Chicano War *(1986). Gault's two main series characters are ex-football player turned private eye, Brock "The Rock" Callahan, and another tough but compassionate Southern California private detective, Joe Puma, whose talents are on display in "The Unholy Three." Like all of Gault's work, this story is an effective blend of realism, fast-paced action, pathos, and in-depth characterization—qualities that have helped make Gault one of the major figures in the crime fiction field for more than forty years.*

I was trying to figure how to pay seven hundred and forty dollars worth of bills with three hundred and twelve dollars I had in the bank when he walked into the office. It was almost dinner time and I was hungry.

So maybe my voice was gruff. "What's your trouble, son?"

His face was thin, his eyes a deep blue, and they considered me with some apprehension. He was about eleven years old. He said nothing.

"Get the wrong office?" I suggested.

He shook his head.

I tried to appear more genial. "You've been watching the private eye shows on TV and you came in to see what a *real* one looks like, huh?"

He took a deep breath and shook his head again, hard.

I matched his silence. I went back to evaluating which bills were most imminently disastrous. A minute of silence moved by.

Then he said, "It's my sister."

I looked up. "Oh? Has something happened to her?"

He frowned. "Well—not yet."

"I see," I said, though I didn't. "How old is your sister?"

More hope in his glance now. "She's twenty-three. She's very pretty."

"And what's going to happen to her?"

"I don't know. But she's going with a guy, a no-good guy."

"What's your name?" I asked him.

"John, John Delavan. My sister calls me Johnny."

"Okay, Johnny, listen carefully. First of all, I generally get a hundred and fifty dollars a day when I work. And second, I can't stop your sister from going with a no-good guy. And third, how do you know he is one?"

"I know all right. And about the money, I thought I could owe you. I've got a paper route. You could investigate the man, couldn't you? There's no law against that."

"If your sister asked me to, I could. What about your parents?"

His face was bleak. "There aren't any. There's just me and Eileen."

Silence for a few moments, and I asked, "Do you live in the neighborhood?"

He nodded. "In the Belvoir Apartments, over on Third. You don't want the business, is that it?"

His steady gaze met mine. "Johnny," I said softly, "I don't want to charge you one-fifty a day for work I'm not authorized to perform. Don't you see my position?"

"I see it. Sitting, that's your position. To heck with you, Mr. Puma." He turned.

"Wait, Johnny," I said. "I'm trying to be honest with you."

He didn't turn back; he continued to walk and the door slammed behind him. The glass in the door rattled, the glass that held the lettering *Joseph Puma, Investigations*.

I sighed and wondered if Eileen's suitor was really a no-good guy or just a guy who didn't like the Giants.

For some reason, I took out a card and typed on it: Eileen and Johnny Delavan—Belvoir Apartments.

Then I looked at my watch, and there was still time . . .

In the House of Genial Lending, Max said, "How much this time?"

"Five hundred," I told him. "She's in good shape, Max. I just put on a new set of tubeless tires."

"And she'd bring six hundred in a quick sale," he said.

"That's more than I'm asking for. Of course, if you want to make it six hundred?"

"Five," he said quickly. He sighed. "Joe, you're too bright a young man to waste your life in such a precarious profession. When are you going to get smart?"

"I'm doing better every month," I told him. "Last time I had to borrow seven hundred, remember?"

He shook his head sadly. "Bright fellow like you, it beats me . . . Where's the pink slip?"

While he was getting the papers ready, I asked him, "Do you know the Delavans who live over in the Belvoir? There's an Eileen and a Johnny."

He looked thoughtful. "Eileen Delavan? There's a girl

at the bank by that name. Beautiful girl. Her parents died a couple of years go, I think, if that's the one."

"That could be the one," I said, "Do you mean the Security Bank?"

He nodded and continued to look thoughtful. "Now, let's see, I think her brother delivers my paper. About twelve, isn't he?"

"I guess you've got the family, all right."

His glance was worried, "They're not in trouble, Joe?"

I chuckled. "I doubt it. Johnny doesn't like his sister's boyfriend. He wanted me to investigate him."

Max didn't smile. "Who's the boyfriend? Maybe I know him, too."

"I didn't ask."

Max shook his head again. "No wonder you're always borrowing money. Some detective." He held out a sheaf of papers. "Sign all three copies."

I signed all three copies and walked out a minute later with a check for five hundred dollars. I was rich again; I went over to Heinie's for some wiener schnitzel.

Somebody had left a paper on the table. I read that the president was giving a policy speech tomorrow and the Russians were arguing about something at the U.N. Locally, the mayor was worried about the increase in the juvenile crime rate.

The vision of Johnny Delavan came to me and I turned to the sport pages. A no-good guy . . . Probably because he could dance, or used slickum on his hair. Kids were too quick to judge their elders.

Reichoff, the beat cop, came in and looked around.

I called over, "Buy you a cup of coffee, Ben."

He came over and took the chair across from me. "Still eating, huh, Joe? That's pretty good, in your business."

"I make out," I told him. "I'm lining up some big accounts right now."

173

"Sure you are," he said tonelessly. "I saw you come out of Max's half an hour ago."

"Do you know the Delavans?" I asked him.

"Eileen and Johnny." He nodded. "Fine people. I wish all the kids in this neighborhood were like Johnny Delavan." He paused. "They're not in any kind of trouble, are they, Joe?"

I smiled. "No, Johnny came into my office about an hour ago. He wanted me to investigate his sister's boyfriend."

"And who would that be?"

I shrugged. "I didn't ask the kid."

"I'll ask him," Ben said. "I'm surprised he didn't come to me in the first place."

I stared at him. "You're kidding. You wouldn't take a kid seriously about a thing like that?"

"I'm not busy," Ben said. "I'll ask him. You never know what a question might turn up, Joe." He yawned. "Thanks for the coffee, Joe. I've got to be getting along."

He smiled and went out, two hundred and twenty pounds of municipal guardian. It has been rumored about him that he is meddlesome and nosy, but a neighborhood cop is supposed to be.

I drank another cup of coffee and went out to face my evening. At thirty-one, without a wife, an evening is something to face when I've nothing to work on.

My kitchenette apartment held no lure for me and I had seen all the movies around. One early star winked down at me.

Well, what the hell, why not? I looked up Delavan in the phone book and found the one who lived in the Belvoir Apartments.

Luckily, Johnny answered the phone.

I said, "Joe Puma, Johnny. You never did tell me the name of that fellow you want investigated."

174

His voice was almost a whisper. "Are you going to work on it, Mr. Puma?"

"I thought I'd give it a free neighborhood routine investigation. Is your sister home? Is that why you're speaking so quietly?"

"That's right, Mr. Puma." His voice was even lower. "The man's name is Jean Magnus and he lives at the Stratford Hotel."

"What don't you like about him, Johnny? What makes you suspicious of him?"

A feminine voice in the background said, "Who are you talking to, Johnny?"

Johnny said, "Good-bye, Mr. Puma. See you tomorrow."

The feminine voice started again before the line went dead.

Well, I knew the houseman over at the Stratford. He'd tried a spell of private work, himself. I drove over there.

Lenny Donovan, the houseman, was in the small office behind the clerk's desk. He was reading a hunting and fishing magazine.

He looked up genially. "A little cribbage, Joe? Or is this a professional call?"

"Semiprofessional," I told him. "I am working free for an eleven-year-old neighborhood client."

He smiled. "Young Delavan, maybe?"

I nodded and sat down. "How did you guess?"

Lenny yawned. "The kid was hanging around here evenings, hanging around the lobby with those big eyes and ears of his wide open. I ran him out."

"His sister's going with one of your guests."

"Oh—?" Lenny looked interested. "He wouldn't tell me why he was hanging around." He pulled at one ear. "Who's the guest?"

"A man named Jean Magnus."

Lenny reached forward to thumb through a card index box. "That would be—let's see—324. Oh, yes, big super-jock type. Real charmer. I can't blame Johnny's sister. This boy's really got it."

"What's his line?"

"Promotion, investments, speculation, You know, Joe, a wheel."

"Self-employed?"

Lenny frowned. "Aren't you getting a little nosy, Joe? This man's got one of the better suites."

"Is it all right if I go up and talk to him?"

Lenny's frown was deeper. "Because a kid doesn't like him? This isn't much of a job, but I'm happy in it. Let's get to the cribbage." He reached into a drawer and brought out a cribbage board.

I shook my head.

I stood up. "Mind if I sit in the lobby for a while?"

"I sure as hell do. You're really reaching for business, aren't you, Joe?"

"It's hard to find," I admitted. "Well, get some exercise; you look a little jowly."

"That's because I eat regular. Good night, Joe." He was chuckling as I left.

There really wasn't any reason for me to feel annoyed. I had made an ass of myself and Lenny had pointed it out. I continued to feel annoyed. I knew what Lenny was earning; maybe $500 a month and his room. He didn't have to be so superior; I'd turned down the job.

I was going through the door to the street, immersed in my own self-pity, when I ran into a large hunk of man.

We both bounced and then he growled, "Why'n hell don't you look where you're going?"

The face was broad, and for a moment a flare of incomplete recognition flickered in my memory, then died.

"Sorry," I said, and tried to recapture the near-memory. "Haven't we met?"

"Head-on," he agreed, and went through the doorway.

Overhead, the star was lost. In front of me, traffic growled and smoked. All around me, the lights were beckoning to buy, drink, dance, or see a movie. The Chevy started with a whine, and I headed her toward the Belvoir.

In the lobby, I took the phone off the hook and pressed the buzzer for the Delavan apartment.

A feminine voice came metallically through the speaker, and I said, "Could I speak with Johnny?"

"He's at a Scout meeting. Who is this?"

"John Foster Dulles," I said, and replaced the phone.

From there, I went to the East Side Station. Buddy Loeske called Headquarters for me and they had nothing on a Jean Magnus. That ended my day; I went home.

It would have ended my involvement with the Delavan problem, except for two things that happened next day. For one thing, Johnny came to see me at noon.

"Sis is burning up," he told me. "When you phoned, I told her you were my route supervisor, but she didn't believe me. And then when you talked to her last night, she knew something fishy was going on."

"I don't blame her for burning. How did she ever meet this Magnus?"

"He came into the bank to rent a safety deposit box and she took care of him. What did you find out, Mr. Puma?"

"Nothing. Except that you'd been hanging around the Stratford lobby. And what did you find out, doing that?"

"I found out Magnus's name isn't Jean. One of his friends called him Nick, right there in the lobby."

"Oh? Anything else?"

He shook his head, his eyes intent on mine.

'Johnny," I said patiently, "what's your real beef with

177

this Magnus? Don't you want your sister to get married? Is that it?''

"That's not it. He's no good. He's got a big lard-bucket friend looks just like a crook. I saw him a lot of times when I was watching the hotel.'' Johnny took a deep breath. "And then there's a little ratty guy he knows, too.''

"Crooks don't look like anything special,'' I told him gently. "You've been seeing too many movies, Johnny.''

He gave me a look of complete scorn. "Okay. So I'm a dope. I've been earning money for two years, but I'm a dope. Okay. So long.'' He turned and went out.

The second thing that happened was that my phone rang, and it was the assistant manager at the Stratford. He wanted to know if I knew where Lenny Donovan was.

I told him I didn't and asked him why he thought I would.

"The clerk told me you came to see Mr. Donovan last night. He didn't show up for work this morning and I've exhausted every other source of possible information.''

"Doesn't he stay there at the hotel?''

"He does. And his clothes are in the room, all except for those he was wearing last night.''

"I've no idea where he is.''

"Thank you, anyway. And incidentally, Mr. Puma, in the event Mr. Donovan hasn't an adequate excuse for his absence, would you be interested in the job here?''

He should have asked me *before* Max lent me the five hundred. I said with simple dignity, "I'm sorry. My living costs are too great for that.''

I thought I heard him chuckle when I hung up. He knew I ate at Heinie's.

So Jean is called Nick and Donovan is missing. Not really important facts, and nobody was paying me. I went out for lunch.

I was halfway through the giant-sized bowl of clam

178

chowder when the girl came in and walked over to Heinie. And then Heinie pointed at me, and she came my way.

Red hair and fine figure and dressed in nice, if modest, clothes. Under other circumstances, a girl it would be a pleasure to meet.

But now her eyes were blazing and the fine body seemed rigid. "Joseph Puma?" she asked me.

I stood up and nodded. "At your service, ma'am."

"I don't want your service. Are you also John Foster Dulles, by any chance?"

I smiled. "Occasionally. I have a lot of disguises."

"I can imagine. Any of them would be better than the one you're wearing. And what gives you the right to establish a residence in my hair?"

"I didn't know I had," I said. "Just exactly what is your complaint, ma'am? And your name?"

"My name," she said evenly, "is Eileen Delavan. Last night, Officer Ben Reichoff interrogated me. He said you had told him something that needed investigating. And you were the one who talked to Johnny on the phone last night, weren't you?"

"No, ma'am. Are you having some kind of trouble, Miss Delavan?"

"Too much. And I'll thank you to stay out of my business. Is that clear?"

"That's clear enough. You're welcome. Believe me, Miss Delavan, you're badly confused, but I haven't the time or the patience to quarrel publicly about it. Could you keep your voice down?"

She glared and glared and then uttered something between a snort and cough and turned and stalked out. The patrons in Heinie's were all smiling; it's a small place and her voice had unusual clarity.

I finished my clam chowder and went over to the Stratford.

Lenny was still missing, the assistant manager told me. That fact hadn't yet been reported to the police.

I asked, "Is Mr. Magnus still occupying Suite 324?"

He nodded. "What would that have to do with Mr. Donovan?"

"I'm not sure it has anything to do with that. Has Lenny been drinking at all?"

The man shook his head. "Not to my knowledge. Not enough to interfere with his duties, at any rate."

"And he left no message behind?"

"None." He paused. "What about this Mr. Magnus, Joe? Why did you ask about him?"

I shrugged. "I was talking to Lenny about him last night. There's a possibility Lenny went to see him and Magnus would then be the last man to have seen Lenny before he disappeared. But that's way out in left field. I haven't any substantial reason for thinking there's anything fishy about Mr. Magnus."

"What insubstantial reason would you have?"

"The dislike of an eleven- or twelve-year-old boy, the brother of a girl Magnus is going with."

The manager looked at me queerly. Then he sighed.

"It's not quite that ridiculous," I protested.

He sighed once more. "We are certainly fortunate we didn't manage to secure your doubtful services, Fearless Fosdick. Well, drop in again, but not soon, please?"

"To hell with you," I said, and gave him my back.

Going through the lobby, I felt an urgent need for a drink. I turned right, into the bar. It was a dim and quiet bar. Two men with briefcases were on stools at the far end, quietly downing an after-lunch drink. In a corner booth, there were three men who interested me more.

One of them was the bulky man I'd bumped into going out of the lobby last night. The other was small, ratty-looking. The third had a dark-haired, dark-eyed charm I could guess would appeal to some undiscerning women.

I thought their talking ebbed when I came within vision and I thought they examined me with interest. There wasn't any doubt in my mind that this was the unholy trinity Johnny had described.

The bartender came up with his smile and I ordered a bourbon and water. The two men with briefcases discussed the merits of term insurance. The three men in the booth directly behind me discussed nothing.

When the bartender brought my drink, I asked, "You haven't seen Lenny Donovan around this morning, have you?"

The bartender shook his head. "And he's usually in by this time."

"If you see him," I said, "you can tell him I got the information he asked me for."

The man nodded. "And your name?"

"Joe Puma. He knows me. My office isn't far." I paused. "I'm a private investigator."

Can a silence deepen? I thought the one behind me did.

The bartender wasn't aware of it if it existed. He said blandly, "I'll be sure to tell him and he's bound to come in. Lenny couldn't go a whole day without a drink."

"He didn't show up for work this morning," I said. "Maybe he's doing his drinking somewhere else. Well, I'll try a couple of his favorite haunts." I finished my drink. "I've got to find him."

In my office, I was looking busy when he came in. He had a rather worried smile on his dark face. "Are you—currently available?" he asked me.

I nodded, and indicated my customer's chair. "Sit down, Mr.—?"

"Magnus," he supplied. "Jean Magnus. I was in the

bar over at the Stratford when I heard you ask about Leonard Donovan.''

"Oh, yes. With a briefcase, weren't you?''

He shook his head, studying me. "I was in a booth right behind you. Maybe you didn't see me.''

"I'll have to admit I didn't notice you, Mr. Mangus. What brings you here?''

"Magnus," he corrected me. "Mr. Donovan's disappearance is what brings me here. Do you know him very well?''

I shook my head. "Very slightly. Through the manager of the Stratford. Is he a friend of yours?''

Magnus smiled. "Hardly. He was married to my sister. He owes her some back alimony.''

"Oh? And you followed him to the Stratford?''

Magnus shook his head. "It just happened that I ran into him there. I tried to reason with him. And now he's disappeared.''

"Leaving his clothes behind.''

Magnus frowned. "Are you sure? That isn't what the manager told me.''

"It's what he told me, an hour ago. Did he tell you anything else?''

Magnus shook his head again. "He just didn't mention it, either way. Well, that would indicate he's coming back, wouldn't it? So I suppose there'd be no point in my hiring you.''

"To find Lenny? If he's an alimony dodger, you wouldn't need me. The police would be happy to look for him.''

"I don't want to make trouble for Lenny. He's lacking in a sense of responsibility, but I think he's open to reason. Jail wouldn't be any solution for him or my sister.''

I said nothing, studying the handsome, grave face in front of me.

Magnus took a deep breath. "I've an idea where Lenny is. But I don't think I should be the one to go out there and find out. Could I hire you for that?"

I nodded.

"It's a cottage at Elk Lake," he went on. "Do you know where Elk Lake is?"

I nodded again.

"A girl lives there—well, a woman, really. Around forty. Very attractive woman, and the reason Lenny left my sister. There's a fifty fifty chance Lenny could be there."

"Her name?" I asked.

"Amalie Johnson, Mrs. Amalie Johnson. She's a widow. The cottage is a fieldstone place, about three houses off the main road on Elk Lane. Her name should be on the mailbox."

"I could check," I said. "And what would you want me to tell Lenny?"

"Tell him I can give him a better job than he has if he is willing to resume his alimony payments. Tell him to use his head for a change. I'll be waiting for his call."

"And wouldn't it be just as simple for you to tell him when he comes back to the hotel? Remember, his clothes are still there; he must be coming back."

Magnus looked at me thoughtfully. "Is business that good, Mr. Puma? Or don't you want *my* business?"

"I can always use the money," I told him. "But I get paid whether Lenny is there or not. That would be one-hundred and fifty dollars, and gas, for the trip."

He reached into his jacket pocket and brought out an alligator wallet. He put two fifties and five tens on my desk. "The gas you can bill me for later."

"Check," I said. "I should be back before midnight. You'll be at the hotel?"

He rose and smiled. "I'll be waiting."

* * *

Once out of town, I ran the Chevy up to a steady fifty-five. Elk Lake was right off the highway and the directions Magnus had given me should be complete enough.

As I drove, I tried to remember where I had seen that heavy man before, the man I'd collided with. The face was ringing a very dim bell in my memory, and I had a vague feeling there had been a number under the face last time I'd seen it.

So Johnny's visit hadn't been completely fruitless. I was now earning one-fifty because of my interest in Jean Magnus. Plus gas. The Chevy doesn't use any oil.

Magnus could be as phony as he sounded. And this could be a wild-goose chase. I'd know when the door opened at Elk Lake. If a woman answered the door, there'd be reason to believe his story.

If a woman didn't answer the door, I wouldn't be too badly off. Because my hand would be on my .38 in my jacket pocket.

At the turnoff, there was a small grocery store and boat rental station and two unattended gasoline pumps. The first mailbox after that was weatherworn and in the gathering dusk I couldn't make out the name.

Three houses up from there, however, the name of Amalie Johnson was blackly clear on an aluminum-painted box. The flag was down.

The lawn was gray and the earth around the shrubs showed no signs of recent watering. It looked like a rented house to me, or the house of an uncaring owner. I touched the bell.

The sound of door chimes and footsteps, the rasp of a latch, and an attractive, dark-haired woman looked at me wordlessly from the open doorway.

"Mrs. Johnson?" I asked.

She nodded.

"I'm looking for a man named Leonard Donovan," I told her.

A few seconds more of silence and then she asked, "Why?"

"I have a message that could profit him. Is he here?"

She shook her head. "He's gone to the store. He's due back any moment, though. Won't you come in?"

I started in and something hit me from behind. I'll never know where the blow came from—maybe someone hiding under the stoop. But as I fell and the skyrockets flared out in my brain, I remembered where I'd seen the face of the bulky man.

I came to, smelling wet sawdust mixed with a faint odor of fish. Under me, I could feel the splintery planking of what seemed to be a thick floor. There was a bitter, bilelike taste in my mouth. My .38 was gone.

The room was completely black, but one guess as to my whereabouts seemed likely. I was probably in one of those lake icehouses, insulated by sawdust, and imprisoned by heavy planking all around. Screaming wouldn't do me a damned bit of good. I moved, and a voice said, "You coming around, Puma?"

"I'm alive. Lenny, is it?"

"Right. They conned me, too."

"You went up to talk to Magnus, then, after I left you?"

"Not right away. When I saw him with Dutch Schroeder I got nosy."

That was the big man, Dutch Schroeder. He was a reformed safe cracker, and he used to give lectures on his former art. I'd heard one of his lectures when I was still with the Department.

"You got nosy, Lenny," I guessed, "and tried to put the bite on them. And they took care of you."

"Now wasn't that a hell of a thing to say. You think I'm a crook, or something?"

"Yup. Or you'd have gone to the police."

"Huh! Like you did? We're sharing this room, honor-bright. How come you didn't go to the police?"

"Well," I said, "I'll tell you how it was. Magnus came to me and said you were his former brother-in-law. And you were behind in your alimony payments and he knew you were shacked up with the Widow Johnson up here. He paid one-fifty to send me up here to reason with you. I didn't believe a word of it, and I'm surprised to find you here, Lenny. You know, I'm beginning to think that kid was right."

Lenny said, "They've got both of us out of the way. They're going to knock off the Third Street Security Bank. Tonight or early tomorrow sometime."

"You're not as lousy a detective as I thought."

"You see, Magnus plans it. Schroeder tackles the safe. The little trigger-itchy punk handles the door, Schroeder's wife out there the car. Quick and easy and off to South America for the sun. Some life, huh, Joe? I heard them discuss it before they threw me in here."

"Lenny, is this an icehouse?"

"It sure as hell is."

"Aren't they usually airtight?"

Lenny said, too quietly, "The good ones are. I noticed I could breathe much easier right after they opened that door to throw you in here. It's a rented cottage, Joe. When they leave, the owner might not be around for weeks."

"Isn't there anything around we could use to batter a hole with?"

"Nothing," Lenny said. "One chance I thought I had— that latch handle pivot goes right through that planking door. But I've torn two fingers to hell trying to turn it."

I got slowly to my feet and inched toward the wall. I

followed it by touch until I came to the door. The nut on this side of the pivot had been pinned to prevent the thread from turning. It was immovable.

I said, "You lived for over twelve hours in this air. Maybe the place isn't airtight."

"Maybe it isn't. But Joe, it's food-tight."

"And if we screamed and hollered and beat on the walls with our shoes?"

"Now? Or after they've gone?"

It was autumn; who'd be around after the quartet left? Who'd be around to hear what little noise that would emerge through those double-planking walls filled with sawdust?

But now? Could we make them nervous with a racket now?

They would come with guns, undoubtedly. We were still alive, but would we be after they came with the guns?

Lenny said, "I figure they'll hole up here for a couple days after the job. This lake doesn't get much traffic in the fall. That Magnus is a cool operator."

"The door is our best bet," I said. "If we kept kicking away right under that latch . . ."

Silence from Lenny.

I reached for a cigarette and then decided not to crumb up the air any more than necessary. My lighter was still in my pocket; I lighted it for a look around.

Planking walls, planking ceiling and floor. Meat hooks were set in rows along the ceiling. Lenny looked pale in the flickering light.

"And there are two walls like that," Lenny said, "with sawdust between."

"The door is only one thickness, though."

"That's right. Two by sixes bolted to the crosspieces."

"How about the ceiling? That's usually single. The

blocks of ice are put in the sawdust around the sides, aren't they?''

"So we can break through the ceiling if our heads are hard enough. Do you want to start?''

"Well, damn it,'' I said, "we can't just sit here! Which way is the lake?''

"Right behind here, about thirty feet.''

"Lenny,'' I said, "I'm going to holler. And if they open that door, I'm going to make a break for it. It should be dark out there. How about you?''

"I'm alive,'' he said. "And I figure if I don't move and keep my mouth shut, I've got a small chance to stay that way. I figure you haven't got any chance your way.''

"Okay,'' I said. "But I don't want to spend the rest of *my* life in an icehouse.'' I began to hammer on the door with a shoe. I had taken both of them off.

In only a little more than a minute, I heard the back door of the house slam and a few seconds after that, a man's voice asked, "What the hell's all the commotion about?''

"I've got a broken arm,'' I said. "I want a doctor.''

"You'll have worse than that if you don't shut up. We're not playing games, shamus.''

"I want a doctor,'' I repeated, and began to hammer on the door again.

"Damn you,'' he said, and then I heard the rasp of the latch.

I slammed into the door as it started opening.

There was a curse and I saw him on the ground as I burst through. He was the little man. He had an awful big gun in his hand and was swinging it right toward my belly. My kick got his hand.

I jumped sideways, raced for the lake. There was a pier leading out about twenty feet.

I heard a big boom and something flicked away the lobe

188

of my ear. As I hit the water, another shot missed me by inches.

I didn't swim out. I stayed under and made the big turn, back under the protection of the pier. The water was clear and calm.

My car burned like fury, my right foot throbbed from the kick. A post of the pier brushed my shoulder, and I came up for air, hidden by the boards overhead.

I heard the woman say, "Did he get away?"

"Nope. I know I hit him. See the blood?"

"But wouldn't he come up, if he was hit?"

The little man said. "Yeah, when he starts to bloat, he'll come up. But we'll be a long way from here then."

"I'm going to watch, anyway," the woman said. "He might just be injured."

My hand went to my ear and came away red. I heard footsteps above me, I went under again.

When my lungs began to burn and spots flared on my eyelids, I came up.

I heard the woman say, "How about the other one?"

"I guess he likes that icehouse. We'll leave him there. How long can he live without food?"

"I see," the woman said thoughtfully. "You've got a point there, George."

"Come on. We'll be late getting into town. That would throw everything out of schedule."

"Just one second. We gotta be sure. I want another look under this pier."

I grabbed a post to hang onto when I went down this time. I was starting to get weak. The bullet that had torn away my ear lobe had creased the side of my jaw and I was losing a lot of blood.

When it was a question of drowning in one more second, I came up for air again. And heard footsteps on the boards above and sent up a small prayer of deliverance.

My handkerchief was wet and cold in my jacket pocket. I put it to ear. Was there an artery running along the jaw line? I didn't know. I wondered if Lenny knew.

The way it turned out, I'm glad I didn't release Lenny first.

When I heard the car start I started for the house. I made it. I couldn't have gone a hundred yards more, but I made the phone.

Captain MacGill in town didn't waste any of my breath with foolish questions. He promised to send the nearest doctor.

Then I turned back toward Lenny. I got through the door and five steps into the front yard before I collapsed.

I came to in an amber room on a hard bed. A face came into focus and it was Johnny's face.

"You're going to be all right," he said.

"Johnny, you're in the Scouts. Is there an artery running along the jaw there?"

He nodded. "You almost didn't make it, Mr. Puma. Mr. Magnus didn't. He got killed when they staked out the bank. Guess that's not much loss, huh?"

"I'm no judge of that. How about Lenny Donovan, that hotel dick?"

"He's trying to cut himself in," Johnny said. "But I got that straightened out. He and those crooks used to huddle plenty. I told Mr. Donovan it would be best if he just kept his mouth shut."

"I'm not following you, Johnny."

"Like I said, he's trying to cut himself in. I mean he was. He isn't anymore, since I told him how often I'd seen him with those crooks."

"On what, cut himself in on *what*, Johnny?"

"On the ten grand reward. That's the Banker's Protective Alliance Security—you know, standard reward. I'm glad the cops didn't get to 'em before they made the try though, huh, Mr. Puma?''

I took a deep breath. "Who did you figure deserved the reward, Johnny?"

"Fifty-fifty, you and me. I was the finger, right? And you were the arm. We're not going to have any trouble about that, are we, Mr. Puma? We're not going to argue some more, are we?"

"No," I agreed. "You're too much for me, Johnny. Where am I?"

"At St. Mary's. I figured this was the best bet. I don't trust those small town hospitals. I'll bet you don't know who's here?"

"I'll bet I do. I'll bet it's your beautiful sister."

He smiled. "Right. And she sure isn't mourning that Magnus slob. Well, I'll bring her in and she can apologize to you, but you'll have to take it from there, Mr. Puma. I can't handle everything."

"Okay, Johnny," I said humbly. "Shoo her in; I'll give it my best."

The Girl Who Loved Graveyards

·

P. D. James

*Twice the recipient of the Silver Dagger Award from the British Crime Writers Association, P. D. James is best known for her widely acclaimed novels about Chief Superintendent Adam Dalgleish (*The Black Tower, Shroud for a Nightingale, Death of an Expert Witness*). But she has also published two mysteries featuring private investigator Cordelia Gray (*An Unsuitable Job for a Woman *and* The Skull Beneath the Skin*), nonfiction about crime, and a variety of series and nonseries short stories. "The Girl Who Loved Graveyards," one of her nonseries tales, contains all the qualities—in-depth characterization, deft plotting, low key but evocative prose—that have won her legions of fans on both sides of the Atlantic.*

She couldn't remember anything about the day in the hot August of 1956 when they first brought her to live with her Aunt Gladys and Uncle Victor in the small east London house at 49 Alma Terrace. She knew that it was three days after her tenth birthday and that she was to be cared for by her only living relations now that her father and grandmother were dead, killed by influenza within a week of each other. But those were just facts that someone, at some time, had briefly told her. She could remember nothing of her previous life. Those first ten years were a void, insubstantial as a dream that had faded but that had left on her

192

mind a scar of unarticulated childish anxiety and fear. For her, memory and childhood both began with that moment when, waking in the small unfamiliar bedroom with the kitten, Sambo, still curled asleep on a towel at the foot of her bed, she had walked barefooted to the window and drawn back the curtain.

And there, stretched beneath her, lay the cemetery, luminous and mysterious in the early morning light, bounded by iron railings and separated from the rear of Alma Terrace only by a narrow path. It was to be another warm day, and over the serried rows of headstones there lay a thin haze pierced by the occasional obelisk and by the wing tips of marble angels whose disembodied heads seemed to be floating on particles of shimmering light. And as she watched, motionless in an absorbed enchantment, the mist began to rise and the whole cemetery was revealed to her, a miracle of stone and marble, bright grass and summer-laden trees, flower-bedecked graves, and intersecting paths stretching as far as her eyes could see. In the far distance she could just make out the top of the Victorian chapel gleaming like the spire of some magical castle in a long-forgotten fairy tale. In those moments of growing wonder, she found herself shivering with delight, an emotion so rare that it stole through her thin body like a pain. And it was then, on that first morning of her new life with the past a void and the future unknown and frightening, that she made the cemetery her own. Throughout her childhood and youth it was to remain a place of delight and mystery, her habitation and her solace.

It was a childhood without love, almost without affection. Her Uncle Victor was her father's elder half brother; that, too, she had been told. He and her aunt weren't really her relations. Their small capacity for love was expended on each other, and even here it was less a positive emotion than a pact of mutual support and comfort against the threatening world that lay outside the trim curtains of their small claustrophobic sitting room.

But they cared for her as dutifully as she cared for the cat Sambo. It was a fiction in the household that she adored Sambo, her own cat, brought with her when she arrived, her one link with the past, almost her only possession. Only she knew that she disliked and feared him. But she brushed and fed him with conscientious care as she did everything and, in return, he gave her a slavish allegiance, hardly ever leaving her side, slinking through the cemetery at her heels and only turning back when they reached the main gate. But he wasn't her friend. He didn't love her and he knew that she didn't love him. He was a fellow conspirator, gazing at her through slits of azure light, relishing some secret knowledge that was her knowledge, too. He ate voraciously, yet he never grew fat. Instead, his sleek black body lengthened until, stretched in the sunlight along her window sill, his sharp nose turned always to the cemetery, he looked as sinister and unnatural as a furred reptile.

It was lucky for her that there was a side gate to the cemetery from Alma Terrace and that she could take a short cut to and from school across the graveyard, avoiding the dangers of the main road. On her first morning her uncle had said doubtfully, "I suppose it's all right. But it seems wrong somehow, a child walking every day through rows of the dead."

Her aunt had replied, "The dead can't rise from their graves. They lay quiet. She's safe enough from the dead."

Her voice had been unnaturally gruff and loud. The words had sounded like an assertion, almost a defiance. But the child knew that she was right. She did feel safe with the dead, safe and at home.

The years in Alma Terrace slipped by, bland and dull as her aunt's blancmange, a sensation rather than a taste. Had she been happy? It wasn't a question that it had ever occurred to her to ask. She wasn't unpopular at school, being neither pretty nor intelligent enough to provoke much interest either from the children or the staff; an ordinary child, unusual only because she was an orphan, but unable to capitalize even on that sentimental advantage. Perhaps she might have found friends, quiet unenterprising children like herself who might have responded to her unthreatening mediocrity. But something about her repelled their timid advances, her self-sufficiency, the bland uncaring gaze, the refusal to give anything of herself even in casual friendship. She didn't need friends. She had the graveyard and its occupants.

She had her favorites. She knew them all, when they had died, how old they had been, sometimes how they had died. She knew their names and learned their memorials by heart. They were more real to her than the living, those rows of dearly loved wives and mothers, respected tradesmen, lamented fathers, deeply mourned children. The new graves hardly ever interested her, although she would watch the funerals from a distance, then creep up later to read the mourning cards. But what she liked best were the old neglected oblongs of mounded earth or chipped stones, the tilted crosses, the carved words almost erased by time. It was around the names of the long dead that she wove her childish fantasies.

Even the seasons of the year she experienced in and through the cemetery. The gold and purple spears of the first crocuses thrusting through the hard earth. April with its tossing daffodils. The whole graveyard *en fête* in yellow and white as mourners dressed the graves for Easter. The smell of mown grass and the earthy tang of high summer as if the dead were breathing the flower-scented air and exuding their own mysterious miasma. The glare of sunlight on stone and marble as the old women in their stained

195

cotton dresses shuffled with their vases to fill them at the tap behind the chapel. Seeing the cemetery transformed by the first snow of winter, the marble angels grotesque in their high bonnets of glistening snow. Watching at her window for the thaw, hoping to catch that moment when the edifice would slip and the shrouded shapes become themselves again.

Only once had she asked about her father and then she had known as children do that this was a subject that, for some mysterious adult reason, it was better not to talk about. She had been sitting at the kitchen table with her homework while her aunt busied herself cooking supper. Looking up from her history book she had asked, "Where is Daddy buried?"

The frying pan had clattered against the stove. The cooking fork dropped from her aunt's hand. It had taken her a long time to pick it up, wash it, clean the grease from the floor. The child had asked again, "Where is Daddy buried?"

"Up north. At Creedon outside Nottingham with your mum and gran. Where else?"

"Can I go there? Can I visit him?"

"When you're older, maybe. No sense is there, hanging about graves. The dead aren't there."

"Who looks after them?"

"The graves? The cemetery people. Now get on with your homework, do, child. I'll be wanting the table for supper."

She hadn't asked about her mother, the mother who had died when she was born. That desertion had always seemed to her willful, a source of secret guilt. "You killed your mother." Someone, sometime, had spoken those words to her, had laid on her that burden. She wouldn't let herself think about her mother. But she knew that her father had stayed with her, had loved her, hadn't wanted to die and leave her. Someday, secretly, she would find his grave. She would visit it, not once but every week. She would tend it and plant flowers on it and clip the grass as the old ladies did in the cemetery. And if there wasn't a stone she would pay for one, not a cross but a gleaming obelisk, the tallest in the graveyard, bearing his name and an epitaph that she would choose. She would have to wait until she was older, until she could leave school and work and save enough money. But one day she would find her father. She would have a grave of her own to visit and tend. There was a debt of love to be paid.

Four years after her arrival in Alma Terrace, her aunt's only brother came to visit from Australia. Physically he and his sister were alike, the same stolid short-legged bodies, the same small eyes set in square pudgy faces. But Uncle Ned had a brash assurance, a cheerful geniality that was so alien to his sister's unconfident reserve that it was hard to believe that they were siblings. For the two weeks of his visit he dominated the little house with his strident alien voice and assertive masculinity. There were unfamiliar treats, dinners in the West End, a visit to a greyhound stadium, a show at Earl's Court. He was kind to the child, tipping her lavishly, even walking through the cemetery with her one morning on his way to buy his racing paper. And it was that evening, coming silently down the stairs to supper, that she overheard disjointed scraps of conversation, adult talk, incomprehensible at the time, but taken into her mind and stored there.

First, the harsh boom of her uncle's voice. "We were looking at this gravestone together, see. Beloved husband and father. Taken from us suddenly on 14 March 1892. Something like that. Marble chips, cracked urn, bloody great angel pointing upward. You know the kind of thing. Then the kid turned to me. "Daddy's death was sudden, too." That's what she said. Came out with it cool as you please. Now what in God's name made her say that? I mean, why then? Christ, it gave me a turn I can tell you. I didn't know where to put my face. And what a place to choose, the bloody cemetery. I'll say one thing for coming out to Sydney. You'll get a better view. I can promise you that.''

Creeping closer, she strained her ears vainly to catch the indistinct mutter of her aunt's reply.

Then came her uncle's voice again. ''That bitch never forgave him for getting Helen pregnant. No one was good enough for her precious only daughter. And then when Helen died having the kid, she blamed him for that, too. Poor sod, he bought a packet of trouble when he set eyes on that girl. Too soft, too romantic. That was always Martin's trouble.''

Again the murmur of indistinguishable voices, the sound of her aunt's footsteps moving from table to stove, the scrape of a chair. Then her Uncle Ned's voice again.

''Funny kid, isn't she? Old-fashioned. Morbid you might say. Seems to live in that bone yard, she and that damned cat. And the split image of her dad. Christ, it turned me up I can tell you. Looking at me with his eyes and then coming out with it. 'Daddy's death was sudden, too.' I'll say it was! Influenza? Well, it's as good a name for it as any if you can get away with it. Helps having such an ordinary name, I suppose. People don't catch on. How long ago is it now? Four years? It seems longer.''

Only one part of this half-heard, incomprehensible conversation had disturbed her. Uncle Ned was trying to persuade them to join him in Australia. She might be taken away from Alma Terrace, might never see the cemetery again, might have to wait for years before she could save enough money to return to England and find her father's grave. And how could she visit it regularly, how could she tend and care for it from the other side of the world? After

Uncle Ned's visit ended, it was months before she could see one of his rare letters with the Australian stamp drop through the letter box without the cold clutch of fear at the heart.

But she needn't have worried. It was October 1966 before they left England, and they went alone. When they broke the news to her one Sunday morning at breakfast, it was apparent that they had never even considered taking her with them. Dutiful as ever, they had waited to make their decision until she had left school and was earning her living as a shorthand typist with a local firm of estate agents. Her future was assured. They had done all that conscience required of them. Hesitant and a little shame-faced, they justified their decision as if they believed that it was important to her, that she cared whether they left or stayed. Her aunt's arthritis was increasingly troublesome, they longed for the sun, Uncle Ned was their only close relation, and none of them was getting any younger. Their plan, over which they had agonized for months in whispers behind closed doors, was to visit Sydney for six months and then, if they liked Australia, to apply to emigrate. The house in Alma Terrace was to be sold to pay the airfare. It was already on the market. But they had made provision for her. When they told her what had been arranged, she had to bend her face low over her plate in case the flood of joy should be too apparent. Mrs. Morgan, three doors down, would be glad to take her as a lodger if she didn't mind having the small bedroom at the back overlooking the cemetery. In the surging tumult of relief, she hardly heard her aunt's next words. There was one small problem. Everyone knew how Mrs. Morgan was about cats. Sambo would have to be put to sleep.

She was to move into 43 Alma Terrace on the afternoon of the day on which her aunt and uncle flew from Heathrow. Her two cases, holding all that she possessed in the world, were already packed. In her handbag she carefully stowed the meager official confirmations of her existence: her birth certificate, her medical card, her post office savings book showing the money painstakingly saved toward the cost of her father's memorial. And the next day, she would begin her search. But first she took Sambo to the vet to be destroyed. She made a cat box from two cartons fitted together, pierced it with holes, then sat patiently in the waiting room with the box at her feet. The cat made no sound, and this patient resignation touched her, evoking for the first time a spasm of pity and affection. But there was nothing she could do to save him. They both knew it. But then, he had always known what she was thinking, what was past and what was to come. There was something they shared, some knowledge, some common experience that she couldn't remember and he couldn't express. Now, with his destruction, even that tenuous link with her first ten years would go forever.

When it was her turn to go into the office, she said: "I want him put to sleep."

The vet passed his strong experienced hands over the sleek fur. "Are you sure? He seems quite healthy still. He's old, of course, but he's in remarkably good condition."

"I'm sure. I want him put to sleep."

And she left him there without a glance or another word.

She had thought that she would be glad to be free of the pretense of loving him, free of those slitted accusing eyes. But as she walked back to Alma Terrace she found herself crying; tears, unbidden and unstoppable, ran like rain down her face.

There was no difficulty in getting a week's leave from her job. She had been husbanding her vacation entitlement. Her work, as always, was up to date. She had calculated how much money she would need for her train and bus fares and for a week's stay in modest hotels. Her plans had been made. They had been made for years. She would begin her search with the address on her birth certificate, Cranstoun House, Creedon, Nottingham, the house where she had been born. The present owners might remember her and her father. If not, there would be neighbors or older inhabitants of the village who would be able to recall her father's death, where he was buried. If that failed she would try the local undertakers. It was, after all, only ten years ago. Someone locally would remember. Somewhere in Nottingham there would be a record of burials. She told Mrs. Morgan that she was taking a week off to visit her father's old home, packed a case with overnight necessities, and next morning caught the earliest possible fast train from St. Pancras to Nottingham.

It was during the bus ride from Nottingham to Creedon that she felt the first stirrings of anxiety and mistrust. Until then she had traveled in calm confidence, but strangely without excitement, as if this long-planned journey was as natural and inevitable as her daily walk to work, an inescapable pilgrimage ordained from that moment when a barefooted child in her white nightdress had drawn back her bedroom curtains and seen her kingdom spread beneath her. But now her mood changed. As the bus lurched through the suburbs, she found herself shifting in her seat as if mental unease were provoking physical discomfort. She had expected green countryside, small churches guarding neat domestic graveyards patterned with yew trees. These were graveyards she had visited on holidays, had loved almost as much as she loved the one she had made her own. Surely it was in such bird-loud sanctified peace that her father lay. But Nottingham had spread during the past ten years, and Creedon was now little more than an urban village separated from the city by a ribbon development of brash new houses, gas stations, and parades of shops. Nothing in the journey was familiar, and yet she knew that she had traveled this road before and traveled it in anxiety and pain.

But when, thirty minutes later, the bus stopped at its terminus at Creedon, she knew at once where she was. The Dog and Whistle still stood at one corner of the dusty litter-strewn village green with the same bus shelter outside it. And with the sight of its graffiti-scrawled walls, memory returned as easily as if nothing had ever been forgotten. Here her father used to leave her when he brought her to pay her regular Sunday visits to her grandmother. Here her grandmother's elderly cook would be waiting for her. Here she would look back for a final wave and see her father patiently waiting for the bus to begin its return journey. Here she would be brought at six-thirty when he arrived to collect her. Cranstoun House was where her grandmother lived. She herself had been born there, but it had never been her home.

She had no need to ask her way to the house. And when, five minutes later, she stood gazing up at it in appalled fascination, no need to read the name painted on the shabby padlocked gate. It was a square-built house of dark brick standing in incongruous and spurious grandeur at the end of a country lane. It was smaller than she now remembered, but it was still a dreadful house. How could she ever have forgotten those ornate overhanging gables, the high-pitched roof, the secretive oriel windows, the single forbidding turret at the east end? There was an estate agent's board wired to the gate, and it was apparent that the house was empty. The paint on the front door was peeling, the lawns were overgrown, the boughs of the rhododendron bushes were broken, and the gravel path was studded with clumps of weed. There was no one here who could help her to find her father's grave. But she knew that she had to visit, had to make herself pass again through that intimidating front door. There was something the house knew and had to tell her, something that Sambo had known. She couldn't escape her next step. She must find the estate agent's office and get a permit to see it.

She had missed the returning bus, and by the time the next one had reached Nottingham it was after three o'clock. She had eaten nothing since her early breakfast, but she was too driven now to be aware of hunger. But she knew that it would be a long day and that she ought to eat. She turned into a coffee shop and bought a toasted cheese sandwich and a mug of coffee, grudging the few minutes it took to gulp them down. The coffee was hot but almost tasteless. Flavor would have been wasted on her, but she realized as the hot liquid stung her throat how much she had needed it.

The girl at the cash register was able to direct her to the agent's office. It seemed to her a happy augury that it was within ten minutes' walk. She was received by a sharp-featured young man in an overtailored pin-stripe suit, who, in one practiced glance at her old blue tweed coat, the cheap case, and bag of synthetic leather, placed her precisely in his private category of clients from whom little can be expected and to whom less need be given. But he found the particulars for her and his curiosity sharpened as she merely glanced at them, then folded the paper away in her bag. Her request to view the house that afternoon was received, as she expected, with politeness but without enthusiasm. But this was familiar territory and she knew why. The house was unoccupied. She would have to be escorted. There was nothing in her respectable drabness to suggest that she was a likely purchaser. And when he briefly excused himself to consult a colleague and returned to say that he could drive her to Creedon at once, she knew the reason for that, too. The office wasn't particularly busy, and it was time that someone from the firm checked up on the property.

Neither of them spoke during the drive. But when they reached Creedon and he turned down the lane to the house, the apprehension she had felt on her first visit returned, but deeper and stronger. Yet now it was more than the memory of an old wretchedness. This was childish misery and fear relived but intensified by a dreadful adult foreboding. As the agent parked his Morris on the grass verge, she looked up at the blind windows and was seized by a spasm of terror so acute that, momentarily, she was unable to speak or move. She was aware of the man holding open the car door for her, of the smell of beer on his breath, of his face, uncomfortably close, bending on her a look of exasperated patience. She wanted to say that she had changed her mind, that the house was totally wrong for her, that there would be no point in viewing it, that she would wait for him in the car. But she willed herself to rise from the warm seat and scrambled out under his supercilious eyes, despising herself for her gracelessness. She waited in silence as he unlocked the padlock and swung open the gate.

They passed together between the neglected lawns and the spreading rhododendron bushes toward the front door. And suddenly the feet shuffling the gravel beside her were different feet and she knew that she was walking with her father as she had walked in childhood. She had only to stretch out her hand to feel the grasp of his fingers. Her companion was saying something about the house, but she didn't hear. The meaningless chatter faded and she heard a different voice, her father's voice, heard for the first time in over ten years.

"It won't be for always, darling. Just until I've found a job. And I'll visit you every Sunday for lunch. Then, afterward, we'll be able to go for a walk together, just the two of us. Granny has promised that. And I'll buy you a kitten. I'll bring it next weekend. I'm sure Granny won't mind when she sees him. A black kitten. You've always wanted a black kitten. What shall we call him? Little black Sambo? He'll remind you of me. And then, when I've found a job, I'll be able to rent a little house and we'll be together again. I'll look after you, my darling. We'll look after each other.''

She dared not look up in case she should see again those desperately pleading eyes, begging her to understand, to make things easy for him, not to despise him. She knew now that she ought to have helped him, to have told him that she understood, that she didn't mind living with Granny for a month or so, that everything would be all right. But she hadn't managed so adult a response. She remembered tears, desperate clingings to his coat, her grandmother's old cook, tight-lipped, pulling her away from him and bearing her up to bed. And the last memory was of watching him from her room above the porch, of his drooping defeated figure making its way down the lane to the bus stop.

As they reached the front door, she looked up. The window was still there. But, of course, it was. She knew every room in this dark house.

The garden was bathed in a mellow October sunlight, but the hall struck cold and dim. The heavy mahogany staircase led up from gloom to a darkness that hung above them like a pall. The real estate agent felt along the wall for the light switch. But she didn't wait. She felt again the huge brass doorknob that her childish fingers had hardly encompassed and moved unerringly into the drawing room.

The smell of the room was different. Then there had been a scent of violets overlaid with furniture polish. Now the air smelled cold and musty. She stood in the darkness shivering but perfectly calm. It seemed to her that she had passed through a barrier of fear as a torture victim might pass through a pain barrier into a kind of peace. She felt a shoulder brush against her as the man went across to the window and swung open the heavy curtains.

He said, "The last owners have left it partly furnished. Looks better that way. Easier to get offers if the place looks lived in."

"Has there been an offer?"

"Not yet. It's not everyone's cup of tea. Bit on the large size for a modern family. And then, there's the murder. Ten years ago, but people still talk in the neighborhood. There's been four owners since then and none of them stayed long. It's bound to affect the price. No good thinking you can hush up murder."

His voice was carefully nonchalant, but his gaze never left her face. Walking to the empty fire grate, he stretched one arm along the mantelpiece and followed her with his eyes as she moved as if in a trance about the room.

She heard herself asking, "What murder?"

"A sixty-four-year-old woman. Battered to death by her son-in-law. The old cook came in from the back kitchen and found him with the poker in his hand. Come to think of it, it could have been one like that."

He nodded down to a collection of brass firearms resting against the hearth. He said, "It happened right where you're standing now. She was sitting in that very chair."

She said in a voice so gruff and harsh that she hardly recognized it, "It wasn't this chair. It was bigger. Her chair had an embroidered seat and back, and there were armrests edged with crochet and the feet were like lions' claws."

His gaze sharpened. Then he laughed warily. The watchful eyes grew puzzled, then the look changed into something else. Could it have been contempt?

"So you know about it. You're one of those."

"One of those?"

"They aren't really in the market for a place. Couldn't afford one this size anyway. They just want a thrill, want to see where it happened. You get all sorts in this game and I can usually tell. I can give you all the gory details if you're interested. Not that there was much gore. The skull was smashed, but most of the bleeding was internal. They say there was just a trickle falling down her forehead and dripping on to her hands.''

It came out so pat that she knew that he had told it all before, that he enjoyed telling it, this small recital of horror to titillate his clients and relieve the boredom of his day. She wished that she wasn't so cold. If only she could get warm again, her voice wouldn't sound so strange. She said through her dry and swollen lips, ''And the kitten. Tell me about the kitten.''

''Now that was something! That was a touch of horror if you like. The kitten was on her lap, licking up the blood. But then you know, don't you? You've heard all about it.''

''Yes,'' she lied. ''I've heard all about it.'' But she had done more than that. She knew. She had seen it. She had been there.

And then the outline of the chair altered. An amorphous black shape swam before her eyes, then took form and substance. Her grandmother was sitting there, squat as a toad, dressed in her Sunday black for morning service, gloved and hatted, prayer book in her lap. She saw again the glob of phlegm at the corner of the mouth, the thread of broken veins at the side of the sharp nose. She was waiting to inspect her grandchild before church, turning on her again that look of querulous discontent. The witch was sitting there. The witch who hated her and her daddy, who had told her that he was useless and feckless and no better than her mother's murderer. The witch who was threatening to have Sambo put to sleep because he had torn her chair, because Daddy had given him to her. The witch who was planning to keep her from Daddy forever.

And then she saw something else. The poker was there,

too, just as she remembered it, the long rod of polished brass with its heavy knob.

She seized it as she had seized it then and, with a high scream of hatred and terror, brought it down on her grandmother's head. Again and again she struck, hearing the brass thudding against the leather, blow on splitting blow. And still she screamed. The room rang with the terror of it. But it was only when the frenzy passed and the dreadful noise stopped that she knew from the pain of her torn throat that the screaming had been hers.

She stood shaking, gasping for breath. Beads of sweat stood out on her forehead and she felt the stinging drops seeping into her eyes. Looking up she was aware of the man's eyes, wide with terror, staring into hers, of a muttered curse, of footsteps running to the door. And then the poker slid from her moist hands and she heard it thud softly on the rug.

He had been right, there was no blood. Only the grotesque hat knocked forward over the dead face. But as she watched a sluggish line of deep red rolled from under the brim, zigzagged down the forehead, trickled along the creases of the cheeks, and began to drop steadily onto the gloved hands. And then she heard a soft mew. A ball of black fur crept from behind the chair and the ghost of Sambo, azure eyes frantic, leapt as he had leapt ten years earlier delicately up to that unmoving lap.

She looked at her hands. Where were the gloves, the white cotton gloves that the witch had always insisted must be worn to church? But these hands, no longer the hands of a nine-year-old child, were naked. And the chair was empty. There was nothing but the split leather, the burst of horsehair stuffing, a faint smell of violets fading on the quiet air.

She walked out of the front door without closing it behind her as she had left it then. She walked as she had walked then, gloved and unsullied, down the gravel path between the rhododendrons, out of the ironwork gate, and up the lane toward the church. The bell had only just started ringing; she would be in good time. In the distance she had glimpsed her father climbing a stile from the water meadow into the lane. So he must have set out early after breakfast and had walked to Creedon. And why so early? Had he needed that long walk to settle something in his mind? Had it been a pathetic attempt to propitiate the witch by coming with them to church? Or, blessed thought, had he come to take her away, to see that her few belongings were packed and ready by the time the service was over? Yes, that was what she had thought at the time. She remembered it now, that fountain of hope soaring and dancing into glorious certainty. When she got home all would be ready. They would stand there together and defy the witch, would tell her that they were leaving together, the two of them and Sambo, that she would never see them again. At the end of the road she looked back and saw for the last time the beloved ghost crossing the lane to the house toward that fatally open door.

And after that? The vision was fading now. She could remember nothing of the service except a blaze of red and blue shifting like a kaleidoscope, then fusing into a stained glass window, the Good Shepherd gathering a lamb to his bosom. And afterward? Surely there had been strangers waiting in the porch, grave concerned faces, whispers and sidelong glances, a woman in some kind of uniform, an official car. And after that, nothing. Memory was a blank.

But now, at last she knew where her father was buried. And she knew why she would never be able to visit him, never make that pious pilgrimage to the place where he lay because of her, the shameful place where she had put him. There could be no flowers, no obelisk, no loving message carved in marble for those who lay in quicklime behind a prison wall. And then, unbidden, came the final memory. She saw again the open church door, the trickle of the congregation filing in, inquiring faces turning toward her as she arrived alone in the porch. She heard again that high childish voice speaking the words that more than any others had slipped that rope of hemp over his shrouded head.

"Granny? She isn't very well. She told me to come on my own. No, there's nothing to worry about. She's quite all right. Daddy's with her."

The Killer

·

John D. MacDonald

John D. MacDonald has been called the consummate story-teller of our time. He learned his craft by writing for the pulps in the 1940s, soon graduated to such slick magazines as Cosmopolitan *and* The Saturday Evening Post, *and turned to suspense novels—beginning his long association with Fawcett Gold Medal—in 1950 with* The Brass Cupcake. *His most celebrated character, Travis McGee, first appeared in* The Deep Blue Good-By *(1963) and has returned for a score of encores since, the most recent being the best-selling* The Lonely Silver Rain. *Among MacDonald's short story collections are* The Good Old Stuff *and* More Good Old Stuff, *which contain some of his best work for the pulps. "The Killer," which first appeared in the digest-sized detective magazine* Manhunt *in 1955, is vintage MacDonald and is reprinted here for the first time since its original publication.*

We certainly got sick of John Lash. A lot of the guys stopped coming after he started to attend every meeting. It's a skin diving club—you know, just a few guys who like to swim underwater in masks and all, shoot fish with those spear guns, all that. We started originally with six guys and we called ourselves The Deep Six. Even when it got up to about fifteen, we kept the name.

When it started we just had masks and fins and crude

rigs. We live and work on the Florida Keys. I work in a garage in Marathon. Dusty has a bait and boat rental business in Craig. Lew manages a motel down on Ramrod. That's just to give you an idea of the kind of jokers we are. Just guys who got bitten by this skin diving bug. We tried to meet once a week. Dusty had an old tub that's ideal for it. We meet and pick a spot and head for it and anchor and go down and see what's there. You never know what you'll find. There are holes down there that are crawling with fish.

Once the bug gets you, you're hooked. There are a lot of little clubs like ours. Guys that get along. Guys who like to slant down through that green country, kicking yourself along with your fins, hunting those big fish right down in their own backyard.

We got better equipment as we went along. We bought snorkel tubes when those came out. But the Aqualungs were beyond our price range. I think it was Lew who had the idea of everybody chipping in, and of putting in the money we got from selling the catches. When we had enough we bought a lung and two tanks, and then another. In between meetings somebody would run the four tanks up and get them refilled. There was enough time on the tanks so that during a full day everybody got a crack at using one of the lungs.

It was fine there for quite a while. We'd usually get ten or twelve, and some of the wives would come along. We'd have food and beer out there in the sun on that old tub and we had some excitement, some danger, and a lot of fish.

Croy Danton was about the best. A little guy with big shoulders, who didn't have much to say. Not a gloomy guy. He just didn't talk much. His wife, Betty, would usually come along when she could. They've got some rental units at Marathon. He did a lot of the building himself, with the help of a G.I. loan. Betty is what I would call a beautiful girl. She's a blonde and almost the same height as Croy, and you can look at her all day without finding anything wrong with her. She dives a little.

Like I said, it was fine there for a while, until Lew brought this John Lash along one day. Afterward Lew said he was sorry, that Lash had seemed like a nice guy. In all fairness to Lew, I will admit that the first time John Lash joined us he seemed okay. We let him pay his dues. He was new to the Keys. He said he was looking around, and he had a temporary job tending bar.

One thing about him, he was certainly built. One of those guys who looks as if he was fat when you see him in clothes. But in his swimming trunks he looked like one of those advertisements. He had a sort of smallish round head and round face and not much neck. He was blond and beginning to go a little bald. The head didn't seem to fit the rest of him, all that tough brown bulge of muscle. He looked as if a meat axe would bounce right off him. He'd come over from California and he had belonged to a couple of clubs out there and had two West Coast records. He said he had those records and we didn't check, but I guess he did. He certainly knew his way around in the water.

This part is hard to explain. Maybe you have had it happen to you. Like at a party. You're having a good time, a lot of laughs, and then somebody joins the party and it changes everything. You still laugh, but it isn't the same kind of laugh. Everything is different. Like one of those days when the sun is out and then before you know it there is a little haze across the sun and everything looks sort of funny. The water looks oily and the colors are different. That is what John Lash did to The Deep Six. It makes you wonder what happened to a guy like that when he was a kid. It isn't exactly a competitive instinct. They seem to be able to guess just how to rub everybody the wrong way. But you can't put your finger on it. Any of us could tell

Dusty his old tub needed a paint job and the bottom scraped and Dusty would say we should come around and help if we were so particular. But John Lash could say it in such a way that it would make Dusty feel ashamed and make the rest of us feel ashamed, as though we were all second-rate, and John Lash was used to things being first-rate.

When he kidded you, he rubbed you raw. When he talked about himself, it wasn't bragging because he could always follow it up. He liked horseplay. He was always roughing somebody around, laughing to show it was all in fun, but you had the feeling he was right on the edge of going crazy mad and trying to kill you. We had been a close group, but after he joined we started to give each other a bad time, too. There were arguments and quarrels that John Lash wasn't even in. But they happened because he was there. It was spoiling the way it used to be, and there just wasn't anything we could do about it because it wasn't the sort of club where you can vote people out.

Without the lung, with just the mask, he could stay downstairs longer than anybody. Longer than Croy Danton even, and Croy had been the best until John Lash showed up. We had all tried to outdo Croy, but it had been sort of a gag competition. When we tried to outdo John Lash some of the guys stayed down so long that they were pretty sick when they came back up. But nobody beat him.

Another thing about him I didn't like. Suppose we'd try a place and find nothing worth shooting. For John Lash there wasn't anything that wasn't worth shooting. He had to come up with a fish. I've seen him down there, waving the shiny barb slowly back and forth. The fish come up to take a look at it. A thing like that attracts them. An angel fish or a parrot fish or a lookdown would come up and hang right in front of the barb, studying this strange shiny thing. Then John Lash would pull the trigger. There would be a big gout of bubbles and sometimes the spear would go completely through the fish so that it was threaded on the line like a big bright bead. He'd come up grinning and pull it off and toss it over the side and say, "Let's try another spot, children."

The group shrunk until we were practically down to the original six. Some of the other guys were going out on their own, just to stay away from John Lash. Croy Danton kept coming, and most of the time he would bring Betty. John Lash never horsed around with Croy. Croy, being so quiet, never gave anybody much of an opening. John Lash never paid any special attention to Betty. But I saw it happen. Betty wasn't going to dive after fish. She was just going to take a dip to cool off. John Lash had just taken a can of beer out of the ice chest. He had opened it and it was a little bit warm. I saw him glance up to the bow where Betty was poised to dive. She stood there and then dived off cleanly. John Lash sat there without moving, just staring at the place where she had been. And the too-warm beer foamed out of the can and ran down his fingers and dropped onto his thigh, darkening and matting the coarse blond hair that had been sun-dried since his last dive. I saw him drain the can and saw him close his big hand on it, crumpling it, before throwing it over the side. And I saw him watch Betty climb back aboard, sleek and wet, smiling at Croy, her hair water-pasted down across one eye so that as soon as she stood up in the boat, she thumbed it back behind her ear.

I saw all that and it gave me a funny feeling in my stomach. It made me think of the way he would lure the lookdowns close to the barb, and it made me think of the way blood spreads in the water.

After that, John Lash began to move in on Betty with all the grace and tact of a bulldozer. He tried to dab at her with a towel when she came out of the water. If she brought anything up, he had to bustle over to take it off her spear.

215

He found reasons to touch her. Imaginary bugs. Helping her in or out of the boat. Things like that. And all the time his eyes burning in his head.

At first you could see that Croy and Betty had talked about it between meetings, and they had agreed, I guess, to think of it as being sort of amusing. At least they exchanged quick smiles when John Lash was around her. But a thing like that cannot stay amusing very long when the guy on the make keeps going just a little bit further each time. It got pretty tense and, after the worst day, Croy started leaving Betty home. He left her home for two weeks in a row.

Croy left her home the third week and John Lash didn't show up either. We sat on the dock waiting for latecomers. We waited longer than usual. Dusty said, "I saw Lash at the bar yesterday and he said today he was off."

There were only five of us. The smallest in a long, long time. We waited. Croy finally said, "Well, let's go." As we took the boat out I saw Croy watching the receding dock, no expression on his face. It was a funny strained day. I guess we were all thinking the same thing. We had good luck, but it didn't seem to matter. We left earlier than usual. Croy sat in the bow all the way back, as if in that way he'd be nearer shore, and the first one home.

Croy came around to see me at the garage the next morning. I was trying to find a short in an old Willys. When I turned around he was standing there behind me with a funny look on his face. Like a man who's just heard a funny sound in the distance and can't figure out just what it was. He looked right over my left shoulder, and said, "You can tell him for me, Dobey, that I'm going to kill him."

"What do you mean?"

"He came around yesterday. He was a little drunk. He scared Betty. He knew I wouldn't be there. He came around and he scared her. The Sandersons were there. She got loose of him and went over where they were. He kept hanging around. She had to stay with them most of the day. He's got her nervous now. You tell him for me if he makes one more little bit of a move toward her at any time, I'll sure kill him stone dead.'' He turned around and walked out with that funny look still on his face. It was the most I ever heard him say all at one time.

At noon I went over to the bar where John Lash was working. He'd just come on. I got a beer and he rung it up and slapped my change down. He seemed a little nervous.

''Get anything yesterday?''

''Les got a big 'cuda. Croy got some nice grouper. Where were you?''

''Oh, I had things to do.''

''You better not have any more things like that to do.''

He looked at me and put his big hands on the bar and put his face closer to mine. ''What kind of a crack is that?''

''Don't try to get tough with me. You messed around Betty Danton yesterday. You scared her. She told Croy. Croy came in this morning and gave me a message to give you. He says you bother her in any other kind of way at any time and he's going to kill you.'' It sounded funny to say it like that. As if I was in a movie.

John Lash just stared at me out of those little hot eyes of his. ''What kind of talk is that? Kill me? With all the come-on that blonde of his has been giving me? Why don't he come here and tell me that? You know damn well why he didn't come here. By God, I'd have thrown him halfway out to the road.''

''He told me to tell you. It sounded like he meant it.''

''I'm scared to death. Look at me shake.''

I finished my beer and put the glass down. ''See you,'' I said.

"I'll be along the next time."

I walked out. One thing about that Lash, he didn't scare worth a damn. I would have been scared. One of those fellows who do a lot of talking wouldn't scare me much. But the quiet ones, like Croy, they bottle things up.

It was nearly three o'clock when Betty came into the garage. She had on a white dress and when she stood there it made the old garage with all the grease and dirt look darker than ever before. She is a girl who looks right at you. Her eyes were worried. I wiped my hands and lit a cigarette and went over to her.

"Dobey, did Croy talk to you?"

"He was in."

"What did he say?"

"Wouldn't he tell you what he said?"

"He just said he gave you a message for John Lash. What was it, Dobey? He won't tell me. He acts so funny. I'm scared, Dobey."

"He told me to tell Lash if he messed around you he was going to kill him. He said Lash scared you."

"Well, he did scare me, sort of. Because he was drunk. But the Sandersons were there. So it was all right. Croy says I have to come along with you next time. What did Lash say?"

"What do you think he said? You can't scare him off that way. I don't think anybody ought to go out next time, Betty. I think we ought to call it off. I think it's going to be a mess."

"Croy says we're going. He's acting funny. We'll have to go. You've got to come along, too, Dobey. Please."

That's the way it was. It was something you couldn't stop. Like one of those runaway trains in the old movie serials. Picking up speed as it went. I had time during the week to get hold of the other guys and tell them what was up. I don't know now why we didn't form a sort of delegation and go see John Lash and tell him to move along, off the Keys. There would have been enough of us. But there was something about Lash. Something wild and close to the surface. You could have done all that to a normal guy, but he wasn't normal. I'm not saying he was crazy.

Anyway, I loaded the little automatic I had brought back from Saipan and put it in the paper sack with my lunch. That's the way I felt about the day.

Dusty and Lew and I were the first ones to arrive. We put the gear in the old tub. Lew had gotten his new Arbalete gun with the double sling and we hefted it and admired it and then we talked about maybe getting our own compressor some time for the two double-tank lungs. I crushed a damp cigarette and rubbed the glass on my face mask. Two more of the regulars arrived. There was the feel of trouble in that day. A different shimmer in the water. A different blue in the sky. A car door slammed and pretty soon Croy and Betty came around the corner of the fish house and down to the dock, laden with gear. For a time I guess we were all hoping that John Lash wouldn't show. It would have been a good day then, like the days before he came along and joined us.

But as hope grew stronger and Dusty started to fool with the old engine, John Lash came down to the dock, walking cat-light, carrying his sack of gear and lunch and beer, his personal Saetta gun in his other hand, looking slimmer and frailer than it was because it was John Lash who carried it, walking toward us, sun picking sweat-lights off his brown shoulders.

I expected it right then and there. I saw Betty hunch herself a little closer to Croy and start to put her hand on his arm and then change her mind. But John Lash came aboard, saying a lot of loud hellos, banging his gear down, opening the ice chest to pile his cans of beer in there. He

219

didn't seem to pay any special attention to Betty, or Croy either. He sat on the rail back near Dusty at the wheel while we headed out and down the coast. It was enough to make you want to relax, but you couldn't. The water had a greased look. We had agreed to try Gilman's Reef. There is good coral there, and rock holes. I don't know whether we were trying to keep a lid on trouble, but the other five of us did more talking than usual, more kidding around. But laughter had a flat sound across the water. Lew checked the Aqualungs. I had me a beer.

When we got close I went up and stood on the bow and had Dusty bring it up to a place that looked right. I let the anchor line slide through my hands. It hit bottom in twenty-five feet, which was about right. We drifted back and it caught and we swung and steadied there, about twenty feet off the reef shallow. No trouble had started and it didn't look like there would be any. Croy and Lew went down first, Lew with a lung and Croy with a mask only, just to take a look around. I noticed that when Croy lowered himself easily into the water he glanced at Betty and then back to where John Lash was working his feet into the fins. He ducked under and one fin swirled the water as he went down.

John Lash got his fins on and flapped forward to where Betty sat on the rail. He laughed out loud and wrapped a big brown fist in that blonde hair of hers and turned her face upward and kissed her hard on the mouth. She struggled and clawed at him and fell to her hands and knees when he released her.

"Hard to get, aren't you, blondie?" he asked.

Dusty said, "Cut it out, Lash. Cut it out!"

"This is nothing to you, Dusty. Keep out of it! This is me and Betty."

"Get away from me," she said. Her eyes were funny and her mouth had a broken look. I picked up the paper sack and put my hand inside and got hold of the automatic. I couldn't tell what he was going to try to do. He stood spread-legged on the deck watching the water. Betty moved away from him toward the stern, beyond me and Dusty.

Croy broke water and shoved his mask up. He was a dozen feet from the boat.

John Lash stood there and laughed down at him and said, "I just kissed your woman, Danton. I understand you got ideas of making something out of it. I got a message from you."

Croy took one glance at Betty. He brought the Arbalete spear gun up almost off-hand and fired it directly at John Lash's middle. I heard the zing and slap of the rubber slings, heard Betty's scream, heard John Lash's hard grunt of surprise as he threw himself violently to one side. I don't know how he got away from it. But he did. The spear hit the end of the nylon and fell to the water on the far side of the boat. John Lash recovered his balance. He stared at Croy as though he were shocked. He roared then and went off the side in a long flat dive, hurling himself at Croy. There was a splash of water, a flash of brown arms, and then they were both gone. I got a glimpse of them under the water as they sank out of sight. Betty screamed again, not as loud.

Nobody was set to go down. We all started grabbing gear at once. I went off the side about the same moment as Dusty, and at the last moment I had snatched up John Lash's Saetta gun. It was cocked and I don't know what I expected to do with it, but I took it. I went down through the deepening shades of green, looking for them. I saw movement and cut over toward it, but it was Lew wearing the lung. He saw me and spread his arms in a gesture that meant he hadn't spotted anything worth shooting. He didn't know what was going on. I motioned him to go up. I guess I looked as though I meant it. He shrugged and headed up.

I looked hard, but I couldn't find them and I could tell by the way my chest felt that it was nearly time to head up. I took it as long as I could. I thought I saw movement below me and to the right but I was close to blacking out and I went up. Dusty was hanging on the side of the boat. Betty stood staring down into the water. I knew from her face that they hadn't come up. I took deep breaths and turned and went down again and got partway down when I saw them. John Lash with a look of agony on his face, was working his way up, kicking hard, one hand holding Croy by the waistband of his trunks. Croy was loose in the water. I went over and got hold of Croy by the wrist. I fired the spear off to the side so the gun would float up. Lash was having a hard time of it. I got Croy up and we got him over the side and put him face down on the bottom and Les, who had the lung and tanks off, began to work on him. Somebody behind me helped John Lash aboard. Dusty had to grab Betty and pull her away from Croy so Les could use the artificial respiration without her getting in his way.

She turned against Dusty and she was crying. Those were the sounds. The small noises she made, and John Lash's labored breathing, and the rhythmic slap and creak of the respiration.

"Tried . . . to kill me." Lash said. "You . . . you saw it. Then . . . tried to drown me. Tried to hold me even . . . after he'd passed out."

Nobody answered him. The boat moved in the offshore swell. Loose gear rattled. Croy retched and coughed. Les continued until Croy began to struggle weakly. Les moved back then and Croy rolled over, closing his eyes against the sun.

Betty dropped to her knees beside him saying words that

did not make sentences. Croy raised his head. He looked at her and then pushed her aside, gently. He got to his knees. I tried to help him up, but he refused the help. He got to his feet with an enormous effort. He stood unsteadily and looked around until he saw John Lash. As soon as he saw Lash, he bent and picked up a loose spear. He held it by the middle, the muscles of his arm bunching.

John Lash moved quickly. He got up and said, "Wait! Hold it! Croy, wait . . ." Dusty tried to grab Croy, but he moved quickly. The spear tip gashed John Lash's arm as he tried to fend it off, and as Croy drew back to thrust again, John Lash hit him flush in the face with one of those big brown fists. Croy bounced back and hit the engine hatch and rebounded to fall heavily and awkwardly, unconscious.

Betty reached him and turned him and sat, his head in her lap, arm curled protectively around his head, murmuring to him. Lew wet the end of a towel and gave it to her. She wiped the blood from his mouth and looked at John Lash and then the rest of us with cold hate. "Why didn't you stop him? Why are you letting him do this to Croy?"

"I had to hit him!" John Lash said, his voice a half-octave higher than usual. "You saw what he was trying to do. Why didn't you guys stop him?"

Croy's mouth puffed rapidly. He mumbled something. Dusty started the engine. "We better get back. You want to get the anchor up, Dobey?"

I broke it free and hauled it in, coiling the line. When I moved back I saw that Croy was sitting up. Betty was holding on to his arm. She was saying, with a gradually increasing edge in her voice. "No, darling. No. No please, darling."

But Croy was looking beyond her, looking at John Lash. Lash was trying to grin. It wasn't a grin as much as it was just a sort of twist he was wearing on his mouth. He'd look at Croy and then look away. Croy got up then with Betty holding on to him. He lurched over toward the rail and grabbed one of the gaffs. Lash came back up onto his feet quickly and said, "Grab him!"

Croy shook Betty loose. Lew and I grabbed Croy. It was like grabbing hard rubber. He lowered his head and butted Lew over the rail. Dusty swung the boat to keep the prop clear of Lew. It made me lose my balance. As I staggered Croy rapped me across my shins with the handle end of the gaff and hot stars went off behind my eyes from the sudden pain of it. When I could see again, I saw him going for Lash with the gaff. They were poised for a moment, muscles like they were cut out of stone, both holding onto the long gaff. Then John Lash, with his greater strength, hurled Croy back toward the stern again. Croy fell, harder than before, but he hadn't been hit.

"Keep him off me!" Lash yelled. "Keep him off me!"

Croy got slowly and clumsily back to his feet and started back toward Lash. I was set to take another grab at Croy. Lew was climbing aboard. The other two guys were having no part of it. They were plain scared. Just as I was about to grab Croy, he put his weight on his left foot and went down. I could see the ankle puffing visibly. He never took his eyes off John Lash. He had fallen near his gear. He fumbled and came out with a fish knife with a cork handle. Holding it in his hand, he began to crawl toward the bow, toward John Lash again, the handle thumping against the cockpit boards every time he put his right hand down. I fell on his arm. I could hear Lash yelling. I couldn't make out what he was saying. I got Croy's wrist and managed to twist the knife out of his hand. Lew had him around the middle. We hauled him over and tried to sit on him. He kept struggling with stubborn, single-minded strength. Once he broke free and started crawling again toward Lash, puffed lips pulled back from bloody teeth, but we got him again.

Dusty helped that time and one of the other guys and we held him and tried to talk sense into him, but he kept on struggling. We finally got heavy nylon line around his wrists and tied his arms behind him. We thought that was going to be enough, but even with his hands like that he managed to get on his feet and, limping badly, try to get at Lash. Dusty put a length of the anchor line around the engine hatch and we tied him there around his chest, sitting on the litter of gear and water and smashed sandwiches and cans of beer, staring at John Lash and fighting the heavy line constantly.

Once he was tied up, Betty kneeling beside him, trying to soothe him, John Lash lighted a cigarette. His hands shook. He grinned. "He get like that often?" he asked. "Look at him. He still wants to get at me."

Croy's shoulders bulged as he fought the rope. Lash kept glancing at him. We were all breathing hard. Dusty examined skinned knuckles. "I never see him like that, not that bad. Old Croy he gets an idea in his head, you can't get it out. No, sir."

"He'll get over this, won't he? When he cools off."

"He's not going to cool off at all," Dusty said. "Not one little bit. Tomorrow, the next day, it'll be just the same."

"What am I supposed to do then?" Lash asked.

"I don't know. I really don't know," Dusty said. "You got to either kill him or he's got it in his mind he's going to kill you. Known him twenty years and he's never gone back on his word one time. Or his daddy before him."

Lash licked his lips. I watched him. I saw him sitting there, nervous. It was something he'd never run into. It was something I guess few men ever run into in their lifetime. I could see him wishing he'd never made any sort of a pass at Betty.

225

Croy fought the rope, doggedly, constantly, sweat running down his face.

John Lash lighted another cigarette. "He'll get over it," he said unconvincingly.

"I wouldn't want to bet much on that," I said.

There was that big John Lash sitting there in the sun, a whole head and forty-fifty pounds bigger than little Croy Danton. And without the faintest idea in the world as to what to do about it. Either way, there didn't seem to be any kind of an out for John Lash.

"He's nuts. You people are all nuts down here," Lash said.

I sensed what was forming in his mind. I said, "When we dock we'll see if we can hold him right here for about an hour. You ought to pack up and take off."

"Run from a character like him?" Lash said.

Croy's arms came free suddenly and he tried to shove the line up off his chest. His wrists were bloody where the nylon had punished them. Three of us jumped him and got his wrists tied again. He didn't make a sound. But he fought hard, Betty kept trying to quiet him down, talking gentle, her lips close to his ear. But you could see that for Croy there were two people left in the world. Him and John Lash.

It took about forty minutes to get back in. Nobody talked. I didn't like to watch Croy. It was a sort of thing I have seen in Havana at the cockfights. I hear it is like that, too, at the bullfights. A distillation, I guess you would call it, of violence. The will to kill. Something that comes from a sort of crazy pride, a primitive pride, and once you have started it, you can't turn it off.

It was easy to see that John Lash didn't want to look at him either. But he had to keep glancing at him to make sure he wasn't getting loose. During that forty minutes John Lash slowly unraveled. He came apart way down in the middle of himself where it counted. I don't think any of us would say he was a coward. He wasn't yellow. But this was something he couldn't understand. He'd never faced it before and few men ever face it in their lifetime. To Lash I guess Croy wasn't a man anymore. He was a thing that wanted to kill him. A thing that lusted to kill him so badly that even defenseless it would still keep coming at him.

By the time we got in, John Lash wasn't even able to edge by Croy to pick up his gear. We had to get it and pass it up to him where he stood on the dock. John Lash looked down and he looked older in the face. Maybe it was the first time he had seriously thought about his own death. It shrunk him a little.

"Hold him for an hour. I'll go away," he said. He didn't say good-bye. There wasn't any room in him to think of things like that. He walked away quickly and a bit unsteadily. He went around the corner of the fish house. We've never seen him since.

Croy kept watching the place where John Lash had disappeared. Betty kept whispering to him. But in about ten minutes Croy stopped struggling.

"There, baby. There," I heard Betty whisper.

He gave a big convulsive shudder and looked around, first at her and then at the rest of us, frowning a little as if he had forgotten something.

"Sorry," he said huskily. "Real sorry." And that is all he ever said about it. He promised that he was all right. I carried his stuff to their car. Betty bound his ankle with a strip of towel. He leaned heavily on her to the car.

That's almost all, except the part I don't understand. The Deep Six is back up to about fifteen again. We have a compressor now, and new spots to go, and we did fine in the interclub competitions this year. We're easy with each other, and have some laughs.

But Croy never came back. He and Betty, they go out by themselves in a kicker boat when the weather is right. I don't see any reason why he didn't come back. He says hello when we see him around. Maybe he's ashamed we saw him like that, saw that wildness.

One morning not long ago I went out alone on the Gulf side. I got out there early and mist hung heavy on the water. I tilted my old outboard up and rowed silently. It was kind of eerie there in the mist in the early morning. All of a sudden I began to hear voices. It was hard to tell direction, but they kept getting louder. There was a deep voice, a man's voice, talking and talking and talking, and every so often a woman would say one or two words, soft and soothing.

All of a sudden I recognized the voices as Croy's and Betty's. I couldn't catch any of the words. I rested on the oars. It made me feel strange. I figured I could get closer and find out what in the world Croy could talk about for so long.

But then understanding came to me suddenly, and it wasn't necessary to listen. I understood suddenly that there was only one subject on which a quiet guy like Croy could talk and talk and talk, and that the situation wasn't over and maybe would never be over. And I realized that embarrassment was only part of the reason Croy didn't come skin diving with us anymore; the rest of the reason was that the sight of us reminded him too strongly of John Lash. I turned the dinghy and headed off the other way until their voices faded and were gone.

Later in the morning after the sun had burned the mist off, I was spin casting with a dude and monofilament line over a weed bed when they went by, heading in, their big outboard roaring, the bow wave breaking the glassy look of the morning Gulf.

Croy was at the motor, Betty up in the bow.

Betty waved at me and Croy gave me a sort of little nod as they went by. I waved back. Their swell rocked me and then they were gone in the distance.

She is the most beautiful woman I have ever seen. You could look at her all day and not find anything wrong.

About the Editors

MARTIN GREENBERG has compiled nearly one hundred anthologies, including nine in Fawcett's Best of the West series. He is a noted scholar and teaches at the University of Wisconsin in Green Bay.

BILL PRONZINI in addition to collaborating with Martin Greenberg on several anthologies, is an award-winning mystery writer, the author of many novels and short stories. He lives in Sonoma, California.